PRAISE FOR SERIES

"For fans of noir mysteries, *Joker Poker* offers a hearty concoction of violence, intrigue, sex, and even a little articulate humor!"
- The Library Journal

"Richard Helms can spin a tale, and he's created some truly intriguing supporting characters in *Joker Poker*, well worth a return visit!"
- Thrilling Detective

"The seminary-trained Irish musician-cum-profiler Pat Gallegher steps out of retirement to smartly solve his third mystery in Richard Helms' tale of serial murder, *Juicy Watusi*. The plot is solid, traditional hardboiled fare, and even better is the middle-aged investigator's snappy observations about the French Quarter's characters."
- Publishers Weekly

Wet Debt is fast-paced and well-written with the gritty kind of straight-up dialogue one expects in noir detective fiction. Readers will notice echoes of Hammett here! There's no lack of mystery and action. For readers of the hardboiled genre, I recommend Pat Gallegher and *Wet Debt*!"
- Mystery Scene Magazine

PAID IN SPADES

OTHER TITLES IN SERIES

Joker Poker

Voodoo That You Do

Juicy Watusi

Wet Debt

PAID IN SPADES

A Pat Gallegher Novel

by

Richard Helms

Clay
Stafford
Books®

Franklin, Tennessee

Published 2019 by Clay Stafford Books

Paid in Spades. Copyright © by 2019 Richard Helms.

Front cover image by Isabella Negrotto
Book design by Clay Stafford Books

This is a work of fiction. Names, characters, organizations, places, events, and incidents are either products of the author's imagination or are used fictiously.

Inquiries should be addressed to:

Clay Stafford Books
P.O. Box 680686
Franklin, TN 37068
www.ClayStaffordBooks.com

ISBN: 978-0-9788427-3-4 (paperback)
ISBN: 978-0-9788427-6-5 (ebook)
Library of Congress Control Number: 2018960147

Printed in the United States of America.

For Jerry Healy

Paying it forward . . .

Prologue

*O*NE THING ABOUT being in a recovery program, you meet the most interesting people.

Cabby Jacks and I couldn't have been more different. I had come up a child of privilege, in a decent home and a decent neighborhood. I'd had a great education—several of them, in fact. I'd had a chance, squandered as it might have been, to make something of myself.

Cabby, on the other hand, was always from the wrong side of the tracks. His own mother told him he was the kind of kid she didn't want her other kids hanging with.

Out of school at sixteen, Cabby worked the back end of a boxing gym handing out towels during business hours and polishing the boxers' knobs after hours, all before age eighteen. Did his first tour in the slam a year later—after cutting up a guy during a bad dope deal over in the Desire housing projects—and sweated out the entire fourteen months bent over at the waist.

Cabby tried to pull things back together when he got out at twenty-one, but by then the call of easy, sleazy money was too loud for him to screen out with yearnings for a straight and narrow life.

Maybe it was some kind of luck that paired him with Mookie Schneider and got him into the mobile poker game business. Mookie set up the games, contacted players he'd heard were visiting New Orleans, and let them know there was good money to be won in a certain hotel room off Poydras Street. Cabby was hired to make sure the players got to the game. That was how he got the name Cabby.

Eventually, Mookie let him into the room to help keep the table clean, refresh the drinks and make the sandwiches, sometimes order up some real food from room service. These games could go on for two or three days, depending on how the cards were falling.

For a long time, Mookie wouldn't get into the game. He was more like a host, assuring all the players were well-tended. Cabby became his number one guy after a year or so. The money was good, the work was easy, and the games got bigger and longer.

That was how I met Cabby. I hit New Orleans about eight years ago at the end of a long downward spiral and in the grips of the worst midlife crisis in human history. I'd been a seminary student, a forensic psychologist, and a college professor—three tragically failed careers in twenty years.

Maybe I had big ideas of making a living as a gambler.

Maybe I was a little delusional.

In any case, I'd had a good, long run of luck at the green felt and had begun to light up the radar screens of guys like Mookie, who approached me one night as I strolled off the Flamingo riverboat, my jacket pockets stuffed with hundreds and twenties.

Next thing I knew, I was sitting in a penthouse room at the Hilton, knocking back Chivas like it was lemonade and watching some real pros gobble up my stake at the rate of five large a hand.

This was months before I was stupid enough to believe I could cover a big marker. I was in the early stages of the gold fever. I still had enough sense to know when the pockets were empty, the night was over.

Oh, well.

Easy come, easy go.

Two years later, I'd advanced to Stage Three Addiction. I'd allowed myself to start piling up some serious gambling debts. Each time, I told myself I'd hit another streak and pay everything off.

There were plenty of stories. Eddie Sakatch had gone in the hole a hundred grand to Lucho Braga. A year later he bought a whole building in the Quarter, turned it into a bed and breakfast, and retired from the game. Guys like Eddie were legends. Every guy like me who was nothing but double-down fodder *knew*, in his heart of hearts, it was only a matter of time before he hit it the way Eddie Sakatch had.

The loan sharks could see us coming a mile away.

I attended my first Gamblers Anonymous meeting one week after I went to work collecting debts for Justin Leduc. I was in to him for twenty thousand, with no real hope of ever paying it down. I figured the only way I could put a positive spin on the situation was to see to it I never—*never*—hit the tables again.

I sat through tale after pitiful tale of wasted opportunities and broken lives, becoming more despondent as I saw my life reflected in each new speaker. Eventually, things wound down and the meeting broke up. I hadn't stood to speak. I figured I could sit in the back, see how things worked, and maybe participate a few meetings down the road when I felt more comfortable.

It was a long meeting. I'd skipped dinner. I was supposed to go on stage at Holliday's, the bar where I play a jazz cornet, in a little more than a half hour, so I dallied at the cookies and punch table waiting for my stomach to quit complaining.

That was when I met up with Cabby Jacks again.

He tugged on my shirt sleeve, trying to get my attention. I looked down at him. Cabby went, maybe, five-seven. He hadn't gained a pound since his stretch in the joint. I put him at a conservative hundred and fifty pounds. I, on the other hand, go six and a half feet and haven't seen the shy side of two-seventy since grad school.

"Yeah?" I asked.

"I know you," he said.

"You look familiar."

"Di'n't you used to play in the games over to the Hilton?"

"That's why I'm here, in part," I said.

"Some kinda Irish name, right?"

"Gallegher."

"Right. Pat Gallegher. Useta live over some dive bar down offa Toulouse."

"I still do. I remember you now. You worked for Mookie. Cabby something . . ."

"Jacks. Cabby Jacks. That's me. You got a good memory, Gallegher. I mean, I wasn't no player or nothin'. I gave rides to the games and helped out in the room."

"You did a good job, Cabby. I remember people who do a good job."

"So, why di'n't you get up and talk or nothin'?"

"My first meeting. I wanted to get the lay of the land, figure out how things worked."

"Oh, man, that ain't gonna do. I mean it. You don't get up and jump right in the first time, you might as well kiss your recovery down the drain. You gotta do it right."

As I said, I'd hung around the snack table for a good long time. The crowd had thinned to me, Cabby, the coordinator of the group, and a couple of dull-eyed stragglers looking for an excuse to go home.

"You gotta do it now," Cabby said. "At least the First Step."

"C'mon," I said. "Meeting's over. Everyone's gone."

"There's still five here," he said.

He turned to the other people there and raised his voice.

"This guy here wants to do his First Step," he said. "He di'n't feel like it wit' a big crowd. You guys got a minute?"

The small group pulled some chairs up, almost in unison. Some of them might have had some place to go, but it didn't seem to matter. A lost soul was looking for a chance to purge, and it was their duty to help, the same as someone had done for them.

"I don't know," I said.

"It's easy," Cabby said. "Anyone can do it. Repeat after me: I got a problem with my gambling behavior."

I looked around at the four other faces. They surveyed me expectantly.

"Look, maybe next time," I said, turning to leave.

Cabby grabbed my sleeve again.

"You can't," he said. It was almost a plea.

"What?" I said, looking down at him.

"You leave now and you ain't never comin' back, you see? People, they come and they either start their recovery, or they don't never come back. You gotta do it. Now, say it: I got a problem with my gambling behavior."

I looked around. Then, almost without my bidding, my lips started to move.

"I . . . have a problem with my gambling behavior," I mumbled.

"And it's taken control of my life."

I gulped.

It hadn't taken control. It *was* my life. I had given over every shred of my meager, failed existence to my gambling addiction. Now, Leduc had a lien on my skin. I never knew when he'd call, but when he did I had to come running. It was like he held the marker to my soul.

"And . . . and it's taken control of my life," I repeated. "I like to play the cards. Like it a lot. Mostly blackjack, but some . . . some poker, too. I've lost . . . too much. Way too much. Can't see how I'm ever going to get even again . . ."

I went on and on, for almost a half-hour, spilling out the story of my depleted and discarded life.

They sat the entire time and listened patiently, until I ran out of gas, sat down, buried my head in my hands. They patted me on the back and told me it would get better.

Within a few weeks, I'd gone through a few more steps, and realized I had been making some serious deposits in the bad karma account of my soul. I had to do something to pull the score even, or I was destined to do some righteous burn time in the afterlife.

That was when I started doing favors.

About six months ago, Cabby Jacks showed up one night at the bar at Holliday's.

He'd put on a few pounds in six years. He was dressed nicely. His smile revealed expensive orthodontic work.

I comped him a beer after my first set and we sat in the back of the bar to hash over old times.

"You still go to meetings?" he asked.

"At least once a week. Sometimes more," I said. "If I don't, I know it. When I start to feel itchy, I double up. You?"

"Oh, yeah. I'm not fallin' in that trap again. You know I don't work for Mookie no more."

"I'd heard."

"I got a sweet deal. Nothin' to do with the games."

"You've gone legit?"

"Well . . ." He smiled.

I understood. I'd gotten into enough mischief over the eight years I'd been in the Quarter that I couldn't pass judgment on anyone else's behavior.

"Can you tell me about it?" I asked.

"I'd rather . . . let's say it's better I don't, you dig?"

"Sure. No problem. Want another beer?"

He handed me the empty. I strolled behind the bar and grabbed another couple of bottles of Dixie.

"Nothin' personal," he said, as I handed one to him.

"It's cool. Let it go."

"Actually, that's kind of why I came by here tonight. You got a reputation around town."

"That so?"

"People say you can find things, even when other folks, the cops even, they can't."

"I'd prefer to stay away from that business, Cabby," I said. "It's been a lot of grief over the years. I figure I've balanced the books by now, done at least as much good as I have bad. I'm trying to start with a clean slate."

"But it's true?"

"I've had some lucky breaks."

He reached into his jacket pocket and pulled out a check. He unfolded it and held it up. It was written out to me, for a thousand dollars. There was no date.

"Time comes, you fill in the date and cash it. I'd like you to find something."

I took a long draw from the bottle and set it down in its wet ring on the tabletop. I left the check where it lay. I wasn't sure I wanted to touch it.

"Not saying I'll do it," I said. "But what do you need?"

He leaned forward, whispering over the top of his own bottle. "I want you to find *me*," he said.

CHAPTER ONE

Six months later

I HAD SPENT TWO weeks in San Francisco with my girlfriend, Merlie Comineau, and was ready to get back home and start earning a living again. I live in an apartment over a bar called Holliday's, which you enter through a door in an alley between Toulouse and Decatur streets in the French Quarter of New Orleans

Farley Nuckolls was waiting for me when I walked in with my bags.

I hadn't seen him in almost a year.

Nuckolls is a gaunt, chinless, bucktoothed guy who always looks as if he's wearing someone else's clothes. He's also the best detective I've ever known. I'd forced him into some desperately uncomfortable corners a year earlier. Part of me considered it justified payback after he hornswoggled me into helping the police find a guy who was ripping strippers in the French Quarter. As a cop, he has a laundry list of ethical constraints on his behavior. I tend not to color inside the lines. It works for me, but it was hell on his conscience.

Before he'd taken an extended leave of absence to pull himself back together, Farley had asked me for a favor. He'd requested—if he ever did come back—that I stay away from him.

Permanently.

I was more than a little surprised when I walked into Holliday's to find him sitting at a table, nursing a Jax and doodling on the spiral notebook he usually carried in his jacket pocket.

I dropped the bags at the foot of the stairs leading to my apartment.

"Detective," I said, as I walked behind the bar to grab an Abita from the ice cooler.

"Gallegher," he said.

"Should I call Cully Tucker before we talk?" Cully Tucker is my attorney.

"No need. As you can see," he said, hoisting the schooner, "this is not an official visit."

"Good."

I twisted the cap off the Abita and sat at the table with him.

"Welcome back," I said, extending my hand. He kept doodling.

"Same to you. How was San Francisco?"

"Well, you know what they say. It's one big cereal bowl. Take out the fruits and the nuts and all you have left is the flakes."

"Sounds like home."

I took a long drag from the Abita. It was smoky and biting and it felt good as it burned the back of my throat a little.

"And how was . . . well, wherever you've been for the last year?" I asked.

"It was nice. You showed up on my radar, and I thought I'd give you a heads-up."

All right. Pleasantries were finished.

"Maybe you should have stayed in San Francisco," he continued. "You are the talk of the town lately. Don't bother telling me why. I'm sick of your stories. But whatever you did before you jetted off to the coast is upsetting people's stomachs."

"Good guys or bad guys?"

"Does it matter? You're an equal opportunity irritant. I know you live by your own rules, have your own code, yada yada yada. If I were you, I'd tread lightly for a while. Keep a low profile. Play your music, mind your own business, and let things die down before you go around yanking chains. That's all."

He drained the schooner of Jax and slipped his notebook back into his pocket, grabbed his Panama hat and dropped it on his bony skull.

"See you around, Gallegher." He walked toward the door.

"Farley," I called.

He turned around.

"It is good to see you again."

He scratched at what passed for a chin and shook his head a little.

"I reckon it's a little too early to say one way or the other," he said.

CHAPTER TWO

I WAS SHOOTING THE breeze with Shorty, my boss at
Holliday's, when Merlie walked in later that evening. It was
almost dark. The nightly revelers had started to parade up and down
the sidewalks on Toulouse and Decatur and Bourbon Streets.

"Good evening, Shorty," she said, as she took the stool next to
mine. Merlie has been the one bright spot in my life for several
years. She is patient and caring, and it doesn't hurt that she fills a
dress like nobody's business. Many a night I fall asleep dreaming of
her auburn hair and violet eyes. I'm just past fifty, and she's a couple
of years younger, but she still turns heads when we walk down the
sidewalk together. I kind of dig that.

"Good evening, Miz Merlie," he said. "Can I get you something
to drink?"

"Nothing, thank you," she said. "I suppose you're glad to get
your cornet player back."

Shorty shook his head. "Can't say I am. Place has been nice
and quiet since he flew off to San Francisco. Gallegher here is like
flypaper for troublemakers."

I glanced over at him. Shorty is a square guy. His body is shaped
like this overly muscled cube, attached to columns for legs and arms

like braided bridge cable. His head is boxy and slightly misshapen from a losing boxing career, with a buzz cut that only accents its angularity. If it came down to me against four bikers with machetes, I'd like to have Shorty on my side to make it even.

At that moment he was grinning, which meant I didn't have to take his abuse personally. I knew him well enough to recognize when it was safe to put distance between us.

"I know when I'm not wanted," I joked back. "I'm taking my girl here to dinner."

"Long's you're back by ten. Sockeye Sam's come down with croup. He's taking a couple of days off."

"Sam?" Merlie asked. "Is he going to be all right?"

"Hard to say," Shorty told her. "You know how it is with these old guys. They're tough as two-dollar shoe leather, but you reach a point where the immune system can't keep up anymore and a head cold can turn into pneumonia. He's moved in with one of his granddaughters for a few days to make sure there's someone to look after him."

Sockeye Sam is a French Quarter relic and a national treasure around Holliday's. He's a wizened black guy somewhere between ninety and a thousand years old who grew his chops in the Storyville whorehouses with guys like King Oliver and Satchmo. Unlike them, he never left the Vieux Carre. He's played a regular gig at Holliday's since sometime in the late eighties, when he took his leave from the Preservation Hall outfit following a dispute over the ownership of a tune he'd written.

"It's going to sound little skinny on the stage," I told him.

"I was gettin' to that. I hired this kid to sit in for a few nights while you was off. He's a guitar player, but I figure jazz is jazz, you know? Name's Chick Kasay."

"Chick?"

"Yeah, I know. Kid's only about twenty, maybe twenty-five. Got this silly little soul patch thing under his lower lip. Thinks he's a shit-hot jazz guitarist. He does all right. You'll see."

I took Merlie to Irene's Cuisine, one of our regular spots. The owners at Irene's usually comps me these days, because I had kept the place from getting shot up about a year earlier by a hype who'd been too long off the spike and who had decided that robbing the place would make his life righteous.

As soon as Merlie and I were seated, the waiter, a guy named Fabrizio, hustled across the floor to greet us.

"Ah, Mr. Gallegher! Ms. Comineau! It is so nice to have you back with us this evening. Can I bring you a carafe of our finest Chianti?"

I thanked him for the offer.

"You are most welcome. Are you ready to order?"

"What do you suggest tonight?" I asked.

"Ah, I'm so glad you asked," Fabrizio said, beaming. "We have some lovely Alaskan salmon, flown in from the west coast. This fish was swimming upstream to spawn yesterday. We are featuring our *salmon en croute* this evening, with a crawfish mousse and sautéed spinach encased in phyllo dough, baked and served with a pinot grigio *beurre blanc*."

"Sounds yummy," I said. "How about you, Merlie?"

"Absolutely."

"Two, then," Fabrizio said. "I'll be right back with your wine."

I watched him trot off to the bar and I turned back to Merlie.

"Did you check in at the shelter?" I asked.

Merlie is the director of A Friend's Place, a refuge for runaways, throwaways, and other destitute children, in the Garden District.

She's a guardian *ad litem,* an angel of mercy, and I could climb into her violet eyes and live there forever.

"I called when I got home. The place doesn't seem to have closed in my absence."

"You're more likely to need a branch office."

"Don't I know it? We've been turning kids away again."

I knew how that broke her heart. The shelter was only licensed to hold nine children at a time. Turning kids away usually meant sending them back to the streets. Tragic as that was, it was a way of life there.

Fabrizio reappeared at the table.

"A carafe of Chianti for the gentleman and the lovely lady. I selected an excellent vintage especially for you, Ms. Comineau, because you are such a special customer."

"Thank you," she said.

"I'll check with the kitchen on your orders," he said, as he turned with a flourish and sashayed toward the back.

Merlie took a sip of wine and placed the glass back down.

"There's a . . . situation," she said.

"Oh."

"One of the kids."

"At the shelter."

"Yes. When I called, Shelley told me she'd been trying to find this kid's father for several days."

"Why?"

"Well, besides the fact that our mission is to get these kids back with their families, this little girl has a medical problem."

"How bad?"

"She needs an operation. It isn't urgent. She isn't going to die if she doesn't have surgery, but we'd like to find her father so we can get him to give consent."

"Couldn't social services take custody?"

"Sure. And she could be placed in a succession of foster homes and spend the majority of her adolescence in a perpetual state of chaos."

I had long since learned that Merlie's inexplicable ardor for me ran a distant second to her passion for the children who were placed, however temporarily, into her care.

"I see. I suppose I could I go look for her father," I said.

"Oh, that's a relief. Thank you for not making me ask."

She placed her hand on the checkered tablecloth near my plate.

I caressed her cool, smooth fingers.

"First night back, and you have me on a missing daddy case."

"Yes."

"Well, this is a hell of a thing," I said.

"Yes," she said. "It's a hell of a thing."

CHAPTER THREE

*A*S WE ROUNDED the corner to front door of the bar, I heard some muted string music coming from the windows. I recognized the warm, resonant sound of a jazz guitar immediately.

"Must be my new partner, Chick," I said.

"What kind of name is that, anyway?" she asked.

"It's the kind young jazz players give themselves, hoping it will stick. Twenty years later, they're sorry they bothered. I'm so happy I never tried to call myself something cheesy, like *Chops*."

"I don't know. Chops Gallegher. I kind of like the sound of it."

"No you don't. Are you staying here tonight?"

"I don't think so. I've been away from the shelter for almost three weeks. I think I should put in an appearance first thing in the morning. You'll probably need to come by around lunch, meet Audrey, and get some information to help you find her father."

"You should have said something. I could have driven you home."

I keep my Pinto parked in the lot built from the courtyard behind Irene's. Now it was five blocks back.

"I'll take a cab. You need to get used to your new partner, anyway."

I hailed her a taxi and stopped her as she started to slip inside.

"Around noon?" I asked.

"Noon would be great," she said.

I kissed her goodnight and watched as her cab pulled out to Decatur and turned right.

By the time I lumbered up to my apartment over the bar and retrieved my cornet, whoever had been playing the guitar had disappeared.

I sat on a stool on the raised plywood platform that serves as a rustic stage in Holliday's, limbering up my chops after a couple of weeks' layoff. I ran through a series of pentatonic scales and lit off a couple of lydians before deciding I hadn't lost it after all.

I was putting the horn on a stand next to my stool when someone called me.

"Mr. Gallegher?"

I turned to find a thin young man, wearing a sleeveless Metallica tee shirt and baggy jeans. His hair had been filled with some kind of goo. It stood straight up in spikes, the ends of which had been bleached pure white. Beneath the freak-show haircut, his face was open and pleasant enough. His eyes were clear, and his nose only slightly protruding, through it was bent slightly to one side in what appeared to be the consequence of some back-alley brawl. He had placed a stainless steel stud through one nostril and another through his right eyebrow. There appeared to be a wooly worm caterpillar perched below his lower lip.

"Chick Kasay, I take it."

"Yes sir. Nice to meet you. Mr. Shorty's told me a bunch about you."

Chick Kasay may have been in his middle twenties, but he

looked like he'd stepped out of a junior high school yearbook.

"So you're my new partner," I said.

"I'm just filling in."

"Where have you played before?"

"All over. I have a hard time staying long in one place. After a while, I get the urge to move along. My last gig was in Pensacola, at a place called Beau's."

"What are you playing?" I said, pointing toward his guitar case.

He opened it and showed me.

"It's a D'Aquisto," he said, proudly, as he held it out the way ancient knights had presented their swords.

I had heard of Jimmy D'Aquisto. He had been the protégé of John D'Angelico, a New York craftsman generally regarded as one of the greatest guitar builders of the twentieth century. After D'Angelico died, D'Aquisto picked up the business and turned out hundreds of artful musical treasures from his lower Manhattan shop before he, too, succumbed to heart ailments in the 1990s.

"That's a lot of axe for a kid your age," I said.

"It belonged to my father. I inherited it from him."

"He played?"

"He taught me everything."

"You warmed up?"

"I played a little before you got here."

"You know Jim Hall's version of *The Answer Is Yes*?"

He smiled, strapped the guitar around his neck and plugged it into an unobtrusive tube amp set in front of Sockeye's piano. After taking a cleansing breath, he launched into the first four bars. He stopped and looked at me.

"That one?"

"It'll do. You lead and I'll follow."

We played about twenty-four bars each, him playing lead the

first go-round, and then some rhythm behind me as I picked up the theme and played with it a little. At the end of my break, I lowered the horn.

"What's your repertoire like, kid?"

"I grew up in jazz bars. What I don't know, I can play by ear."

"Okay then," I said. "Let's earn our keep."

It isn't easy to make decent music when both of the instruments are intended to be solo players. Chick could back me up relatively well, but when it came time for him to cut loose he had to play rhythm and lead—a feat he somehow managed with amazing dexterity. About all I could do during his breaks was play some counterpoint on the cornet.

Even so, we did all right. I would have enjoyed having a competent drummer or maybe a bass to back us up, but Shorty wouldn't take well to the idea of shelling out for a third musician. The bar wasn't *that* successful. With any luck, Sockeye Sam would be back in a few days.

Around midnight, we put the instruments down and grabbed a beer. I wasn't sure Chick was old enough to drink, until he produced a North Carolina driver's license showing him to be twenty-seven. Shorty was skeptical. He glowered at the license long enough to make the kid nervous before uncapping a Dixie and sliding it across the bar. We sat on the stools at the bar and drank a little.

"So," he said, after killing a third of his beer. "Are all the stories true?"

I stared off into space before I said, "Don't know what you're talking about."

"They say you're some kind of detective."

"*They* tend to run off at the mouth."

14

"The way I heard it, you had to skedaddle to San Francisco after you got tangled up with some mob business a few weeks back."

"The story loses something in the translation. The official line is this: builders found a body buried in the concrete floor of the building next door, and Shorty asked me to find out who he was. Along the way I pissed off some people who like to play with guns and push their weight around. I'm a big guy. I don't push easy."

"You're big enough, all right. Like a halfback I knew in the . . . well, a few years back. You look kind of funny playing a little cornet."

"I'm not compensating for anything."

"Word has it you killed one of the bad guys."

"You must not read the papers. A police detective named Cal Nucci got the credit."

"Or maybe the blame. I suppose I could be wrong."

"You could be," I said.

"You think the rest of the people in this bar are wrong, too?"

I glanced over at Shorty, who had been standing close enough to hear the entire conversation.

He shrugged.

"Drink your beer," I said.

We knocked off around one in the morning so Shorty could start clearing the bar to close. I blew out my spit valves and placed the cornet back on the stand, as Chick laid his D'Aquisto lovingly back in the velveteen compartment of the hard-shell guitar case.

Shorty crooked a gnarled finger at me. I walked over to the bar.

"See that kid sitting over in the corner?" he said, pointing toward a shadowy figure across the bar.

"Sure."

"He came in about a half hour ago, asking after you."

"What does he want?"

"Didn't say. He seems a little . . . you know."

He waggled his hand back and forth.

"Well, let's see what he's after," I said.

I fished a Dixie out of the beer tank and tossed the cap in the trash on the way to the visitor's table.

He saw me coming and stood to greet me. He was in his early thirties, about six feet tall, thin as a rail, and dressed like he put a lot of time into thinking about it. A real slave to fashion. He had a hundred-dollar haircut working hard to look rumpled, and couple of rings on each hand. His nails were manicured and polished. He wore thin eyeglasses.

"Mr. Gallegher?" he asked, as I shook his hand. His voice was distinctly southern, with an erudite, almost feminine lilt I'd heard often in the home decorating shows on television.

"Yes. What can I do for you?"

He gestured for me to sit, so I did.

He pulled a card from a chrome metal case he carried in his pocket and handed it across the table to me. It read *Ross Duncan, Antiques*, with an address in the Garden District. I pocketed the card.

"Something I can help you with, Mr. Duncan?"

"I'm not sure. I'm a friend . . . a *special* friend, of Cabby Jacks."

"I know Cabby. How's he doing?"

"I haven't heard from him for about a week. I think, maybe, something's happened to him."

"Like what?"

"I don't know. Cabby and I have known each other for almost a year. We met at a party down on the Riverwalk. He's a sweet guy, lots of fun, but he doesn't like to talk about his work. One thing he told me was that, if anything ever happened to him, I should look up a guy named Pat Gallegher at Holliday's in the French Quarter and you'd know what to do."

I took a sip of the beer and visualized the check Cabby had written me, now thumbtacked to a corkboard on my refrigerator upstairs. Was his sudden disappearance the realization of the fears that had led him to ask me to find him?

"Maybe he took off on business for a few days," I said. "Forgot to tell you where he was going."

"That isn't something he'd do. Like I said, we've gotten . . . well, *close*. He might not tell me what he was planning to do, but he would tell me if he wasn't going to be around for a while."

"When did you see him last?"

"Friday, a week ago. He showed up at my studio. I sell antiques. We made a date for dinner that night. He seemed all right when he left, but he never showed up later."

"And he hasn't called or anything since then?"

"Not a peep. I have to tell you, I'm a little worried."

The check notwithstanding, Cabby had exacted a promise from me. The money was immaterial. The promise was backed by my obligation to him for forcing my recovery from gambling addiction. I owed Cabby Jacks almost everything. Ross Duncan was calling in the marker.

"Where has Cabby been crashing lately?" I asked.

"He has an apartment about halfway down Bourbon Street."

"I suppose you have a key."

He blushed a little. "Yeah. I have a key."

"Have you been there?"

"I dropped by a day or so ago. I didn't see anything out of the ordinary."

"Maybe you didn't know what to look for."

"Maybe I didn't."

I breathed heavily. Following so closely on the heels of my scrape with the Anolli family, this Cabby Jacks situation sounded like the kind of oven I didn't want to stick my head into.

On the other hand, I did owe him.

"Give me the address and the key," I said. "I'll look around there tomorrow, see if there are any leads I can follow up. I'll also put out some feelers with other people who know Cabby. Maybe one of them has heard something."

He slid the key across the table to me.

"I appreciate this," he said. "I'm sure Cabby would, too."

CHAPTER FOUR

I GUESS SHORTY'S DEAL with Chick Kasay didn't include helping to shut down the bar for the night, because the kid lit out during my conversation with Ross Duncan. I helped Shorty close and fell into bed around four.

I had promised to meet Merlie at A Friend's Place at noon, so I set the alarm clock for nine. That gave me five hours of sleep on top of flying the wrong way across the country the day before, which made it damned hard to wake up.

I threw myself into the shower and nearly dozed off somewhere in the middle of washing my hair, but shook myself awake long enough to towel off, wander across the apartment, and fall back into bed.

I awoke again shortly before eleven, which gave me an hour to dress, grab a bite, and get to the shelter. Fortunately, I'm a rough-and-tumble sort of guy. I was up to the challenge.

I parked my dilapidated Pinto by the curb at A Friend's Place. It chugged on for a few seconds after I pulled out the key. I had lost count of the times it had rolled over the odometer. I figured it had done its duty several times in the course of its long and poorly-maintained life. I probably should have dumped it years ago, but I couldn't see shelling out almost twenty large for some new over-engineered piece of crap when I could continue to set the points and gap the plugs every couple of years on the Explode-A-Ford until it wheezed itself into scrap.

As always, there were three or four kids lounging on the deep, shady gallery of the shelter, some of them plugged in to music players, the rest staring off into space. The kids who wound up there tended to arrive with a ton of heavy baggage and not a great wealth of options. Sometimes it was a chore for them to see farther than the next meal.

I didn't recognize any of them. That's not unusual. The maximum stay at the shelter, except in the most extraordinary circumstances, is only two weeks. The roster in the place had probably rotated a couple of times since my last visit.

Shelley, the counselor who had stuck it out with Merlie the longest, was working on some charts in the front room when I opened the screen door. She glanced at the clock over the fireplace mantel and shook her head. It was a quarter after twelve.

"Why she puts up with you . . ." she said.

I was fairly certain she was joking.

"I'm jet lagged," I said. "She's lucky I made it at all."

"Can you keep a secret?"

"No."

"I'll tell you anyway. She came in a half-hour late this morning. If she gives you any shit, you can hit her with that."

"They're going to love you at the unemployment office," I said. I pointed toward the parlor French doors that Merlie used to shut out the world when she needed time to think.

"She's in there." Shelley said. I shot her the okay signal.

Merlie was sitting at her desk. Her eyes were closed. She snored softly. I cleared my throat. Her eyes snapped open and her head jerked up.

"Damn," she said. "I can't believe you caught me dozing."

"For what it's worth, I'm fifteen minutes late."

"I'm happy you're here. I could use a diversion."

She pulled herself from her chair and came around her desk to lay a quick kiss on me.

"How'd it work out with Chick last night?"

"He's talented. He's also inquisitive."

"He wanted a peek under your cape?"

"Something like that. I blew him off. I think Shorty's been filling the youth's head with tall tales."

"Sweetie, they ain't tall if they're true."

"Speaking of which, I believe you wanted me to do a little sleuthing?"

She turned and grabbed a folder from her desk.

"Have a seat," she said. I dropped into one of the two seats in the office and gave her my *all ears* look.

"The girl's name is Audrey Sharp. She's thirteen."

"Tough age."

"And how. She's had it tougher than most. Parents are divorced. Her mom's nowhere to be found. Took off for parts unknown years ago. Dad's not much better, but at least he's been around for most of her life, when she wasn't shuffled off to relatives."

"Ping-pong kid."

"You got it, Ace."

"Why does she need surgery?"

"She has some floating cartilage in her knee. It interferes with walking great distances. Otherwise, she's healthy as a horse and cute as a button. She needs arthroscopic surgery to clear away the cartilage and restore full movement in her knee."

"Preferably with her father's permission, to keep social services

21

out of the picture."

"Yes."

"Do we know anything about Dad?"

"Not a lot. I have his name and approximate age. Audrey knows what his last semi-permanent address was, but otherwise she's a little light on information."

"Does she know her mother's name?"

"Yes."

"So, how did our little waif end up here?"

"The usual. Some kind-hearted individual found her dumpster-diving for dinner and brought her to me."

"No fair," I said.

A couple years earlier, I had found a young girl named Louise Onizuki scrounging in the trash behind Holliday's for food. I had brought her to A Friend's Place on the recommendation of my friend, Father D'Agostino. That was how I met Merlie.

"There are a number of ways to do this," I said. "As it happens, I have something else I need to handle. It came up last night. An old friend has gone missing. His boyfriend wants me to find out what happened."

"Is it dangerous?"

"Does it matter?"

She took on an expression I hate—the one that seems chiding and judgmental at the same time.

"I promised I'd do this if he disappeared," I said. "This guy got me started going to meetings, and he kept me going when I got weak. I owe him."

"I suppose you'd still do it even if you didn't."

"Yes. I probably would. I'll find Audrey's lost dad, too. Under the circumstances, I should probably look at doing it the fast way."

"Which is?"

"You don't want to ask questions like that," I said.

CHAPTER FIVE

*A*UDREY SHARP WAS thirteen years old and thirty years shopworn. She had all the makings of a beauty, if the streets or some predator didn't intervene while she was waiting to grow a little more. She was slight, only a little over five feet tall. I could tell she'd grow some more. She was coltish, all legs and arms and hair, but she had deep blue eyes and full lips and an expression on her face that belied her youth.

"When did you see your father last?" I asked.

"About a month ago. He left me with my aunt, but I don't think she's really my aunt. I think she's just this woman he dated once who told him she liked me."

"Why aren't you still with her?"

"She's a bitch."

I tried to look unconditionally accepting and non-judgmental, the way they taught me when I was in graduate school learning to be a psychologist.

"What kind of work does your father do?" I asked.

"I'm not sure. I think he builds things."

"Like in construction?"

"I think. He's never taken me to work with him. I remember he had a hard hat in the back seat of his station wagon and some boxes of equipment."

"Do you know what kind of car he drives?"

"It's blue."

I nodded sagely, as if she had provided me with the Rosetta Stone to her entire life. An idea occurred to me.

"Do you have any health insurance?" I asked. "You know, in case you get hurt or something?"

Her eyes brightened.

"Yes! Dad gave me a card to keep in my wallet, in case I ever had to go to the hospital."

"Can I see it?"

She looked at the floor. "I . . . I left it."

"Left it?"

"At Carly's house."

"Who's Carly?"

"My aunt who probably isn't my aunt."

"Do you know where she lives?"

Audrey's eyes clouded over.

"What is it?" I asked.

"You aren't going to make me go back there, are you? She's mean to me. I don't want to live with her again."

I glanced over at Merlie. She shook her head gently.

"I'm not going to make you do a thing you don't want to do," I said. "Where you go and who you live with isn't up to me. I was thinking this Carly woman might know where I can find your dad."

She bit her lower lip while she wrestled with the decision. I tried to give her my trustworthy face, the one I used on the IRS when they audited me.

"Okay," she said, after mulling it over.

24

She wrote the address down on a notepad Merlie placed in front of her and wrote the name *Carly McKee* underneath it.

"Tell you what," I said. "How about I drop by and talk with Carly, maybe see if she has any idea where I can find your father?"

The address Audrey gave me for Carly McKee was north of the French Quarter, near the interstate highway. It was in entirely the opposite direction from Cabby's place on Bourbon Street. I did a little moral triage. Cabby was missing, and Audrey's knee could wait.

I parked my Pinto in the lot behind Irene's Cuisine and walked up Bourbon until I found the house.

Cabby's place looked as if a set straight out of a production of *Streetcar Named Desire* had undergone gentrification. It was a cluster of apartments situated around a courtyard that had been carefully tended and restored to antebellum grandeur. The center of the courtyard sported an elegant wrought-iron table and set of chairs. Someone had placed Cinzano umbrellas strategically around the perimeter of the terrazzo, under which stylish young men lounged in rattan chaises, reading books and chatting.

A couple of them ogled me as I walked through the gate. I don't go that way, but it was nice to know I still had it.

I quickly found Cabby's apartment number on one of the stairway posts and shambled up the steps to a landing overlooking the courtyard. When I looked down, a couple dozen eyes looked back up as I opened the front door to Cabby's home with the key Ross Duncan had given me.

I don't know what I had expected, but given what I knew about Cabby it took me a few moments to adjust to his apartment. While, like many of the pre-war pensions in the French Quarter, the exterior of the building had a sort of chic shabbiness attached to it, Cabby's apartment looked like it had been prepared for a *Southern Living* cover shoot.

Someone had put a lot of effort into the décor and the design. The walls had been painted in faux stonework, and false windows had been installed high on the twelve-foot walls. The furniture was custom-built to fit the space. What wasn't built to suit consisted of fine antiques which I imagined might have found their way to Cabby's apartment by way of Ross Duncan's studio. This hardly seemed the haunts of an ex-con, but I guess people can change.

Change, I reminded myself, was the foundation of Gamblers' Anonymous, to which both Cabby and I owed much of our lives.

I wandered through the digs. The kitchen was sanitary and well-appointed, right down to the gleaming copper cookware hung from a central rack over the island separating the range from a breakfast nook. The sink was empty. The dishwasher likewise. When I looked in the cabinets, the glasses and plates and cups and saucers were arranged with almost military precision. Everything shone as if it had been polished minutes earlier.

I made a mental note to ask Duncan whether he had tidied up when he had checked Cabby's place earlier in the week.

In the living room, Cabby had placed a forty-two-inch flat screen television right over the mantel. To the side of the fireplace was a teak glass-door cabinet containing an expensive stereo outfit, a DVD recorder-player, and a satellite receiver.

Behind the sofa was a roll top desk with ornate woodcarvings on either side of the framework supporting the tambour cover. It was finished in a red oak stain that made the wood grain pop like a 3D movie.

I tested the tambour cover, which gave way easily, sliding upward with barely a rattle, assisted by cleverly hidden counterweights in the back of the desk. I sat in the hardwood banker's chair and began rooting about in the various cubbies and drawers at the back of the desktop.

Like the rest of the house, the desk was neatly organized, with little clutter on the desktop. The drawers were arranged by intent— receipts in one, bankbooks in another, and one wide drawer holding three or four greeting cards. I opened one. It read: *Thinking of you– Ross*.

Rifling through other people's most personal stuff always makes me itchy. I placed the card back in the drawer, peeked under the desk blotter, and saw a piece of paper.

It said: *D. Nigra*, followed by a date. The date was the previous Friday. Ross Duncan had told me Cabby had missed their dinner date that Friday. Had he missed it because he was meeting this person Nigra?

I stashed the slip of paper in my jacket pocket and continued looking through the cubbies. After exhausting them and finding nothing of any real interest, I started in on the desk drawers, beginning with the center one. I found a day planner. I riffled through it to the previous Friday's date and was rewarded with the words *D. Nigra, 6:34 pm*.

The time was interesting. It suggested something more than a casual meeting. It was more like a schedule, the kind you'd find at an airport or a train station. Perhaps Cabby was supposed to meet Nigra's plane.

Maybe someone else met them, too.

I was interrupted by a cough at the door. I quickly placed the day planner on the desktop as I turned. A man stood in the doorway, staring at me. He held a wicked-looking pump shotgun and an even nastier scowl on his face.

CHAPTER SIX

"**Y**OU WANT TO keep your hands where I can see them," he said.

"No problem."

The man was in his early sixties, with a slight paunch and jowly cheeks crisscrossed by burst capillaries. He sported a thick salt-and-pepper moustache and gold wire-rim glasses. His hair was cropped short, but clearly styled with considerable effort and attention. He wore a lavender tee shirt and tight jeans.

"My name is Gallegher," I said. "I've been asked by Ross Duncan to look for Cabby Jacks. Duncan gave me Cabby's key."

"What are you, some kind of detective?" the man said.

"Not exactly. Sometimes I help people who don't think they can turn to anyone else. It's sort of a hobby gone bad."

"Why are you looking for Jacks?"

"He's missing. Has been for over a week."

"So why didn't Duncan call the cops?"

"It's complicated. I kind of promised Cabby I'd look for him if he ever disappeared. The cops would take a missing person report and pass it along to some overworked detective with five other cases. I can give it my sole attention."

I didn't mention I was actually working two cases myself and it was only a little past one in the afternoon. Who knew what the evening might bring?

The man seemed to relax a little. He didn't lower the shotgun.

"Take out your wallet," he said. "Slowly."

I reached into my pants pocket and extracted my billfold. I held it up for him to see.

"Toss it over this way."

I shrugged and flung the wallet across the floor. The guy grasped the shotgun by the pistol grip, his fingers on the trigger, as he knelt to pick up the wallet. He flipped it open and glanced at my driver's license, then back at me quickly.

"You live on Toulouse?"

"Above a bar called Holliday's."

"Says here your name's Roy Patrick Gallegher."

"Yes."

"And you say Ross Duncan told you to come up here and root around?"

"Not exactly. I asked him for the key. The rooting was my idea."

"You find anything?"

"Nothing substantial. Cabby's a friend of mine. I've only started looking for him. Maybe you can tell me a little bit about him."

"You keep talking about this Cabby fellow. Who in hell is he? Mr. Jacks' brother or something?"

I never imagined the entire world might not know Cabby by that name.

"That's what I call the guy who lives here," I said. "It's a nickname. I've never heard him called anything else."

"His real name is Brian. Brian Jacks."

"Okay. What can you tell me about Brian?"

"Don't know whether I ought to be telling you anything at all,

Gallegher. Maybe I ought to call the police on you."

"Before you do," I said, holding up Ross Duncan's card, "maybe you should call Ross Duncan. He can explain."

"Oh, I will, all right. Might call the cops anyway."

"Then call the Rampart Station. A detective there, guy named Farley Nuckolls, knows who I am. We've worked together before."

"You said you aren't a cop."

"I'm not. I consult with them sometimes. Would you at least not point that cannon at me? It makes me nervous."

"Don't you worry yourself about this shotgun. I got your wallet and your ID here. I reckon you aren't going anywhere. You sit tight while I make a couple of calls."

He stepped out onto the landing and pulled a cell phone from his pants pocket. I heard him make a couple of calls. When he was done, he stepped back inside. I was relieved to see him hold the shotgun at trail arms.

"You done here?" he asked.

"For now."

He tossed my wallet back to me.

"Come on downstairs. Doesn't seem right to sit around a man's home talking about him when he isn't here."

I pocketed my wallet and followed him out onto the front landing. He waited as I carefully locked the front door, and then led me down the steps into the courtyard.

"My name's Cook," he said. "Tyler Cook. I own these buildings."

"You're the landlord."

"I suppose. Never thought about it that way. I know every boy who rents from me. In a way, they're like my sons. Their welfare is important to me. Here's my apartment. Let's step inside and discuss Brian Jacks."

His apartment was on the ground floor, facing the courtyard.

Many of the young men who had been sitting in the courtyard had vanished. Those who remained watched us carefully as I followed Cook into his apartment. I didn't dwell on what they imagined to be happening.

Cook's place was a lot like Cabby's. It was tastefully decorated, clean as an operating room, filled with pastel shades and expensive furnishings. Despite the occasional frills, the apartment decidedly lacked a woman's touch.

"Are all your tenants gay?" I asked.

"I suppose. Never gave it a lot of thought. Tea?"

"No thanks."

He stowed the shotgun in the cleaning closet.

"I was brewing a pot when one of the boys told me you were ransacking Brian's place. Probably way too strong by now."

He gestured for me to sit on the sofa and disappeared into the kitchen. I heard him open and close a drawer and a cabinet. After a couple of minutes, he reappeared with a large teacup on a saucer.

"I know Brian as Cabby," I said. "It's going to be hard to call him anything else."

"Understandable. Ross Duncan told me you could be trusted. Is Ross a friend of yours?"

"I met him for the first time last night."

"So he must have heard that from Brian."

"Stands to reason."

"Your Detective Nuckolls, on the other hand, seemed a little irritated when I called. He didn't seem happy to vouch for you."

"I don't suppose I could blame him."

"He said I should shoot you and call animal control."

I chuckled.

"I wasn't at all certain he was joking," Cook added.

"Farley and I have a complicated relationship."

"He did tell me whatever you said you were doing, it was probably true."

"It's nice to know he hasn't completely lost faith in me."

Cook sipped at the tea and placed the saucer down on a coaster.

"Brian has lived here for about a year," he said. "I've known him for, maybe, three years total. He was introduced to me at . . . a meeting."

I pulled my bronze three-year medallion—in Gamblers' Anonymous, it seemed a little risky to call it a 'chip'—from my pocket and showed it to him.

"Strange I've never seen you," I said.

"Not so strange," he said. "New Orleans is a gambling town. This would have been a seven-year medallion if I hadn't stumbled onto a riverboat a few years back. There are a lot of meetings. Besides, we might have attended the same meetings for a long time and we wouldn't recall each other. No reason to, I suppose. You're not exactly my type."

I pulled the slip of paper from my shirt pocket.

"I found this under Cabby's . . . Brian's desk blotter. It says 'D. Nigra' and '6:34 pm.' Does that mean anything to you?"

"Nope."

"He also had the same notation in a day planner in his desk, on the page for last Friday."

"Still doesn't ring a bell."

"You've never heard of anyone with the last name Nigra, I suppose."

"No."

"Any chance some of your tenants might have?"

"I don't know," Cook said. "I could ask around. You think Brian was meeting this person Nigra last Friday?"

"I can't say for certain. The time is peculiar. Who sets an

33

appointment for six-thirty-four?"

"Trains and airplanes do."

"I suppose it would be easy to find out whether there were any trains or airplanes scheduled to arrive at that time last Friday night. How has, um, Brian been as a tenant?"

"Hasn't given me a moment's difficulty," Cook said. "A model resident. He's also been helpful around the place. He maintains a lot of the plants out in the courtyard. Helps the boys moving in or moving out. Always happy to grant a favor."

"Does he have a lot of visitors?"

"No more than anyone else. In fact, now that I think of it, he doesn't have many at all. Ross Duncan I've seen a number of times. Before Ross there was another boy, but I can't recall his name."

"Maybe it was Nigra."

"I might forget the occasional Smith or Jones, but I'd recognize a name like Nigra."

I placed the slip of paper back in my pocket.

"At least I found a starting place," I said. "I know he was supposed to meet this Nigra person last Friday, on the night he disappeared. I know who and I know when. Now all I need is where."

"I do hope nothing's happened to Brian," Cook said. "That man has traveled a hard road. Things seemed to be turning right for him."

I stood to leave.

"It's been my experience," I told him, "that when things are turning right, you have to be most careful. I'll let you know if I find anything else."

CHAPTER SEVEN

I CALLED A GUY in my usual Gamblers Anonymous group who seems to know where every meeting is in town. He told me a church about two blocks from Cabby's apartment held a meeting twice a week. He gave me the telephone number of a woman named Emily Battaglia who ran the meeting.

It was mid-afternoon. I'd skipped breakfast to sleep in, so I ducked into a muffaletta shop to grab a sandwich and a beer. For those outside New Orleans, the muffaletta might be an unknown delight. Imagine an Italian loaf round, sliced in half and filled with ham, mustard, pickles, and a salad made from five or six different types of cured olives chopped and mixed with extra virgin olive oil and red wine vinegar. It's the heart attack you eat with your hands. I don't mind living dangerously, so I stuff back one or two every week. Each one probably cuts a week off my life expectancy. I don't care. I wasn't planning anything particularly exciting that week anyway.

I savored the sandwich, and then called Emily Battaglia while I sipped my beer. She answered on the third ring.

"You don't know me, Ms. Battaglia," I said after introducing myself, "but I attend the GA meeting at St. Anselm's on Decatur."

"You in crisis?"

"Thankfully, no. But one of your members might be. I'm trying to find a man named Cabby Jacks."

"You aren't a cop, are you?"

"I'm a musician."

"Oh," she said, in the way people do when they've heard something disquieting.

"You don't like musicians?"

"I remember who you are. I've heard of you."

"From Cabby?"

"No. Well, yes, partly. You're the guy who was all over the news last year. I saw you on TV and mentioned it to Cabby. He told me stuff about you."

I stifled a sigh. A year earlier, I had become temporarily famous during a major police case. My ugly face had been plastered on the front pages of the newspapers and on the six o'clock news. I was hoping people had forgotten. For most of the world, the case had gone unsolved. Only four people knew otherwise, and I was one of them.

"It was a temporary gig. I try to keep a low profile these days. You see Cabby a lot?"

"Sure. He's a regular, but you know we aren't supposed to talk about it. That's why they call it anonymous."

"I understand. Cabby may be in trouble. A friend of his has asked me to look for him."

"Gambling trouble?"

"Gone missing trouble. Maybe he's on a cruise to the Caribbean, blowing his life savings in the casino. Maybe it's worse. His friend is worried."

"But he didn't go to the police."

"The police would take a report, put out a BOLO, and file the papers, never to be seen again. I have a talent for finding people, and I'm motivated. Cabby and I go way back, all the way to Mookie Schneider's poker orgies in the Hilton. Cabby got me into the program. I owe him."

There was a long silence on the other end. I took the opportunity to drain my beer.

"How can I help?" she said, finally.

"How long has it been since Cabby hit a meeting?"

"About two weeks, but that's nothing new. Cabby attends several different meetings, different places. Sometimes he'd come to three meetings straight and then disappear for as much as a month. I don't worry about him. I know he's hardcore into his recovery. If he isn't coming to our meetings, I know he's going somewhere else."

"I don't want you to betray a confidence, but do you have a member with the last name Nigra?"

"I wouldn't tell you if we did, but I don't mind telling you we don't. I mean, not that I know of. Some people come and don't tell their last names. The anonymous thing again, you know. I never met anyone by that name at our meetings."

"Was Cabby close to anyone at the meetings? Was there anyone he hung out with more than others?"

"There's his sponsor."

"You have a name?"

"We've reached the limits of what I'm comfortable divulging, Mr. Gallegher. You obviously know Cabby, but I'm not interested in outing other members."

"Sure. I get it."

"I have your telephone number on my phone. I'll do this for you. I'll call Cabby's sponsor and see if he wants to talk with you. If he does, I'll give him your number. Have you ever been to one of our meetings?"

"It's a little far from my place," I said.

"We have one scheduled for tomorrow night. You want to drop by, you're welcome. If you give a testimony, maybe some of the other members will feel comfortable talking with you about Cabby."

Ross Duncan hadn't filed a police report, but that didn't stop me from doing so. I had little reason to believe going through usual channels would do any good, but I had a little more pull with some segments of the NOPD than your average bear.

Farley Nuckolls' office was in the Rampart Street Station, between the Ursuline Convent and the Iberville projects. I hesitated at the front door, wondering whether I dared to impose on our troubled truce so early after his return. I finally decided the worst thing he could do was throw me out.

The guy who'd covered desk sergeant duty the last time I'd been there had either died or retired. In his place was a black woman who smiled at me as I walked up.

"Help you?"

"I'm looking for Detective Nuckolls. He's been away for a while, and I don't know whether he has the same office he had before."

"He expecting you?"

"No."

She picked up the phone and punched in a couple of numbers.

"There's a man here to see you," she said.

"Yeah . . . . Tall . . . . Big . . . . Yep, Saints cap . . . . You sure you want me to tell him that?"

Her eyes widened a little, and she hung up the phone. "I'm a Christian woman. I am not interested in repeating what Detective Nuckolls said."

I started to thank her and walk away, but she held up a visitor's badge and slipped it across the desk. "Room twenty-seven. If I were you, I'd take a whip and a chair."

Farley was in the same office, after all. I clipped the badge to my jacket and walked down the hall. I found him standing with his back to the door, staring out the window. He didn't turn around when I walked into his office.

"Sea of Cortez," he said.

"Come again?"

"I spent the last year on personal leave, basking and fishing and drinking tequila in the Sea of Cortez."

"That's in Mexico, right?"

"The Baja Peninsula. Specifically, a small town called Todos Santos near La Paz. Rented a cottage about two blocks back from the water, because I'm a cop and I couldn't afford oceanfront. It's an artists' colony, of sorts. I even tried my hand at painting, since everybody else there painted. Discovered I don't have the soul of an artist. Some days I wonder whether I have any kind of soul at all anymore. What do you want, Gallegher?"

"A friend is missing."

"File a report."

"I'd kind of like him found."

"You're looking for him yourself?"

"You remember Cabby Jacks?"

Farley turned around and stuffed his hands in his pants pockets. "Short, wiry dick-smoker."

"Not especially politically correct, but yes."

"Ran him in a couple of times on vice charges a few years back over that floating poker game he helped run at the Hilton."

"He's the one."

Farley crossed the office, sat at his desk, and drummed his fingers on the blotter.

"What will get you out of my office fastest?" he said.

39

"You could tell me to leave."

"Never works. I kick you out, you always bounce back, like a bad reputation. What have you learned so far?"

"Cabby was supposed to meet his partner, a fellow named Ross Duncan, for dinner Friday before last. He never showed. His landlord, the guy you talked with earlier . . ."

"Tyler Cook."

"Right. Cook hasn't seen him for a couple of weeks. Cabby last attended a GA meeting about two weeks ago. I'm waiting to hear from his sponsor. I found a slip of paper under Cabby's desk blotter and a notation in his appointment book for the Friday he disappeared, at 6:34."

"Morning or evening?"

"Duncan saw him that afternoon, so I'm figuring it was evening. The notation included a name. D. Nigra."

"Dee, like in Sandra Dee?"

"No. Just the initial. There may be some connection between Cabby's disappearance and this D. Nigra character. It occurred to me Nigra might have a jacket."

Farley turned to the computer and tapped a few keys.

"I got two Nigras in the system. One's been dead for five years. You didn't have anything to do with that, didja? No, reckon not. The other is in the state prison up in Avoyelles. Has been for twenty years and will be for another eight to ten. Other than those, I got nothing. You want my advice?"

"Sure."

"File a missing person report. You do, the next time you wander into my office I can pretend I'm doing my job."

"Um, there's something else."

He laced his fingers in front of his chest and glowered at me.

"There always is."

"Merlie has a kid at her shelter who needs a knee operation. We'd prefer to keep her out of the system. I'm trying to find her father to give consent. He's been AWOL for a while. Might be incarcerated somewhere."

"What's his name?"

"Garry Sharp. Two 'r's in Garry. He's around forty."

Farley checked the computer again. "Nothing here but a couple of outstanding parking citations. I have a last address."

He read off the address I had for Carly McKee.

"His girlfriend's place. I'm going to meet with her next."

"Got a little warning I'd like to pass on," Farley said.

"Okay."

"I learned a little more about your escapades before you flew off to the coast. There are a few bent-nose types around town who are not happy with you. Apparently, you have information that could inconvenience them. Got a call from our obnoxious buddy in Baton Rouge, looking for you."

"Boulware?"

"Yeah."

Chester Boulware was an agent with the Organized Crime Division of the DOJ. He was a major pain in the ass with a badge that allowed him to fuck with anyone he chose. Abusing privilege was his favorite hobby.

"If memory serves," Farley said, "last time you hooked up with Boulware was over in the Atchafalaya Basin, where he took a couple of loads of double-ought in the vest. Put him on the injured list for a month."

"I recall. On the other hand, we got the girl back."

"I suspect Boulware keeps a different sort of win-loss tally than the rest of us. He's more likely to remember getting sixty percent disability pay for a month. If he holds a grudge, your mob acquaintances may be the least of your problems."

"Thanks for the tip."

"All part of the service. Now blow. I got police work to do."

CHAPTER EIGHT

*I*T WAS LATE in the day. I didn't want to face Merlie without having at least made a stab at finding Garry Sharp, so I headed across town to have a conversation with Carly McKee.

I was on the I-610 loop headed toward Metairie, trying vainly to avoid the rush hour traffic, when my cell phone buzzed. I was in-between exits and couldn't pull over, so I risked a ticket and answered it. It was Albert Somerville, Cabby's GA sponsor. He had one of those magnolia-dripping voices you hear in a lot of 1930s movies, where every word gets an extra syllable or two.

"Emily Battaglia gave me your number," he said. "Is Cabby in some kind of trouble?"

"Thanks for calling. I'm in the program myself. I know how you want to respect his privacy, but Cabby has been missing for over a week. I was hoping you might be able to help me figure out where he's gone."

"Gosh, Mr. Gallegher, I don't have a clue. Fact is, I haven't spoken with Cabby in over a month. He's been doing great on his recovery. Hasn't had a lapse in over a year."

In recovery lingo, a 'lapse' is when you're tempted to gamble, or drink, or do drugs, or have sex, or whatever your program is supposed to prevent. A 'relapse' is when you actually do it. Lapses are the reason you need a sponsor. A relapse will cost you your recovery medallion. You'd have to start the whole process all over.

"I'm glad to hear it. Doesn't explain why he's missing."

"Mind if I ask why you're looking for him? I mean, isn't this a matter for the cops?"

I was getting tired of this question. I explained my relationship with Cabby again.

"I think he might have been afraid something might happen to him," I said. "About six months ago he hired me on a retainer to look for him if he were to disappear."

"You're some kind of detective?"

"Sans portfolio. Let's say I'm not without experience in this sort of thing. You're his sponsor. I'm sure you know a little about his history."

"I know he's an ex-con."

"That's part of it. In the old days, before he got in the program, Cabby ran in a crowd in the employ of a crime family here in New Orleans name of Anolli."

"I heard of them. Wasn't one of them killed in a shootout a couple of weeks ago?"

"Yes," I said. Strange how life kept conspiring to remind me. "They aren't terribly powerful anymore, but that doesn't mean they aren't dangerous. Cabby's been out of the life for quite a while, but when he hired me he implied he was engaged in some kind of enterprise you couldn't call one hundred percent legal."

"You think you ought to be telling me this stuff? Seems like it's part of the man's private life."

"Normally, you'd never hear any of this from me. Cabby's missing, and he trusts me to find him. I've resigned myself to divulging information about him I'd usually keep close to the vest.

I don't know what he was involved in, but it obviously posed some risk to him or he wouldn't have taken the precaution of hiring me. Tell me, do you know anyone named Nigra?"

There was a brief silence on the other end. Then Somerville said, "Doesn't ring a bell."

"As far as you know, there aren't any members of your GA group by that name?"

"No. I'd recall a name like that. Kind of a strange name. Who is this Nigra person?"

"I don't know. Cabby had the name and a time in his appointment book for the night he disappeared. It might be important. It might not. Can't tell until I know who he . . . or she . . . is."

"You know," Somerville said. "I'm Cabby's sponsor, but I'm not the only person he hangs with at the meetings. He tends to spend a lot of time talking with one or two other regulars. Maybe they know what he's been doing outside the group."

"Do you know how to contact them?"

"I bet both of them will be at the meeting tomorrow night. You say you're in recovery?"

"Yeah. I usually attend the meetings over at St. Anselm's."

"I been there. Nice group. Great cookies. Why don't you drop by our group meeting tomorrow night? If Cabby's friends are there, I'll introduce you. Maybe they can tell you something I can't."

It was the second invitation to the meeting I'd received in three hours. It felt like a good time to exercise Gallegher's Rule Number Seven. *When a door opens, walk through.*

"Sounds like a good idea," I said. "I'll be the big guy wearing a Saints cap."

Carly McKee lived in a post-war rambler on a quiet street a few hundred yards outside the Metairie city limits. The red bricks had wear spaces in the mortar and there were missing shingles on the roof. There was an eight-foot, square, plate glass picture window beside the front door, but the rest of the windows were short, rectangular jobs situated high on the walls, and looked as if they cranked out from inside. There was a carport on one side of the house, walled in painted plywood. I could see an old Toyota Camry four-door parked there. According to Audrey, Garry Sharp drove a station wagon.

I parked on the street and walked up to the door. I only needed to ring once before the door opened.

Carly McKee wasn't half-bad-looking if she was over forty. If she was younger, the world had not been kind to her. She wore a faded chambray shirt over a tank top and cutoff jean shorts frayed at the thighs. She was barefoot. Her toenails were painted four different colors of chipped polish, which I'd noticed was sort of a fashion that year. For the life of me, I never understood why, but I've always been a bit of a stodge. She needed a new bleach job on her hair, judging by the half-inch dark roots. She wore three earrings in each ear and a nose stud only slightly smaller than a baby's fist. There was some kind of cheap Asian symbol tatted on her hand that she probably had been told meant "peace" or "love," but actually read "mu shu pork."

"Help you?" she asked, after looking me up and down a couple of times.

"Carly McKee?"

"The one and only. You aren't a process server, are you?"

"No."

"Good, one of those in a week is enough. What do you want?"

"I'm here about Audrey Sharp."

"Find her, did you?"

"Not exactly. I'm working for a shelter over in the Garden

District. She's been staying there the last several days."

"Social worker, then?"

"Me? No. I am, or was, a psychologist."

"Well, then, Audrey ought to keep you real busy Mr. . . . ."

"Gallegher. Pat Gallegher."

"You wanna come in, Pat Gallegher?"

There was more than a hint of seductiveness in her voice. I'm a tough guy. I can handle it.

"Sure."

She led me into the living room, which was surprisingly better kept than the exterior of the house. She noticed me looking around.

"The house is a rental," she said. "Asswipe landlord doesn't do shit about the outside. Doesn't mean I can't be comfortable inside. You thirsty? I got some fresh iced tea in the fridge."

I thanked her, and she disappeared around the corner.

"Make yourself at home," she called from the kitchen. I took a seat in a chintz-covered wing chair next to the picture window. There was a pile of mail accumulated on the table next to the door. I noticed a couple of bulk mail fundraising brochures from A Friend's Place in the stack. That explained how Audrey knew to run to Merlie's shelter.

One question answered.

Carly walked back into the living room and handed me a glass of tea that was already sweating. She placed a cork coaster on the table next to me.

"I suppose I should ask how Audrey's doing," she said.

"Mostly okay. I'm looking for her father. Audrey needs medical permission for some work on her knee."

"The old knee story, eh? Got her out of a lot of gym classes at school. I've always suspected it was a dodge, myself."

"Not according to the doctor she saw last week. Mind if I ask your relation to Audrey?"

"I don't mind. I have no relation to the little twerp at all, except that I bounced bones with her dad for a few months last year. Garry got a job outa town and couldn't take Audrey with him, so he asked if I'd look after her for a week or two. He left me a couple hundred dollars for food and stuff. That was two months ago. The money ran out about four weeks before Audrey did."

"When did she leave?"

"A week ago this past Monday."

"You didn't contact the police? File a runaway report?"

She took a sip of the tea and swirled the glass a little, tinkling ice against the glass.

"No," she said.

"Mind if I ask why?"

"First, I was glad to be shut of her. Kid was a pain in the ass. Second, I had no legal standing. Garry didn't leave me with any power of attorney for Audrey, or any guardianship papers. I took her to school and I fed her, but I had no legal responsibility for her. She takes off, I figure it's her business."

"When she left, did you try to contact her father?"

She snorted and scratched at her chin.

"You ask me," she said, "Garry wanted about as much to do with that girl as I did. I have a cell phone number for him. I called it a couple of times the night I found out Audrey had skipped, but it was out of service. He hasn't called to check on his daughter since two nights after he left her here. Like I said, that was two months ago. You think, if he was interested, he'd have made a little more of an effort."

"Unless something happened to him. Audrey says he's in the construction business."

"In a way. He doesn't actually build anything. He's a nondestructive engineer."

"I don't know what that is."

"Not completely sure I understand it, either. It has something to do with welding. The way Garry told it, back in the day if you wanted to check a welder's work, you had to actually cut it open to make sure the weld went all the way through the metal. That was destructive technology, and it was wasteful. Nowadays, there's this new x-ray and ultrasound equipment that can check the weld without destroying the work. Non-destructive testing, you see? That's what Garry does."

"Does he work with a company specializing in these kinds of jobs?"

"No. He's freelance. He hires onto a construction project and when the job's done he moves on to another one."

"What about the job he started two months ago?"

"It was a pipeline deal, down on the Gulf. I got a card in the kitchen. Hold on."

She handed me a card after she came back from the kitchen. It read "Holbrook Transport Systems," with an address in Algiers, across the Crescent City Bridge.

"You called them?" I asked.

"I tried. Didn't get far. Every time I phoned, I got one of those automated systems—punch one for information, punch two for billing, you know. I punched every number on the phone, never got up with a human. Finally thought fuck it. I didn't want to talk to them, either."

"Do you know what kind of work he was supposed to do for them?"

"Like I said, some kind of pipeline deal. Something to do with offshore oil drilling. Supposedly he was gonna check the welds in a pipeline headed to a refinery in Biloxi. From what he said, it was

49

gonna be a six, eight-month gig for him. Maybe longer. He said he'd get settled in a few weeks and then come by to get Audrey. Last I heard from him."

"Excuse me," I said, pulling a notepad from my pocket. I started to copy the information from the card.

"Keep it," Carly said. "I got no use for it. Audrey ain't coming back here. You can bet on that. After dumping his kid on me, I don't care whether I ever see her father again either, fuckin' deadbeat."

I pocketed the card.

"Audrey had a medical insurance card," I said. "It was in her billfold. She left it here when she ran away. I'd like to collect it, if you don't mind."

"You can take all her stuff. Come on, I'll show you her room."

I followed Carly down a dim hallway to a bedroom at the back of the house. Audrey's room, like the rest of the house I'd seen, was nicely furnished. There was a double bed with a bookcase headboard. The carpet was clean, and the room was as bright as you could expect from the narrow jalousie windows set inches down from the ceiling. Unlike a lot of teen rooms I'd seen over the years, there were no clothes lying on the floor or junk piled on the desk.

"I cleaned up the room after she left," Carly said. "She wasn't messy, but I like to keep things neater than she did. Her suitcase is in the closet."

She pulled a sliding door on the wall and yanked a faded hard-shell American Tourister suitcase from inside. In the age of rolling soft bags, I hadn't seen a case like hers in quite a while. About a quarter of the closet was filled with hanging clothes, which Carly pulled and began to pile on the bed, removing the hangers. She started folding the clothes.

As she packed the bag, I said, "So I take it you and Audrey didn't hit it off."

"She's okay, for a teenager," she said. "That's the problem. Teens are a pain. All whiny and argumentative, and they think they know everything. I got better things to do with my time than raise some other person's brat. I liked her father, up until he dumped his kid on me. Maybe I even hoped there might be some kind of future there, you know? I could put up with Audrey if there was some kind of payoff with Garry. He was gone a month, and I hadn't heard from him, I figured I was free to look around. Having a teenager I didn't whelp lying around the house was kind of a deal-breaker for the guys I met, except for one particular perv who hinted we ought to consider a three-way. He's probably still nursing the bruise I kicked into his backside tossing him out the door."

"I see."

She stopped packing the bag and took another look at me.

"What about you, Pat Gallegher? Looks like it would take some work to toss you out the door. You seeing anyone regular these days?"

"I am."

"Sorry to hear that. What's a psychologist make, anyway?"

"I wouldn't know. I haven't practiced in years. I feed myself playing a jazz cornet in a bar over in the French Quarter."

"How did get you involved with a runaway shelter in the Garden District?"

"The person I'm seeing? Director of the shelter. I help her out with some of the kids."

"Is it serious?"

"The poets have not yet devised language of sufficient beauty to describe our love."

She chewed absently at her left thumbnail. "So . . . um, tight then?"

I had to smile. The more I saw of Carly McKee, the more I

understood why Garry hadn't come back.

"The tightest," I assured her.

"What a shame. We could have some fun, you and me."

"Believe me, we couldn't."

She pulled some more folding clothes from the dresser.

"Here's the billfold," she said, handing it to me. I found the insurance card inside, along with some pictures. One showed Audrey with a man I presumed to be her father. He stood about five-nine. In the picture he wore a plaid flannel shirt, jeans, and a pair of work boots. His hair grew over his ears and was combed back, graying at the temples. He had a round moon face and nice smile. He and Audrey were sitting on a park bench in Washington Square, judging by the view in the background, which included The Cabildo Museum. They looked happy together.

I held up the picture.

"This is Garry Sharp?"

She glanced at it.

"Fuckin' deadbeat."

"Maybe you're being a little tough on him. Construction's a hard business," I said. "For all you know, he's been injured on the job. He might be lying in a hospital somewhere."

"I sure wish I had your faith in humanity, Gallegher."

I noticed—now that I was clearly unavailable—I had stopped being "Pat." I had a feeling Carly McKee's affections were as constant as a strobe light. She finished packing the suitcase. I hefted it and started back down the hall.

"If you find Garry, you tell him I kept all the receipts for the money I spent on the girl," Carly said. "I expect him to pay me back."

"I'll pass it along. Any message for Audrey?"

"No. I reckon she wouldn't expect any. She tell you much about me?"

"Mostly that she didn't consider you Mother of the Year material," I said, as I opened the front door and stepped back out onto the porch.

"Well, I reckon she might be decent judge of character, if nothing else," Carly said.

CHAPTER NINE

MERLIE AND I decided to eat in that night. It was my usual night off at Holliday's, so I was able to stay over. She made spaghetti at her place. I brought along a nice bottle of Valpolicella. As she cooked, I opened the wine. Then I told her about my visit with Carly McKee while I chopped veggies for the salad.

"She came on to you?"

"Modestly. I fended her off with my infinite devotion to you. She cooled quickly."

"Good. I am in no mood for a cat fight this week."

"Believe me, nothing would have happened even if you weren't in the picture. She'd have driven me back into the seminary. The woman is the poster child for celibacy. Given her personality, I can only think of one thing which might have attracted Garry Sharp to her."

"Being?"

"Desperation and easy accessibility."

"That's two things, dearest."

"But together they can add up to one major headache. Gonna go easy on the radishes. They give me gas."

"The last thing I want. What do you think about this job Garry took with the pipeline company?"

"Hard to say. According to Carly, the job could last for months. Maybe he's so tied up with it he lost track of time. I'll check with the company tomorrow, see if they know where he's currently working. More wine?"

"Absolutely."

"I have Audrey's clothes and stuff out in the trunk of my car. I can drive you over to the shelter tomorrow and give them to her. How much longer can she stay with you?"

"About a week. After that, I have to find another place for her."

"I should be able to track her father down long before then."

"Famous last words."

"Meaning?"

"When was the last time one of these gigs turned out easy?" she said. "I figured you'd have him by now. The longer he stays missing, the more I regret asking you to look for him. The fact that nobody has heard from him in weeks worries me. I might have involved you in something dangerous."

"I'll keep my head down."

The next morning, I drove out to the shelter with Merlie to deliver Audrey's suitcase.

She was sitting on the front porch and reading a magazine when I pulled up. She dropped the magazine and limped gingerly down the steps toward me as I opened the trunk to grab her case. Merlie headed into the house.

"Did you find him?" Audrey asked.

"Sorry, sweetie," I said. "Not yet. I got your things, though. Your knee bothering you?"

"It's bad today. I took a walk with a couple of the other kids last night. Stepped off the curb the wrong way and wrenched it. I guess I should have stayed home and watched TV."

"Probably best to stay off it today. Let's take this up to your room and make sure I got everything."

She led me inside. I gave Shelley the high sign and she waved back. Merlie was already in her office talking on the phone, but she paused to blow me a quick kiss. Audrey led me up the stairs to a room she shared with another girl. I dropped the suitcase on the bed and threw the latches. She checked the contents.

"Looks like everything's here," she said. "Oh. Except . . ."

"What? Did I forget something?"

"My Elmo," she said.

"Elmo?"

"It's a doll, sort of. It used to laugh and say things when you tickled it, but the motor broke or something. I've had it a long time, long as I can remember. If I'd known when I left that I wasn't coming back, I'd have brought him with me."

"I'm sorry," I said. "I didn't know. We packed everything in your room."

"It was under the bed," she said.

"I did get this." I held up the billfold with her health insurance card. "Maybe we should give it to Merlie for safekeeping."

"Good idea. So Carly didn't know where my dad is?"

"Not for certain. She did give me some information I can use to help find him. I'm going to check it out later this morning. And, tell you what. When I get a chance, I'll drop by Carly's again and pick up your Elmo."

"Gee, Mr. Gallegher, you're the best."

"If I were the best, honey, I wouldn't have missed it the first time. Let's head downstairs and give your wallet to Merlie, and I'll head out to look some more for your dad."

I dropped by my apartment for change of clothes before striking out to talk with the folks at Holbrook Transport Systems in Algiers. Holliday's doesn't open until happy hour, so the place was dim when I walked in and headed for the stairs to my second-level apartment. From the darkness in an alcove near the front door I heard a voice.

"Gallegher."

In my experience, voices from the dark tended to be followed by fists or brickbats, so I spun and dropped into a defensive crouch. The voice chuckled.

"You know how silly you look? If I wanted to hurt you, I'd have shot you without saying a word. Relax."

My eyes began to adjust to the dim light. I saw a large, broad figure sitting at one of the tables.

"Boulware? Who let you in?"

"I did. I have my ways."

"You can let yourself back out again. I have things to do."

"Indeed. That's exactly why I'm here."

I flipped a breaker box switch in the stairway and the room instantly flooded with light.

Chester Boulware was about my size, maybe six and a half feet tall. He favored the dress and mannerisms of a sports commentator. His hair was cut in a half-inch flattop butch cut, with the front waxed into a wall. He wore suits worth a month of my tips, and Maui Jim sunglasses everywhere he went, indoors or out. He reached up and lowered the shades as he looked me over.

"Gotta say it," he remarked. "I am more than a little surprised to discover you are still alive."

"I am easily underestimated."

The last time Boulware had been in Holliday's, I'd split his lip and flattened his nose, risking a visit to a federal prison. He didn't seem in the mood to return the favor, so I drew up a chair and sat across the table from him.

"You here for a reason, Boulware, besides jerking my chain?"

"I'm clearing up loose ends. There are a lot of them surrounding an incident a few weeks back involving bribery at the city Public Works Office."

"Nasty business," I said. "Read about it in the papers. Imagine. Corruption in New Orleans. Boggles the imagination."

"You've been out of town ever since."

"Vacation. My lady love and I decided to visit San Francisco."

"Maybe you should have stayed there."

"You are not the first to make the suggestion."

"I talked with a woman named Shirley Wheems. Know her?"

Shirley Wheems had been a secretary at the office of Safety and Permits.

"Know her? No."

"But you've met."

"I'm in the hospitality business here. I meet a lot of people. Our paths might have crossed."

"Miss Wheems distinctly remembers seeing two gentlemen who bear a strong resemblance to you and that nutcase Scat Boudreaux in her boss's office not long before he got chucked out a window."

There were a lot of things you could say about Scat. "Nutcase" adequately summed them up.

"Some coincidence."

"It is. Look Gallegher, there are going to be a lot of heads rolling downtown once this deal is all sorted out. You can bet the city has no interest in involving some slacker jazz trumpeter and a whack job 'Nam vet in the narrative. You get a pass on this one, much as I hate to say it."

"I play a cornet, not a trumpet."

"Details."

"Not admitting anything, but why are you here then?"

"I have a vacation coming up. Don't want it to be interrupted by petty civic corruption bullshit. I want to wipe my plate clean of this one. You could make my life infinitely more convenient if you could fill in some blanks. If you turn state's evidence, I can promise you federal protection until the trials are finished."

"Protection."

"If we're going to wrap this case up tight, we need help. In return we'll keep the bad guys from doing some serious zippage on your ass."

I stood, walked over to the bar, and pulled a cold Dixie from the beer cooler.

"Get me one too," Boulware called out.

"You're on the clock."

"Fuck it. I'm federal. I don't give a damn. Don't have to."

I grabbed another bottle and returned to the table. We ceremoniously clinked the longnecks, and each took a sip.

"Let's say I know something," I said. "How are you going to keep the gangs off my back?"

"We could do a relocation until the trial."

"Won't flush. I'm in a relationship and she can't go along. Besides, I have a couple of things I'm wrapped up in right now. Looking for some people."

"Shit, dude. Back in town two days and you're already in trouble?"

"It's a gift. Maybe you can help with one of them. Maybe we can do some kind of trade. Have any dope on an outfit named Holbrook Transport Systems over in Algiers?"

"Not my territory, man. I can look into it."

"You ever run across a guy named Cabby Jacks?"

"Strike two."

"He was a gopher for Mookie Schneider."

"Schneider, I remember. Too low on the totem for us to worry about, but we knew about him. What about this Jacks guy?"

"I can't say much, because I don't know much. He's missing. Before he went missing, he hired me to find him."

"Wait. He hired you to find him *before* he disappeared?"

"About six months ago."

"Well, I'm only a dumb public servant stacking time on a federal pension, but that suggests to me some expectation on his part that badness might happen to him."

"Yeah."

"And he worked for the same people we're after?"

"A long time ago. I don't think he's involved with them anymore, but he did intimate he was working on some *sub rosa* shit. He didn't want to talk about it."

"Not good."

"The night he disappeared, he had some kind of appointment with someone named Nigra. The name mean anything to you?"

"I'm getting no hits today. I can look into it, if you have something worth trading. You know anything else?"

"Not a thing. I'm talking with some of his buddies in a twelve-step group tonight. I'm hoping they can send me in the right direction. Look, you know me. I try to keep a low profile. I enjoy playing music for a living. Every time I've aligned with law enforcement, it's turned out badly for someone, usually someone close to me. Let's say I know a thing or two about the bad business down at Public Works. Anything I do know I came across incidentally. Sometimes you stumble onto a piece of information, and along the way you unintentionally fall into someone else's garden party. Being there doesn't mean I have any understanding of the entire picture. What would it be worth if I could turn you on to a guy who was smack dab in the middle of the conspiracy? Someone who could give you names and dates and dollar amounts?"

He rolled the bottom of his beer bottle in the water ring on the table, as he stared me down. Then he said, "You can do this?"

"I think I can. Would that get you out of my life for a while? You wouldn't need me to testify. After all, I don't know anything first hand."

"I could live with that. Can you? If you know half what I think you know, giving me information is going to piss off some very nasty people. If they come gunning for you, you'll need more than Boudreaux to cover your ass," he said.

"Let me worry about that. What do you say?"

He shook his head. "Not so fast, Quickdraw. Show me your cards."

"You want a man named Gary Tate. He works as a record keeper in the Safety and Permits office. He actually handled the payoffs. He took off for Mexico, supposedly on vacation. Should be back any day now. Tate's a whiny little guy, a real Casper Milquetoast. You could turn him with a raised eyebrow. I think he'd jump at the chance for a little federal protection in return for telling you everything he knows."

"And what do you want in return for Tate?"

"I don't know what Cabby Jacks was involved in, but it was dangerous, and he had a history of mixing with people who consider the law a list of suggestions. If I discover he was mobbed up again, I may need some information."

Boulware drained his beer. "I could live with that arrangement."

CHAPTER TEN

MOPPING UP THE flood of troubles stemming from my life before I flew off to San Francisco was interfering with my new obligations. It was time to get back on the trail of Garry Sharp.

I paid my toll on the bridge and exited I-90 shortly into a densely-populated industrial park. The directions I'd written down before leaving Holliday's pointed me toward a cluster of prefabricated warehouses and truck farms, about a mile off the main highway.

I found Holbrook Transport Systems nestled between a small engine repair shop and a novelties distributor. It took me a few minutes to locate, as it was marked over the door by a screen-printed metal sign only slightly larger than a sheet of loose-leaf paper. Carly McKee had told me she had a hard time getting a human on the telephone when she called them. Apparently, they weren't actively trolling for visitors, either.

The front door opened into a waiting area about the size of a walk-in closet, at the end of which, behind a metal office desk, sat a woman about thirty years old. She had red hair and freckles and wore a pair of oversized glasses. She had one hand on top of the desk. The other was hidden underneath. A panic button? Sawed-off shotgun? The possibilities boggled.

Merlie had printed cards some months earlier that identified me as working with A Friend's Place. They were for occasions like this, when I might need some sort of bonafides to explain why I was nosing around. I handed the woman one of the cards.

"Okay," she said. "What can I do for you?"

"One of the kids at the shelter has some medical needs. I've been told her father is working for you on a pipeline project. He's a nondestructive examiner."

I tried to make the term roll of my tongue as if I actually understood completely what he did.

"I'm afraid I wouldn't be much help to you. I only answer phones and take messages. You'd need to speak with Mr. Holbrook."

"Is he in?"

"Sorry. He's almost never in. Fact is, I sometimes sit here for a week or more without seeing a single person. It's not like we get a lot of walk-in business."

"Know where I could find him? It's kind of important. Like I said, it's a medical issue regarding an employee's daughter."

Throughout our entire conversation, her hand had remained hidden under the desk. It was beginning to make me nervous.

"He's probably out at the worksite. He likes to keep a close eye on the projects."

"Perhaps I could contact him there."

"You might." She didn't elaborate.

"You know where I could do that?" I asked. The conversation was about as tedious as pulling porcupine quills from your hide. Either this girl behind the desk had no idea what Holbrook Transport Systems did, or she was being intentionally cagey.

She pulled out a printed sheet of paper from the top drawer of her desk.

"You know anything about oil pipelines?" she asked.

"Virtually nothing. Not my field."

"The pipeline begins at Port Fourchon, at the LOOP."

"Loop?"

"L-O-O-P. All caps. It's a centralized port for offloading oil and natural gas from the offshore rigs. Here." She circled an area on the map, on the Gulf of Mexico. Port Fourchon was to the east of New Orleans, near Gulfport. The pipeline on the map snaked along the coast, passing between New Orleans and the Gulf of Mexico. "One of the major oil processing companies is building a new refinery outside Biloxi. We've been awarded the contract to build a new twelve-inch pipeline from Port Fourchon to the refinery. They've been at it for a little over a year, with another year to go on the contract. As of three days ago, they were here." She circled another point on the map, about midway between Slidell and New Orleans. "They tend to lay about an eighth of a mile of pipe each day, so figure they're somewhere in this circle."

"Only about forty minutes from here, driving," I said. "That's convenient. Think I'll head out, see if I can find Mr. Holbrook on the work site. I suppose you can contact him by phone, let him know I'm on the way?"

"Oh, you can count on it. Mr. Holbrook doesn't care for surprises."

Using the map, it took me a little over an hour to locate the Holbrook worksite. They were on an island off Lake Catherine, near Bayou Platte. The place was essentially a huge mosquito farm with sandy soil that frequently gave way to marshes and bogs. There were a number of hand-painted signs along the sand-swept, two-lane blacktop running through the area that said simply "Holbrook," with arrows pointing through the trees. I took the third one I saw. It looked newest.

It placed me onto a rutted, oiled dirt road meandering through stands of moss-covered live oaks, cypress bogs, and brushy meadows. In several places, the road—if you could call it one—was washed by small creeks filled with black water, maybe three inches deep. At one point, I feared I might have lost my way, but then I saw another crudely painted "Holbrook" sign, pointing to my left.

Half a mile farther down this path, I broke through the trees into a clearing dotted with mobile office units and heavy equipment. Someone had posted a sign on one of the trailers that read "Supervisor," so I decided to start there.

I stepped out of the car. The humidity slapped me like a wet palm. A smell like rotting detritus mixed with diesel fumes burned my nostrils. A couple hundred yards away, a backhoe clawed at the soft, sandy soil, digging what looked like a trench that stretched off around a stand of trees.

I knocked on the door at the supervisor trailer and walked in before anyone could answer. A blast of cool air from an overworked window unit washed over my face. A man sitting at a desk inside glanced up at me as I closed the door behind me.

"I'm looking for Mr. Holbrook," I said.

"You Gallegher?" he asked.

I pulled another of the cards from my pocket and handed it to him. He read it carefully and placed it on his desktop before standing and extending his hand.

"Bob Holbrook. My girl in Algiers told me you might drop by."

"I'm sorry to disturb you, but I'm in a bit of time crunch. One of the kids at the shelter needs an operation. The doctors need permission from her dad. According to the dad's girlfriend, he's a contractor working on your pipeline."

"What's his name?"

"Garry Sharp."

"Sharp. Doesn't ring a bell. It probably wouldn't. The sign on this building says supervisor, but my primary duty is signing the checks. All the real hiring and firing is done by my foreman, Aldous Garlock."

"Even the contractors?"

"Sure. I'll be honest with you, Mr. Gallegher. I'm only on the job site one or two days a week. The rest of the time I'm off on the gulf on my boat fishing, or in the city. You were lucky to catch me here today. One of the benefits of owning the business. I can delegate the real work to my subordinates and let them do the heavy lifting while I enjoy the perks. Let me call him in, and we'll see if we can locate your fellow Sharp."

He keyed a walkie-talkie. Seconds later a tinny voice answered. "Yeah?"

"Al, there's a man here who is looking for one of our contractors. Could you come by the trailer?"

"Sure. Be there in five. Over."

Holbrook set the radio back on the table.

"You're building out in the boonies," I said. "I won't say this place is the middle of nowhere, but you can sure see it from here."

"It's economical," he said. "Land out here in Bayou Platte is only fit for predators and parasites. The soil is mostly sand, and the water table begins about six inches above ground. To reclaim this kind of land for houses or businesses would cost a fortune. Because it isn't worth anything to anyone else, the pipeline rights-of-way can be purchased for a song. The oil barons don't become immensely wealthy by wasting money."

"I see. By running the pipeline through marshes and snake

farms, I'd imagine you also don't have to deal with a lot of flak from environmentalists."

"You'd be wrong, there. Seems the more desolate some scorched piece of earth is, the more endangered it is to the tree huggers. Don't get me wrong, Gallegher. I like clean air and water as much as the next guy, but I don't consider quicksand to be wetlands. Fortunately, dealing with that sort of hassle is for people who make a lot more money than I do. They own the rights-of-way. I'm happy to let them deal with the environmentalists."

"Which company is that?"

"Kenzie Petroleum. They're building a new refinery in Biloxi."

"Yes, your secretary told me. She didn't mention the company."

Kenzie Petroleum had become a lightning rod for the left over the previous decade. Its owner, Kellen Kenzie, was a New Orleans native who had inherited the company from its founder, his father, about thirty years earlier. He had parlayed it into a multinational megacorporation. Kenzie had his fingers in tankers, offshore drilling, refining, and distribution to a chain of gas stations he owned. When it came to petroleum, the only part he hadn't played a role in was growing the trees and animals that cooked in the earth for millions of years to become oil. With money from his oil and gas empire, he'd branched out into broadcasting, movie theater chains, real estate, publishing, and even owned a couple of major league sports teams.

Beyond their business interests, Kellen Kenzie and his wife Claudine had become darlings of the far right, actively fighting anti-pollution legislation, battling environmental regulations, and opposing almost all attempts to provide education, healthcare, and even food to the poor. They stated openly that helping people less fortunate only fostered dependence, and it would be better for the poverty-stricken to die than it would be for them to live as slaves to the welfare state. Obviously, the poor had other opinions on the matter, but that didn't sway the Kenzies at all. It was well known that, besides their corporate interests, the Kenzies had invested heavily in several K Street lobbying agencies in Washington, D.C. It was widely believed they effectively owned two or three key senators, maybe a dozen members of Congress, and at least one Supreme Court justice."

Kellen Kenzie and his wife, in other words, were heavy hitters.

I didn't care one way or the other. Despite being shanghaied from time to time into the middle of other people's nightmares, I tend to live a sheltered and cocooned life, buffered from the geopolitical gravity that fascinates most of the world.

Many years ago, as a young psychologist, I'd had a colleague whose sister had Down Syndrome and an IQ of fifty, which put her in the severely mentally handicapped range. I talked about her with my colleague from time to time. At one point I asked whether her sister saw all the world events surrounding her with awe, or with confusion.

"She doesn't see them at all," my colleague had said. Those things are so far beyond her understanding, she disregards them entirely. They have nothing to do with her physical comfort or emotional happiness, so they aren't part of her world."

This was more or less the way I felt about the Kenzie family. They weren't part of my world. They existed in some Olympian realm far removed from my day-to-day experience. I didn't think of them at all, beyond what I read occasionally in the papers or in magazines. They might as well have been Martians.

"Big money," was all I said.

"Oh, yes. I don't have to like their politics or their morals. They make their payments on time, which means my employees and contractors get paid and I get to enjoy myself. The Kenzies' money spends as well as anyone else's. Let's face it. I'm in the pipeline business. You don't see a lot of environmentalists building pipelines. You go with the folks who pay for the groceries, right?"

"Sure," I said, as the door opened.

A man wearing a sleeveless T-shirt, filthy jeans, and a yellow hard hat stepped into the trailer. His face was leathery from years working in the hot sun and crisscrossed by deep crags and crevasses. His upper arms and shoulders were covered with hair almost thick enough to qualify as fur. He had maybe three days of beard growth, which only made him look angry and intimidating.

"Al Garlock, Pat Gallegher," Holbrook said. "Mr. Garlock is our site foreman. He actually runs the show here."

I grasped Garlock's extended hand. It was strong and calloused, a roughneck's hands. I could tell he could have crushed my hand with ease, but he only applied enough pressure to be respectful.

"I represent a runaway shelter for kids over in the Garden District," I said, showing Garlock another of my cards. He didn't take it, so I shoved it back into my pocket. "There's a child staying there whose father is a contract worker on this pipeline. The girl needs parental permission to get an operation on her knee. The director of the shelter has asked me to track down the father. His name's Garry Sharp. He's a nondestructive engineer."

Garlock glanced over at Holbrook, then took off his hard hat and wiped at his brow with a rag he pulled from his back pocket.

"Wish I could help you," he said. His voice was deep and coarse, like his features. He had a strong south Texas accent, the kind you'd expect from a movie cowboy or a beef commercial. "We had a guy by that name here, a few weeks back. He left one night and never came back. I had to hire a replacement for him a few days later. Got his equipment out in one of the trucks, if you want to take it with you."

"Wait," I said. "You say he was here, but he isn't anymore?"

"That's about the size of it. Can't say I'm happy about it, either. Walking off the job the way he did, he put us several days behind."

"How so?"

"You know what a nondestructive engineer does?"

"Something to do with welding."

"Sort of. Better if I show you. If it's okay with you, Mr. Holbrook."

"Sure," Holbrook said. "If it will help Gallegher here find the girl's father."

"Don't know if it will or won't," Garlock said. "You need a hard hat."

He pulled one from a rack in the trailer, handed it to me, and held the door open. I stuffed my Saints cap into my jacket pocket and donned the hard hat. He'd parked a four-wheel-drive truck in front of the trailer.

"It's about a half-mile," he said. "We could walk it, but it's quicker to take the truck."

I slid into the passenger side. Garlock took the wheel.

"We need four-by-fours out here," he said, as he swung the truck around. "Regular two-wheel drive will get bogged down in the sand. Like I said, Sharp was here. I hired him about three weeks before we started this stretch of the pipeline. The last guy before him was a drunk, only showed up for work half the time. Sharp seemed like a reliable type, sober and even a little educated. He did a good job for us for a couple of weeks, but then things began to go south."

"How do you mean?"

"Little things. He started to take twice as much time to inspect the work. He became argumentative. He rejected some completely acceptable work because it didn't meet *his* standards."

"Maybe he was a perfectionist," I offered.

"Maybe he was a pain in the ass. No offense intended, Mr.

Gallegher, but work like we do out here has hard deadlines. You miss the deadlines, you lose money. There are penalties. Mr. Holbrook pays me to keep the work on schedule. Anything that slows us down is a problem. Sharp started to slow us down."

"And then he left."

"Took off one night. Never came back. Left his rig and everything."

"That didn't seem suspicious to you?"

"Sure it did. I was more concerned about the job. Without an NDE on site, everything slows to a crawl. We can dig the trenches, for sure, but laying the pipe is another matter. No inspections means no pipe. I gave him a couple of days to come back, like I said, and then I processed his contract termination papers and hired another guy to take his place. Here we are."

He pulled the truck alongside another trailer, this one still attached to the trailer hitch on a huge diesel truck. The sign on this trailer read FOREMAN. Behind us, workmen wrestled a twelve-foot long length of cast iron pipe toward a four-foot deep trench.

"C'mon," Garlock said. "I'll show you what an NDE does."

He led me over to the trench. By the time we got there, the men had lowered the pipe into place. An enlarged flange on the back end of the pipe fit over the un-flanged end of the one before it. A man wearing a leather apron and gloves, who held a welding wand in one hand, slid down into the trench.

"Better look away," Garlock said. "Arc welders are brighter than looking at the sun. It'll blind you if you look it too closely."

I moved my gaze above the trench as the welder struck an arc and began welding the two pipes together. There was a sound like rapidly frying bacon. Sparks and smoke rose from the trench and, despite the fact I wasn't looking directly at it, the flare of the arc made me squint in the noonday sun.

He finished his work in a couple of minutes. After the welder climbed out of the trench, a truck backed up to it, and a man wearing blue coveralls and a blue hard hat jumped out. From the back of the truck he pulled several instruments. One of them looked like a huge horse shoe, only thicker. It was tethered to another machine in the back of the truck with several heavy-gauged wires, thick as battery cables.

I followed Garlock to the trench. He called out to the man in the blue coveralls as we approached.

"Wayne, hold up a minute."

Wayne had knelt down next to the pipe weld but looked up as Garlock called.

"Yeah? What's up?"

"Pat Gallegher, this is Wayne Falkner. He's our nondestructive engineer now. Wayne, Gallegher here's interested in what you do. Can you explain it?"

"I guess."

Wayne sat on the edge of the trench and pointed toward the recently joined pipe flange.

"Welding can be an inexact science," he said. "Too hot, and you can burn right through the work, or create pinholes that can lead to failure later. Too cold, and you don't get good penetration of the weld, which means the joint can fail later. Either possibility can mean digging up the pipe and fixing the weld, which costs a lot of money. You know what they say? Nobody seems to have time to do it right the first time, but they can always find time to fix it later. Well, with pipelines, it's better to do it right the first time around. I come behind the welder and inspect the joinery to make sure it meets standards."

"Who sets the standards?" I asked.

"ASME, the American Society of Mechanical Engineers,"

Wayne said. "A good weld is as strong as or stronger than the steel surrounding it. A bad weld is a problem waiting to happen. Was a time, some years back, when we'd have to cut through every ten pipe joints or so, to ensure the welds were fully penetrated. Cutting it destroyed the work piece. It slowed the pace of the job. What I do is every bit as effective, and we don't have to ruin the welder's fine work to do it."

"How exactly do you inspect it?" I asked.

"This is a portable digital X-ray unit," he said, holding up the U-shaped device. "I run it around the weld and it records an image on the computer up in the truck. A good weld won't show any voids. A bad weld will show gaps or bubbles in the metal. You want to back off a few meters here. I'm wearing lead shielding, so I'm safe. This thing could fry your junk if you got close enough."

Garlock and I retreated to his truck as Wayne examined the pipe. I could hear a faint buzz from the trench as he manipulated the X-ray wand around the pipe joint. He stood in the trench and waved us back over.

"It's okay. I've turned the unit off. Now, I take a look at the images on the computer."

He checked the screen, manipulating a touchpad to scroll through the picture of the weld.

"Kind of like a CAT scanner," I observed.

"Almost exactly," Wayne said. He reviewed the images, and then looked up. "Problem. Gimme a second."

He pulled another device from the equipment in the truck. This one looked like a microphone, again on a long, cabled tether. He climbed back down into the trench.

"Uh, need us to back up again?" I asked, a little concerned for my junk.

"No, no. This is an ultrasound wand. Completely safe. Relax."

He held the wand against the flange and slowly dragged it around the weld. This time he had taken his laptop computer into the trench with him. He watched the image on the screen carefully as he manipulated the wand against the cast iron. Then he shook his head.

"This is a fail," he said. "There are bubbles midway through the weld. We'll have to redo this joint."

"How do bubbles get in there," I asked.

"Contamination," Garlock said, before Wayne could answer. "The best welds are made in a vacuum. We don't live in a vacuum. When air gets incorporated into the joint, it gets trapped, creating bubbles. In the old days we used flux to keep the contaminating air out. These days we use carbon dioxide or some other kind of inert gas like argon injected through the welding gun. Sometimes it works, sometimes it doesn't."

"What happens when it doesn't?"

"We cut off the pipe right behind the joint and replace it with another one."

Garlock stepped away and gestured for his work gang to assemble. He explained the problem to them. A couple of the men groaned but didn't delay in getting to work. The welder climbed into the trench with a cutting torch and started to burn through the pipe to remove the faulty joint. Wayne started to replace his equipment in the back of his truck. I walked over to him.

"You've been on this job for how long?" I asked.

"About two weeks. No. Three weeks tomorrow."

"Do you live in the city?"

"Me? Lord no. I'm from Gulfport."

"You live on site here?"

"Yeah. We have several trailers back a mile or so. Some are for sleeping, some are for showering. We have a cook trailer that provides our food, and even a rec trailer with a TV and some video games."

"How often do you get home?"

"Maybe once a month. Sometimes less frequently."

"Know anything about the guy you replaced?"

"Nope. Sorry. Can't help you."

I hadn't heard him walk up, but suddenly Garlock was at my side.

"I told you I had Sharp's gear in a truck. I'll show it to you."

He shot a look at Wayne I couldn't completely figure out. It looked a little angry, but also a little scared. I wasn't sure what it meant, but I've studied human nature long enough to recognize when I had suddenly become unwelcome. It usually happened when I asked questions other people didn't want answered.

Garlock didn't look at me as he started the truck to drive back toward Holbrook's trailer.

"So, how did you like Garry Sharp?" I asked. "What kind of person was he?"

"He seemed okay. Kept to himself. He was good at his work. He didn't drink much, which is good on a crew like this. Fewer chances for accidents and injuries."

"Have you always worked on pipelines?"

"No," Garlock said. "Army Corps of Engineers. Twenty years in, building all sorts of shit in every armpit country on earth. I'd spend six months tossing up a bridge in some godforsaken jungleville, and the bad guys would blow it up six months later. I mustered out as soon as I could draw a pension. You ever try living on a military pension?"

"No."

"You can't. I lounged around for a while, drank a bunch, did some fishing, watched a lot of TV. Mostly I got bored. So, I took a job here and there, but I didn't fit at any of them. I only know how to do one thing, Gallegher. I build. So, I cast about looking for a job where I could build something."

"How's Holbrook to work for?"

"Holbrook's worthless, except when it comes time to sign checks. Wasn't for his wife, he'd be a beach bum somewhere."

"Who's his wife?"

"You don't know?"

"Wouldn't have asked if I did."

"He's Kellen Kenzie's son-in-law."

Garlock pulled into a complex of trailers clustered on the edge of the woods, surrounded by a number of trucks and cars, and shut down the truck.

"This is the crew quarters," he explained. "I put all of Garry Sharp's gear in the panel truck over there.

He pointed toward a yellow truck with a twelve-foot-long box on the back of it. It had clearly started life as a rental moving van.

"Which trailer did Sharp live in?" I asked.

Garlock pointed to the third one down from our position. "He was in Trailer Six."

"How many other people stay there?"

"We sleep six to a trailer."

"And where are the men who shared the trailer with him?"

"Three are back in the field, working. Two are gone."

"Gone?"

"One quit, one fired. They didn't like the conditions. The guy we fired was slacking off, not pulling his weight. The other didn't like working in the heat and humidity and spending the day fending off black flies and mosquitoes."

"Would it be possible to talk with the three men who are still working here?"

"Why?" Garlock asked.

"Because they lived with Sharp. They may know things. He might have told them he was leaving, or where he was going."

"We talked with all his bunkmates after he disappeared."

"But I didn't. I've had a lot of experience finding lost people and lost things. I've learned it's a lot better to know something than it is not to know it. I'd appreciate it if I could talk with those men."

Garlock rubbed at this chin. I could hear his palm rasp against the stiff bristles of his whiskers.

"I don't know," he said. "We lost three days replacing Sharp. We've been hauling ass to catch up. Pulling three guys off the line would push us back further."

"I don't have to see all three at once. One at a time will work."

"I'm inclined to say no. Fact is, you don't have any real legal standing here, Gallegher. I don't have to let you talk to anyone. Come to think of it, since this worksite is on the Kenzie Oil right of way, I could run you off for trespassing."

"Or, we could run it up the line and let Mr. Holbrook decide. That'd take you off the hook, wouldn't it, Boss Man?"

His eyes narrowed.

"What did you call me?"

"You heard me. I recognize your look. Between mustering out of the army and going to work for Holbrook, I'm betting you pulled a gig as a gun bull. You still stand around watching the guys work the trench line as if you were cradling a twelve-gauge in your arms."

"You need to watch what you say," he said. "Some of our workers have pulled time. They aren't partial to people who wore a badge, no matter how short a time or how long ago it was."

"None of my business, Boss Man," I said. "I only want to ask a few guys some questions. So, do we run it by Holbrook, or not?"

CHAPTER ELEVEN

MIKE NAVVO WAS the kind of guy who'd spent most of his life looking at a tiny piece of the sky from the bottom of a hole of poverty. He was wiry thin, with veins that popped on the back of his sunburned hands and his forearms like drinking straws under the skin. His pockmarked face framed ice-blue eyes. His hair had been shaved maybe two weeks earlier and had grown back to a quarter inch in length. Like a lot of the work gang on the Holbrook project, he wore a sleeveless t-shirt and overalls and thick-soled, steel-toed leather work boots. A sour smell rose from his body, as if he hadn't showered in two or three days. He had a lump in the side of his jaw from the wad of chewing tobacco he'd stuffed there right after taking a seat in Trailer Six.

"Nice to get out of the heat," he said, his voice dripping with Alabama or maybe the Ozarks. "Scorcher today out on the line."

I introduced myself and told him why I was there.

"Sure," he said. "I remember when Sharp took off. Four, five weeks ago, I reckon."

"How well did you know him?"

"Not so well. I mean, we bunked here in the same trailer, but we didn't talk a whole bunch. He tended to keep to himself. Read a lot."

"What did he read?"

"Hell, mister, I don't know. Books. Not much of a reader myself. I kind of wish I'd spent a little more time at it in school."

"How was he right before he left?"

"How do you mean?" Navvo asked.

"Did he seem worried about anything, or agitated?"

"Well, now you mention it, he did seem kinda out of sorts. I recall he got into it a coupla times with Mr. Garlock."

"Got into it? You mean they argued?"

"Oh, yeah. They argued. At one point it looked like they was gonna throw down right there on the line."

"What did they argue about?"

"Can't rightly say. Gets noisy out there, what with the backhoe and the bulldozers. I do recall, the day before he took off, I saw him and Mr. Garlock out on the line. Garry was waving his arms around like a wild man and pointing toward the truck he used. Mr. Garlock looked like he was fit to bust. His face got all red, and I thought he was gonna blow a blood vessel—not that I would have minded."

Garlock hadn't mentioned this. I made a mental note to ask him about it.

"Did Sharp stay on the worksite the entire time he was here, or did he go into the city at all?"

"Well, we all get two days off a week. There's a van we can use to go into the city if we want to, but it's a long haul. I do seem to recall he went off site once or twice. One of them, I think he was gone overnight."

"Did he talk about anything he did in the city?"

"Naw. Like I said, he was pretty close-mouthed. He didn't talk about much of anything, at least not to me."

• • •

"Sure, I remember Sharp," Stu Stuyvesant said. He was like the Mutt to Mike Navvo's Jeff. He was a short, thick man with a moon face and squashed black eyes set deep into his skull. He had a thick red mustache and stringy limp hair matted with sweat on his forehead. "Quiet guy. Didn't mix well with the rest of the men here in the bunk."

"How's that?"

"Look at us, man. We're a bunch of roughnecks. Most of us didn't finish high school. I didn't get past tenth grade. Ain't a one of us ever gonna have two nickels to rub together for more than a day. Sharp had education. He'd gone to college, always had his nose buried in some damn book or another."

"What kinds of books?"

"Here, he gimme one of them before he took off."

Stuyvesant crossed to his bunk and pulled a tattered paperback from the rack next to it. He showed it to me. It was a science fiction novel by some author I'd never read.

"Only got a little way into it," Stuyvesant said. "Seems fun enough, but they use a lot of words I don't understand."

"I heard Sharp and Garlock didn't get along," I said.

"Hell, Garlock don't like anyone. He's the foreman. On a job like this, he's the man. Don't pay for the foreman to get friendly with the line workers. I'd like to be a foreman one day. They make a lot more money."

"I heard about a particular argument between Sharp and Garlock out at the worksite. From what I heard, they both got hot under the collar."

"Yeah, I recall that. About two days before Sharp took off. Got no idea what it was about. They was both steamed, that's a fact."

"So Sharp didn't talk about it later, here in the trailer."

"No. I could tell he was upset. He looked like he wasn't ready to

81

let go of whatever it was, but he didn't talk about it to anyone far as I know. Like I said, he kept mostly to himself. Strange sort of guy."

"How so?"

"He not only read a lot, he also wrote a bunch. He wrote every night in this notebook he kept in his gear. Sometimes he'd write a page at a time. I glanced at it once when he didn't know I was looking. There was some math and a lot of figures I didn't recognize. I do recall there was a drawing on one page."

"A drawing?"

"Yeah. He drew one of the flange attachments, like we got out on the line. Now, how do you figure that? Guy looks at the damn things all day long and then he draws one in his notebook at night. You'd think he'd want to think about something else on his own time."

"And he didn't say anything about where he might be going before he left the last time?"

"Not to me. Wish I could help you, sir, but there wasn't much to know about Sharp."

Marshall Dinkins wiped at his face with a rag. He was almost my height, but rail-thin. His skin was the color of coal and his arms were ashen from the sun. He opened a bottle of chilled water and took a long swig from it.

"I talked with Sharp once or twice," he said. "But we wasn't friends or nothing."

"Did he say anything to you about why he was leaving?"

"Nope. He was here one day, gone the next. I don't even recall when he left the camp. I remember it was hot as blazes, 'cause I got me a touch of heat exhaustion. I came back to the trailer, grabbed a shower to cool off, and hopped right into the rack without even eating supper. That's how tired I was. Don't even recall whether Sharp had come back to the trailer by then. When I woke up the next morning, his rack was empty. Didn't even look like he'd slept in it. I never saw him again."

"How'd he get along with the other guys here in the trailer?"

"Okay, I reckon. Don't think he was buddies with anyone. He wasn't unfriendly or nothin', but he didn't mix it up a lot neither. Tended to eat by himself, usually reading some book."

"Did you ever see him writing in a notebook at night?"

"Sure did, sir. I even asked him about it once. Know what he said? Sounds strange, but he said he was writing out his retirement account."

"What did he mean?"

"Damned if I know. He didn't let me look at the notebook, but he was sure intent on putting something down on paper."

"Was the notebook still here after he left?"

"Don't recall as it was. Damnedest thing. Guy ups and leaves, doesn't take his clothes or his fancy testing equipment, but he takes some cheap notebook. What do you make of that?"

"I have no idea," I said. "But I plan to find out. There were two other men living in the trailer at the time Sharp was here. Remember their names?"

"Sure. Truluck and Hines."

"Remember their first names?"

"As I recall, it was Will Truluck and Yancey Hines."

"I need contact information for Will Truluck and Yancey Hines," I told Bob Holbrook.

He didn't look happy. Al Garlock glowered at me from the corner of the room.

"I think we've been accommodating enough," Holbrook said. "I didn't have to let you talk with anyone here. Maybe it's time you left."

"A man's missing," I said. "His daughter needs him."

"I'm sympathetic," Holbrook said. "But there's a limit to sympathy. Garry Sharp took off without notice and left me in a bind. I have a deadline to meet with this pipeline. I'm not interested in taking time away from the work to deal with some missing malcontent."

That struck me oddly.

"Malcontent?" I said. "Could you explain that? Did Garry Sharp have any specific complaints he registered with you?"

Holbrook had his hands flat on the desk. He looked down at them and then began worrying at a hangnail.

"Perhaps I misspoke," he said. "An assumption. Guy takes off in the middle of the night and never comes back, you have to figure he isn't happy with the work."

"Hell of an assumption," I said. "He left his means of making a living behind. Doesn't that strike you as strange?"

"If I cared, it might. I have bigger concerns."

"Like not upsetting your parents-in-law by falling behind schedule?"

His ears reddened, and he drew in a quick breath. For a second, I worried he might go ballistic. Garlock fumed in the corner.

"Time for you to go, Gallegher," Holbrook said. "You've worn out your welcome here."

"C'mon," Garlock said. "I'll let you take Sharp's equipment. If you ever locate him, you can see he gets it."

"I don't think so," I said. "According to your friend Wayne out in the field, some of this equipment is radioactive. Between you and me, I think the trunk of a forty-year-old Pinto might not be the safest place for it. Besides, I have a feeling it's rather expensive gear. I don't feel comfortable taking responsibility for it. Why don't you continue to store it until I can locate Sharp?"

"To be honest with you, I don't want it lying around here," Holbrook said. "I might have to dump it."

"I'd check with the EPA first. I hear there are specific laws about disposing of radioactive materials. I like to think positively. I plan to find Garry Sharp. When I do he'll probably want his gear back. If I were you, I'd take good care of it."

"Show Gallegher to his car," Holbrook said.

"Wilco," Garlock said, and held the door of the trailer open. I walked down the steps toward my car. I was halfway there when Garlock tugged at my shoulder. I had half expected it. I grabbed his hand, spun on my pivot foot, and bent his wrist backwards, almost forcing him to his knees.

"What the fuck, man?" he growled.

"Grabbing me is a bad idea."

"Let go, damn it! I only wanted to know why you threw me under the bus in there."

I released his hand. He rubbed at his wrist.

"You some kind of tough guy?" he said.

"Yeah. I'm The King of Thugs."

"Well, you could have cost me my job. Not a lot of folks around here know about Holbrook and the Kenzies. He'll figure only one or two people could have told you."

"Sorry. He pissed me off. What did you and Sharp argue about out on the trench line the day before he left?"

"What?"

"Two people told me you and Sharp got into it with lots of arm waving and yelling at each other."

"Hell, I don't remember. It was weeks ago. I'm the foreman on this job. I yell at a lot of people. Sometimes they take it personal."

I walked over to the panel truck where Garlock had stored Sharp's gear.

"I'd like to take a look at his personal effects." I said.

"You said you didn't want that equipment."

"It's not the equipment I'm interested in. You have his clothes and books and stuff in there?"

"Sure."

"Can I look at them?"

"Will you leave and not come back if I let you?"

"I'll leave," I said. "Can't guarantee I'll stay away."

Garlock sighed and lifted the sliding tailgate to the panel truck. There were several boxes in the back labeled SHARP. Two of them held his nondestructive testing equipment. Remembering the potential radioactivity, I shied away from them. The third box held a military surplus duffel, a few pairs of shoes, and some books. I rummaged through it and found some more paperbacks, but I didn't see any notebook. As I searched the boxes, Garlock stared over my shoulder.

"You looking for something in particular?" he said.

"No," I lied. I checked the duffel, but found nothing inside but a lot of shirts, pants, socks, and underwear. To be thorough, I checked the shoes to see if anything had been stuffed into them. I came up empty.

Whatever Garry Sharp had been writing in the notebook, it was important enough for him to take it with him when he left, even as he abandoned all his other possessions.

"How often did Sharp go into the city while he was here?" I asked.

"Couldn't tell you. Don't know whether I would if I could. You're turning into a real burr under my saddle, Gallegher. I don't think our welcome mat applies to you anymore. Might be healthier for you to drive back to the city and stay away."

"Can't imagine why Garry Sharp might hightail it out of here,"

I said. "Seems like such a friendly place. Word of advice. I usually find the people I'm looking for. If you're involved in anything illegal, or if you had anything to do with Sharp's disappearance, you might want to come clean now."

I took one of my cards from my jacket pocket and wrote my cell phone number on it.

"If you have a change of heart, give me a call," I said.

He took the card and slid it into his pocket as I folded myself into my car. He watched as I waved and headed back out toward the highway. He was still watching as I turned the corner and lost sight of the trailers.

I had a sneaking suspicion I'd see them all again.

CHAPTER TWELVE

I GOT BACK TO Holliday's around four o'clock. I still had four hours until the Gamblers Anonymous meeting and I'd missed lunch. I had two priorities—grab a bite, and track down Will Truluck and Yancey Hines.

The first part was a cinch. I walked several doors down to The Gumbo Shop and ordered a jambalaya plate and a takeout container of red beans and rice.

Shorty was behind the bar when I walked back inside. I waved at him and started to head upstairs to my apartment.

"Hold up," he said. "Need to talk with you."

I took a seat at the bar. He uncapped an Abita and slid it across the mahogany to me. He was halfway through one of his own.

"How's it working with Chick?" he asked.

"Only did the one night with him so far. He has good technique and a relatively decent repertoire. He's doing okay. Why?"

"You know he trained at Juilliard?"

"Didn't come up."

"You gotta wonder. What's a kid who studied at a first-class joint doing playing down here for tips?"

"Not as strange as it seems. Schools like Juilliard crank out hundreds of graduates. There aren't enough musician gigs out there to support them all. Had a friend back when I worked in New Hampshire who decided he wanted to get married in New York City. Picked out a place in Central Park. Figured he'd like to have a little instrumental music. He put an ad in the *Times*, saying he'd pay fifty bucks for two hours of work by a classical guitarist. He got fifteen responses. Nine of them were Juilliard alumni. They were carrying hundred-thousand-dollar college loan debts and two-thousand-dollar a month apartment rents, and they were whoring themselves out two hours at a time for a picture of Ulysses S. Grant. Supply and demand, my friend. Too much supply and damned little demand."

"I reckon."

"I notice you never wondered why *I* work here."

"Well, you ain't no fuckin' Juilliard graduate."

"No. I'm not. Anyway, Chick will do until Sam gets back on his feet."

"Yeah. Sam ain't doing so well. Got a call from his daughter. She says whatever he's got has gone to his chest. The doctors are talking about pneumonia. They moved him to the VA Hospital over on Perdido. Didn't even know he was a vet. I asked about it. Turns out he was in the Navy in the South Pacific. The things you don't know about people."

"He's going to be okay. Right?"

"From what I hear, it's touch and go. When I was a kid, my ma used to say pneumonia was an old man's best friend. You're sick for a while, and then you drift off to sleep real peaceful like and never wake up. They don't get much older than Sam."

"Merlie and I will try to get by to see him. Maybe tonight. I have a meeting at eight, but—"

"Don't bother. He's on some kinda seclusion. Family only. Maybe if he gets better. Anyway, I need you here tonight. This thing at eight, it's one of your twelve step meetings?"

"Yeah, but I'll be back here by ten for my shift."

According to the telephone directory, there were three William Trulucks in the greater New Orleans area. I called each of the numbers listed. Two were disconnected. On the third, a woman answered.

"I'm looking for a William Truluck who worked on a pipeline for Holbrook Transport Systems," I said.

"Wrong number," she said, and hung up.

I wrote the addresses for the other two Trulucks and moved on to Yancey Hines. With a name like that, it was a sure thing I'd only get one hit in the directory. I dialed the number. This time a man answered.

"Is this Yancey Hines?" I asked.

"Who's asking?"

I introduced myself. "Did you work for Holbrook Transport Systems on a pipeline for Kenzie Oil?"

"Sure did. Why?"

"I'm trying to locate a man who also worked there. I understand you both shared a sleeping trailer."

"Which one?"

"Garry Sharp."

"Who is this?"

"I'm exactly who I said I was. I'm working on behalf of a children's shelter in New Orleans. Sharp's daughter is living there. I've been trying to find him for her."

"So, who told you to call me?"

"I was at the Holbrook worksite today. I talked with several of the people still on the job there. One of them gave me your name."

"Which one?"

"A man named Marshall Dinkins."

"Old Marsh? Hell of a guy."

"I also spoke with Mike Navvo and Stu Stuyvesent. It was Dinkins who gave me your name. According to the foreman there—"

"Garlock?"

"Yes."

"I'm surprised someone hasn't run him over with a backhoe."

"Dinkins said, besides Garry Sharp, two other men in the trailer had also left the worksite. One of them quit and the other was fired. I was wondering which one you are."

There was a long pause. "I'm not comfortable talking about this over the phone."

"We could meet somewhere."

"Where are you?"

"In the French Quarter. I work at a bar called Holliday's."

"On Toulouse. I seen it before. When do you work?"

"I'm here six nights a week, ten to two."

"You work four hours a day? Not a bad gig."

"I'm a musician. I also work another two hours cleaning up the place after closing."

"You get any breaks?"

"Sure. More or less whenever I want."

"I'll come by tonight. We can talk there, where I know there won't be people listening in."

Obviously, people were "listening in" on his phone calls.

"Okay," I said. "When you get here, talk to a short, square guy behind the bar, looks like a former Marine gunny. Tell him you're here to see me. He'll give me the high sign and I'll take a break."

"You're on the level? Garry Sharp's gone missing?"

"Yes."

"Then we do need to talk."

92

CHAPTER THIRTEEN

*S*UPPORT GROUP MEETINGS everywhere are mostly the same. A lot of people desperate not to make the same mistake twice show up in one place and talk about it. In most of the twelve-step programs, you're allowed to use only your first name. Identities aren't as important as recovery, which is the real goal.

I'd never attended a meeting at Cabby's usual location, but I recognized the surroundings and the people by type. There's always a table with cookies, coffee, and punch near the front door. Sometimes there are doughnuts.

Not tonight.

The first time I'd attended a Gamblers Anonymous meeting, I was content to sit in the back and twiddle my thumbs as I watched others engage in emotional self-evisceration in front of a crowd of strangers.

It wasn't until I made a few more meetings and became more comfortable talking about my addiction that I began to understand. You'd think, since I perform in front of people for a living, I would have no problem confessing my shortcomings in public. There's a difference between art and therapy. It was quite a while before I could step up to a microphone or move my seat to the middle of a circle at a meeting without a racing heart and flop sweat soaking my scalp and armpits.

I figure I've attended more than a thousand meetings over the years. With time, I've become more comfortable with the process. I'd been stuck on Step Nine, in which I try to make amends to everyone I've harmed with my risky behavior, for quite a long time. There were a lot of people on the list. It seemed to grow with each passing year. Any time I met with a new group, I considered it a good idea to treat things as if I were starting all over.

"Hello, I'm Pat," I said, as I stood in the circle of people in the church social hall, "and I'm a gambling addict."

Now this is the part in the movies where everyone says, "Hi, Pat." It doesn't always work that way in real life. This time, the group stared at me, waiting for some new story of personal failure. I wondered how many of them were there for the first time.

"I have a particular affection, and a weakness, for blackjack," I continued. I pulled my two-year medallion from my pocket. "I've been coming to groups for five years. You all know what this little guy means, so you can also figure out it's been a tough road. I last gambled on the Flamingo Riverboat a few years ago. I've had some lapses since then, but with help I haven't relapsed. Next month I get my three-year medallion. I also know I could lose it all in a second with one bad decision."

Several of the people in the big circle nodded to one another. They'd been there.

"Fact is I might not be here at all if it hadn't been for one of your regulars. I owe him a lot. When he talked me into getting serious about recovery, I'd graduated from piling up gambling debts to working as a collector for a loan shark. You can look at me and understand. When I knocked on your door, you paid up."

A couple of people chuckled. A few looked scared. It had been a long time and I couldn't remember everyone I'd shaken down. For all I knew, there were a few of my old acquaintances in the crowd.

It had happened before.

"I'm on my Ninth Step. If any of you were among those people I visited, I apologize. We all know how desperate a person can get when we think there's no way back up. I was hopeless when I attended my first meeting. Some of you know Cabby. Maybe you know him as Brian. I've always known him as Cabby and old habits are hard to break.

"I get to meetings once or twice a week these days, even when I don't feel the urge to splurge. I've never been to this meeting before. I probably wouldn't be here tonight, except Cabby, or Brian, might be in trouble. I could use some help finding him."

Several of the people in the circle turned and whispered to one another. Emily Battaglia, who was acting as facilitator, held up her hand and asked for quiet while I was speaking.

"Thanks, Emily," I said. "Those of you who know Cabby may have noticed he hasn't been at meetings for a couple of weeks. I don't want to alarm you, but nobody has seen him since Friday before last. One of his close friends has asked me to help find him. I'm not a cop, but I have some experience finding people. I have no idea where he is, but we all know what can happen to an addict when he falls off the radar, so it's possible he could use your help. If any of you know Cabby, I'd like to talk with you after the meeting. I'll hang at the goodie table for a bit. You don't have to tell me your name if you don't want. I won't hassle you. I just need more information than I have now if I'm going to help one of our fellow travelers. Thanks."

I put my Saints cap back on and took my seat.

• • •

Searching for lost people is a lot like fishing. Sometimes you splash your bait across the top of the water and bass climb all over each other to strike at it. Other times you dangle the lure in the water for hours without a nibble. Then there are the days when you straggle home with an empty creel, skin tight and itchy from sunburn, and a headache from pounding back too many beers waiting to land the big one.

I started to worry this night might be one of the latter as I hung out around the snack table scarfing cookies and washing them down with watery punch. A couple of people sidled up to me, thanked me for my testimony, and wished me luck in finding Cabby, but they didn't offer any assistance or useful tips. I checked my watch. It was already nine thirty. I had to be on stage twenty blocks away in a half hour. I couldn't dawdle much longer.

A tall, skinny guy with a fringe of graying hair circling his otherwise bald head like a victory laurel stepped by me and grabbed a chocolate chip cookie.

"So you're Gallegher," he said, after taking a bite of the cookie.

I recognized his voice. "Mr. Somerville?" I asked.

He extended his hand. "Call me Bert. Want you to meet someone."

I looked around. Except for Cabby's GA sponsor, Emily Battaglia, and myself, everyone else had left.

"Is he in your pocket?" I asked. "Because I don't see anyone else here."

"Out back. This guy values his privacy."

"Why?"

"He didn't say. I told him you wanted to talk with anyone who knew Cabby, and he got this look on his face like he was gonna bolt. I talked him into staying around, but he doesn't want to be seen talking with you. Can't say why. He's paranoid like that."

"Where's the back door?"

"I'll show you."

Somerville led me to a two-foot-high stage at the back of the church rec hall. We took some side steps and he walked me through a narrow backstage area to a steel security door with a bar latch.

There was a second parking area in back of the rec hall, but it was mostly deserted. A man of average height, maybe thirty-five years old, wearing a Grateful Dead tee shirt and jeans, stood beside a dumpster. I recognized him from the circle in the meeting. I remembered he hadn't gotten up to talk. His hands were crammed into his back pockets. Nearly finished remains of a cigarette dangled from his lips. Both his arms were inked from wrist to shoulder with elaborate sleeve tattoos. His head whipped around as we walked out the back door. He reached up with his left hand, took the butt, and flicked it into the lot before walking toward us.

"This is Nate," Bert told me. "He and Cabby are kind of tight."

"Got a last name, Nate?" I asked.

"Don't know whether I want to tell you," Nate said. "Are you cop?"

"I'm a cornetist."

"What in hell is a cornetist?"

"I play cornet. It's a horn."

"A musician?"

"That one's up for grabs. I play while people drink in a bar. If they get drunk enough they sometimes give me money."

"So how come some musician is looking for Cabby?"

"I'm his friend, Nate. I think he might need one."

"Who you working for?"

"Cabby dropped by my place a few months back and gave me a retainer check, asked me to find him if he disappeared. I suppose that means I'm working for him, but it was a close friend of his who told me he was missing."

"Ross Duncan?"

"Yes."

"It's okay," Nate said to Bert. "I think I want to talk to Gallegher alone."

"I'll be right inside if you need me," Bert said.

"Bert's all right," Nate said. "He ain't my sponsor or nothing, but I could do a lot worse if he was."

"He's Cabby's sponsor," I said. "He wants what's best for Cabby."

"Yeah. I know. Maybe Ross Duncan should've kept you out of this. I like Ross. He and I went out a couple of times, but it wasn't happening for us, y'know?"

"Okay."

"Yeah, I know. I don't look it. Ross is sweet, but he's a bit of a twink. I look like I spend my days cleaning sewers."

"Why should Ross have let Cabby's disappearance go?"

Nate pulled a hard pack of Marlboros from his pocket and lit up another cigarette with an old-fashioned Zippo flip top lighter. I could smell the kerosene from two feet away. He closed the lighter with a well-practiced snap of his wrist and stowed it in his pocket as he took a long drag and exhaled a cloud of smoke into the humid night air.

"I don't know details," he said. "I don't know much of nothing, understand? I like Cabby. He got me a couple of jobs over the years. I was two quarters away from starving about a year ago. He introduced me to a friend who gave me some work. You say he saved you by getting you into the program? Well, maybe he saved me by getting me a job."

"The lad is generous to a fault."

"You bet he is. Here's what I know. I was at a meeting here a while back. I was talking with Cabby afterward, shooting the shit, killing time so I didn't have to go straight home and stare at the television while I played solitaire. So, we're chatting it up, and this other guy walks up and gives Cabby a look. He tilts his head toward the door, like to say, 'Let's take it outside.'"

"Did you recognize him?"

"Never saw him before. He sure wasn't a regular at the meeting. Cabby looked a little embarrassed, and he apologized. I told him no problem. He and this other guy walked out to the parking lot."

"Can you describe him?"

"Taller than me by three or four inches, so he was maybe six feet tall. He had long, dark hair, combed back. Looked like he used half a bottle of product on it. He had some kind of accent."

"Strong accent?"

"Not like he walked off the boat this afternoon or nothin', but you could tell he wasn't from around here. Sounded Mexican or Cuban at first, but I spent my time around beaners and he talked differently. He was dressed nice. White pima cotton shirt open two buttons down, twill slacks with a nice sharp crease. Italian loafers, no socks. Lightweight herringbone jacket."

"You have good eyes, Nate."

"Yeah, well maybe I was checking him out a little. He was good looking, except for the scar."

"What kind of scar?"

"It was on the side of his face. Began under his ear and ran along above the jaw line before turning up toward the corner of his mouth. Looked like he finished second in a knife fight. Kind of thick, like it didn't heal well. I didn't see it at first because he was turned away. From the left side, he's like some kinda movie star. The right side's like Frankenstein, dig?"

"How'd Cabby react toward him."

"Like I said, he was embarrassed at first when the guy horned in on our conversation. Didn't give the guy the brush-off, like I know Cabby can. I seen him give guys in the bars a look that made them run for the bathroom before they crapped their pants. Cabby can look dangerous if he wants."

Were we talking about the same person? The Cabby Jacks I'd always known had been almost too eager to please. I'd never found him anything approaching intimidating. Time changes people, I suppose.

"Anything else?"

"After a few minutes I decided to take off. I walked out to the parking lot, where Cabby and this guy was having some hellacious argument. I couldn't catch a lot of what the other guy was saying, on account of this accent he had, but I could hear Cabby okay. He pointed his finger at the foreign guy's chest and jabbed at him a couple of times. Then he said, 'Don't you worry about my end. I know better than to piss in the Brazilian's grits.' Right about then he must have seen me, and I could tell even in the dim light he wasn't happy I was there. The other guy turned and looked at me. He reached into his jacket and Cabby grabbed the guy's arm. 'Ignore him,' he said. 'He don't know nothing.' Then he looked past the guy and yelled to me, 'Have a great night, Nate. See you next meeting.' And that was it. The other guy, I could have sworn he was getting ready to pull out a gun. I walked away, fast as I could without trying to look like some kinda punk. I ain't seen Cabby since."

"When was this?" I asked.

"About three weeks ago."

"Would you recognize this other man again if you saw him?"

"Shit, man, I been having nightmares about that dude. I hope I never see his goddamned face again."

"You know anyone named Nigra? First name might start with a 'D.'"

"Doesn't ring a bell. Strange sorta name."

I pulled one of my cards from my jacket pocket and wrote my cell phone number on the back.

"If you see this man again, or if you think of anything else that might be helpful, you call me."

I was going to be late for work. Shorty would give me a little shit, but everyone knows musicians don't keep bankers' hours. Even the regulars didn't care whether the show started on time as long as the beer well didn't run dry.

On the brisk walk back toward Toulouse Street, I replayed the conversation with Nate in my head. From his description of the stranger who had waylaid Cabby at the meeting, I think *I'd* recognize him. You don't see a lot of matinee idols sporting a six-inch scar on their faces traipsing around the Quarter. I was particularly interested in what Cabby had said: *Don't you worry about my end. I know better than to piss in the Brazilian's grits.*

Was D. Nigra the man with the scar? Or was that the Brazilian's name?

When Cabby had visited me, months earlier, I'd asked him if he was keeping his nose clean. He'd implied he was involved in some sort of shady business he didn't want to divulge. "It's better I don't tell you about it, dig?" he'd said. Cabby had been involved over the years in any number of activities that fell on the dingy side of grace, from fixing fights to running card games to briefly working as a bag man for the Anollis. It was likely he'd never held a completely legitimate job in his life.

The last time I'd seen him, he had been dressed in expensive clothes, and had cleaned up nicely. He had a good haircut. His hands were clean, and his nails manicured. Some of that might have been Ross Duncan's influence on him, but I had also gotten the impression he was engaged in a lucrative racket, whatever it was. In New Orleans, it could have meant he had some connection with one of the mobs.

I'd had more than my share of experience dealing with gangsters. For the most part, they weren't much like what you see in the movies. In the age of technology, it's extremely difficult to hide or launder large sums of illicit cash, so most of the syndicates had diversified. Chris Anunciato, the latest *capo* of the Sicilian-linked gangs, made more money from his string of French Quarter restaurants and bars than he did running numbers or dealing drugs on the street. I'd played no small role in putting a renegade Vietnamese mobster behind bars several years earlier before he could start a gang war in the Quarter, and in the course of doing it I'd earned the gratitude of his boss, who was now rolled up in far more semi-legitimate business ventures than purely illegal ones. Most of the gang members I knew were, for the most part, ordinary guys ninety percent of the time. You've probably run up on them in the grocery store or at the movies. They like to keep a low profile. Business runs much more smoothly if you don't always have the police breathing down your necks. The days of drive-by shootings and barbershop assassinations were more the stuff of legend than a resemblance of anything that takes place today. The local street gangs in the housing projects didn't mind taking frequent potshots at one another to maintain their turfs. Sometimes their violence spilled over into the streets of the French Quarter, but they weren't part of the mainstream of organized crime.

Brazilians were a new twist on me. I wasn't familiar with any significant criminal activity involving their particular demographic. I made a note to call Boulware the next day, as repugnant as the notion was to me, to see if he had any background information on them he could share.

Chick was already on stage playing when I walked into Holliday's. Shorty shot daggers at me with his eyes. I shrugged and ran upstairs to grab my horn.

CHAPTER FOURTEEN

*Y*ANCEY HINES WANDERED into the bar a few minutes before the end of our first set. He strolled over to the bar, had a couple of words with Shorty, and then took a seat on one of the stools. Shorty drew him a draft, caught my eye, and pointed at Hines.

After we finished the song, I told the crowd we we'd be back in a few minutes. Chick looked a little surprised, since we'd planned to play for another ten minutes or so.

Shorty already had a Dixie popped open for me when I got to the bar. I took the stool next to Hines. He looked on the short side of forty. He'd let his hair grow down past his shoulders, and wore it pulled back and tied with an elastic band. It was graying at the temples, but the rest was dark brown and frizzy. He had about two week's growth of reddish-brown beard. His eyes were so dark they were almost black. It was difficult to see where his pupils ended and his irises began.

"You aren't bad," he said, after we introduced ourselves. "I mean, you ain't no Al Hirt or nothin', but you got some talent."

"Hirt plays a trumpet," I said. "Don't worry about it. Everyone makes that mistake."

"I played a clarinet in high school. Still noodle around with it from time to time. I remember enough theory that I can jam if I want to. You guys ever have an open mike night here?"

"Sorry. Shorty here wants to get every penny's worth of work out of his players."

"So you think they'd show up on time once in a while," Shorty chimed in.

Hines leaned in toward me.

"Someplace we can talk in private?"

"Sure," I said.

I led him up the stairs to my second-floor apartment. He reacted more or less the same way everyone does when I open the door. My place isn't large—a living room with a small kitchen in an alcove, a bedroom, and the bath. Every inch of the wall in the living room is filled with bookcases, and every bookcase overflows with books.

"This some kind of fuckin' library?" Hines asked.

"Of a sort."

"You've read all of these?"

"Not all of them. I like to leave some things in my life for anticipation. If I live long enough, I'll get to all of them. Have a seat and let's talk."

As he sat on the couch, I finished my Dixie and grabbed another from the refrigerator. I plopped down into my sprung-out recliner and tossed the cap from the beer onto the coffee table.

"Funny thing, you calling me the way you did. I been giving this Garry Sharp fella a lot of thought over the last couple of weeks."

"Why?"

"Some people stick in your head. God knows why, but they do. Sharp was a weird one. Didn't fit in. Half the guys working the Holbrook job are old-line roughnecks. Some of them worked the offshore rigs until they got too old or too blown out to cut it anymore. Others have spent their entire lives on the sweaty end of a shovel or a mattock or a pickaxe. Sometimes I'd watch these guys and wonder how many tons of dirt they either dug up or spread back down over the course of their lives. Sharp wasn't one of them. He was an oddball. For one thing, he was educated. Don't see a lot of college dudes humpin' a backhoe or layin' oil pipe."

"According to Marshall Dinkins, three of the six people who lived in your trailer on the Holbrook site don't work there anymore. Besides Sharp, there was a man named Truluck, and there was you. Dinkins told me, between you and Truluck, one quit and one was fired. Which one were you?"

"I quit."

"Any particular reason?"

"You mean besides slaving under the sun while fighting off water moccasins and mosquitoes the size of crows? As a matter of fact, yeah. I had a good reason. I saw a guy get killed on the job."

"Killed? How?"

"Not keeping his head up. Got caught between the backhoe and a length of pipe. Wasn't watching what he was doing. Crushed his head like a pumpkin. Poor bastard never knew what hit him. You think something like that happens, the boss would want to take a few hours off to let the line workers deal with it. Instead, they called the ambulance and let the poor bastard lie there in the dirt until it got there. The rest of us were ordered to keep working, with this guy bloating up only few yards away. Finally, that asshole Garlock covered him with a tarp, but it didn't help. I took off that night. Told Garlock to send me my check and I hit the road."

"Tough deal," I said.

"Well that ain't the half of it. I could tell you stuff, Mr. Gallegher. I mean, stuff would make it hard for you to sleep at night. I don't mind admitting I done some time a few years back. Got busted on an assault and battery beef in Alabama. I was young, I was stupid, and I figured I could get away with anything. Wound up working a road crew, which taught me a few things I was able to use to get this gig with Holbrook. I gotta tell you, there ain't a whole hell of a difference between the two. You ever ask yourself why the gulf coast is so littered with oil refineries and offshore drills and pipelines?"

"I figured it was because that's where Mother Nature put the oil."

"That's part of it, yeah, but there's oil other places too. All the states surrounding the Gulf are right-to-work, which means no unions. North Florida, Alabama, Mississippi, Louisiana, they're all at the bottom of the charts when it comes to household income. People around here are desperate for work and they ain't particular about what kind of work it is. They only want to eat. People like Holbrook know they can replace any worker in a matter of hours. When people get expendable, the bosses tend to treat 'em like garbage. OSHA don't give two shits about some work crew off in the sand dunes south of New Orleans. There ain't no inspectors touring the site handing out citations for workplace safety violations. Between that and the fact the fuckin' Kenzies own every politician from Texas to Tallahassee, a working man ain't gonna get any breaks. I saw that poor bastard lying on the ground with his brains leaking into the dirt, and I decided I could find plenty of better jobs. That was the last straw, man."

"What was the first one?"

"Beg pardon?"

"Sounds like you'd been thinking about leaving for some time."

"You got another beer in the fridge?"

I stepped into the kitchen and got him a bottle of Dixie.

"Yeah," he said. "There's something shady going on with Holbrook."

"Shady?"

"I don't think his operation is on the up and up. I'm no cop, and despite the fact I got a prison record, I ain't no criminal, either. I did my time standin' up and I walked out determined never to go back. I got no interest in getting tied up with anything illegal."

"What is it you think Holbrook's doing?"

"Maybe it ain't him. Maybe it's Garlock. I don't know. Garry Sharp had an idea. Like I said, he's educated. I think he had suspicions. I think maybe that's why he disappeared."

"Seems you're leaving out part of the story, Mr. Hines."

"I gotta be careful. I made the mistake of mouthing off to Garlock before I walked away. Told him he could keep his crooked operation. He didn't like it, but what was he gonna do? Shoot me and dump me in the pipeline trench? I was packed and out the door. I figured that would be the end of it. Man was I wrong."

"About what?"

"I came back to New Orleans. Been looking for a job for a couple of weeks. A few of the prospects looked promising. I even had one guy tell me I was perfect for the job. Said I could start the next Monday. Next day, I get a phone call from him. He says he can't hire me. Won't tell me why."

"Maybe he found out about your prison record," I said.

"Naw. He already knew. I put it on my application. I'm up front about my past. Don't want no misunderstandings. No, something else soured him on me. I think someone is trying to drive me out of town."

"Because one potential employer backed out on a job offer?"

"It's more than that. I think my phone is tapped. I'm an old-fashioned guy. I still got a land line phone hanging on my kitchen wall. I was talking to my mom the other day and I heard this weird clicking noise on the phone. I looked it up on the Internet, figured maybe it was something I could fix. Found a bunch of listings talking about how clicking noises can mean there's a tap on the line. I took the phone apart, but I didn't see anything suspicious. Also, I think I'm being followed."

"Followed?"

"Yeah. I've seen the same car behind me several times over the last couple of weeks, ever since I quit the Holbrook job. It's a tan Ford. There's a place broken out of the grille, so I know it's the same car."

"Probably someone who lives in your neighborhood."

"Maybe. But if it is, then why was it behind me on Decatur Street here in the French Quarter not twenty minutes ago?"

CHAPTER FIFTEEN

"*I*T FOLLOWED YOU here?" I asked.

"If I'm lyin', I'm fryin'. It followed me here. It followed me to a job interview the other day. I saw it in the parking lot at the grocery store last Friday. I'm telling you, someone's keeping tabs on me."

"But why?"

"Think about it. Who is Holbrook building the pipeline for?"

"Kenzie Oil."

"That's right. Kellen Kenzie is the fuckin' devil, man. His wife ain't much better. You ever see those spy movies, where some dude is always plotting to take over the world? Well, that's Kellen Kenzie. You know Holbrook is Kenzie's son-in-law?"

"I'd heard."

"From the talk on the trench line, Kenzie thinks Bob Holbrook is five kinds of idiot inside one head, but his daughter seems to love the guy. Holbrook knows which side his bread's buttered on, so he does whatever Kenzie tells him. With Kenzie paying the bills and Holbrook running the pipeline project, who's gonna speak up if illegal shit is going on?"

"You've said that before. What kind of illegal shit? What do you think Kenzie and Holbrook are up to?"

"I'm not sure. You know they sleep us six to a trailer on the site, right?"

"Yeah. I was inside one of the trailers today."

"It ain't bad. Air conditioned, and the showers are all right. The beds are kind of ratty, but I've slept on worse. Hell, it's a lot better than sleeping in the barracks in prison. Here's the thing. Once you're on the site, there ain't much to do, and ain't much of anywhere to go. We had our cars, and they gave us a night off in town once a week if we wanted it, but who can afford the gas? Holbrook even had a van brought in to take us into Biloxi once. All in all, it could be worse, right? So how come, every once in a while, they lock us in?"

"What?"

"You heard me. Okay, it's not like they use real locks or nothin', but they might as well. I wanted a smoke one night. This was, maybe, three or four nights before Sharp took off. A couple of the other guys in the trailer smoked, but Sharp and Truluck didn't, and they didn't like breathing it in. They're good guys. I didn't want to upset them, so I'd step outside the trailer and smoke on the steps. This one night, I was dozing in my rack when I heard an engine outside. It was a low, rumbling sort of sound, like a diesel on a boat or a bus. At the time, we were near the Old Pearl River, which empties into the inlet from the gulf into Lake St. Catherine, so it could have been either one. The noise woke me up and I couldn't go back to sleep. When I tried to open the door to take a smoke, it was blocked."

"Blocked?"

"Actually, there was someone leaning against it. I pushed, and when I did Al Garlock opened the door halfway and told me to stay inside. I asked him why. He told me to ram it. Said he didn't owe me no explanations. Said I'd better stay inside if I knew what was good for me. So the conversation woke up Garry. He asked me what was going on. I told him I only wanted a smoke and Garlock wouldn't let me out of the trailer. Garry tried to look out the window, but someone had turned out the lights on the work site. I couldn't get my smoke, so I hopped back in the bed, but Garry got out his notebook and wrote some stuff down before turning out his light."

"Did you see what he wrote?"

"Not that night, but I did happen to get a look over his shoulder once or twice when he was writing. I couldn't make it out. It was mostly a lot of numbers and formulas and stuff. I never did get beyond elementary algebra in school. What he was writing was way beyond that."

"One of the other men in the trailer said he saw Sharp make drawings of the pipes."

"If he did, I never saw one. Why on earth would he want to draw the pipes?"

"You said it yourself. What if something was wrong with them? Maybe, somewhere along the line, either Holbrook or Kenzie was cutting corners and Sharp figured it out. The same guy who told me about the drawings asked Sharp about the notebook. According to him, Sharp said he was writing his retirement plan."

"You think maybe he found something hinky and planned to shake Holbrook down?"

"Holbrook or Kenzie."

"Then he was stupid. You ain't gonna shake Kenzie down. Guy's got too damned much juice. Try to squeeze a guy like Kenzie, you might as well shoot yourself in the head to save someone else the time."

"Or," I said, as I considered all the possibilities, "he might make you disappear."

Hines stood and headed for the door.

"I don't think I like the way this is going," he said. "Getting followed and blackballed is one thing, but getting killed ain't on my dance card. I'm thinking maybe I shouldn't have come here. Do me a favor, Gallegher. Forget I was ever here. We never talked. I dropped into the bar, pounded back a couple of brews, and went on my way. I'd rather you didn't call me again."

"One more thing," I said.

He stopped, his hand on the doorknob. "What? Make it quick."

"When you wanted that smoke and Garlock wouldn't let you out of the trailer, were there any bus or truck tracks in the sand? Tracks that weren't there the day before?"

"Now that I think of it, there weren't."

"The land near the water there is awfully sandy. A vehicle the size of a bus would leave some deep impressions. It might even get stuck, if it was off the oiled track, which it would almost have to be if it were to turn around before leaving. What does that suggest to you?"

He said, "A boat."

"A boat wouldn't leave any tracks. Makes me curious as to what was on it."

"Curiosity is gonna get you killed."

I had to smile a little. "You might not believe this, Mr. Hines, but you aren't the first person to suggest that. You wouldn't happen to know why Will Truluck was fired, would you?"

"No. He was still there when I walked."

"Thanks for coming by," I said.

"What in hell are you talking about?" Hines said. "I was never here."

First thing the next morning, I drove over to A Friend's Place in the Garden District. Merlie had one of the kids in her office, so I sat in the living room and read a relatively new copy of *Reader's*

Digest. The only other option was *Highlights*. I had no real interest in the antics of Goofus and Gallant.

As I was reading, I became aware of someone standing behind me. I turned and found Audrey Sharp staring at me.

"You found my dad yet?" she asked.

I gestured for her to come around and have a seat, which she did.

"Not yet," I said. "Yesterday, I visited the place where your father was working. I'm sorry to have to tell you this, but he left the job several weeks ago. I talked with his boss and a few of the men he worked with, but they don't know where he is. I'm still looking for him. Don't worry about that."

"Miz Merlie told me I could stay here for two weeks. What happens if you don't find him by then?"

I didn't have the heart to tell her the truth. If I couldn't locate him by then, he was probably never going to turn up at all.

"I don't know, sweetie," I said. "Miss Merlie is the expert in those matters. You'd be better off asking her."

I lied. I'd spent too much time with Merlie not to know the way things were going to roll. If her dad couldn't be found, Audrey's problems were only beginning. If she reached the end of her two weeks, and no legal guardian was available, Merlie was required by law to turn the matter over to the Department of Social Services. They'd get a court order to take custody of Audrey. They'd try to find a good foster home, but placements for teenaged girls were few and far between. Most foster parents wanted young children and babies. Placing a teenaged girl in a home-like setting was almost as difficult as placing a teenaged boy, which was damned near impossible.

The other option was a group home, which wasn't so terribly different than staying at A Friend's Place, if you could find one where the people working there were as caring and warm and involved as Merlie—which was a tall order—and if the other kids there accepted her and didn't see her as an interloper trying to cadge a small slice of their ever-shrinking pie of attention and affection.

Not finding Garry Sharp meant tossing his daughter into the maw of The System. Some kids got lucky, and the experience turned out to be a positive one. For most, it was a nightmare of monthly moves to a new house with new staff and new roommates, or foster placements with occasionally abusive or exploitative caretakers. It meant the loss of an entire normal adolescence.

Audrey didn't need to hear any of this from me. If I failed to find her father, she'd learn it the hard way soon enough.

"I'm sure Miss Merlie has already asked you this," I said. "I need to ask again, though. Do you have any other relatives your dad might have contacted after he left this job? Any aunts or uncles?"

"I don't have any aunts or uncles," she said. "Dad was an only child, like me. My mom's been dead since I was barely able to walk. I don't think I've ever met any of her folks. I wish I could help, but there's nobody."

"How about close friends? Do you know any people your dad liked to spend time with?"

"Well, there's Carly, but you already talked to her. You know the kind of work my dad does. He used to say growing up with a man in that line of work was like being a military brat. Here today, gone tomorrow. We haven't stayed in any one place long enough to wear out a magazine subscription, let alone make a lot of friends."

"I see."

She chewed on her thumbnail, and bent forward, putting her hands on her knees, staring at the floor.

"Miss Merlie says you're a hero," she said. "She says you do things most other people can't."

"She told you that?" I asked.

"No. I overheard her talking with Miss Shelley yesterday. They didn't know I was listening. I was sitting right here on the couch when Miss Shelley went into Miss Merlie's office. She looked at me, and she closed the door, so I figure they were talking about me. I walked over to the stairway next to her office, like I was going upstairs, but I stood there and tried to hear what they were saying."

"You know Miss Merlie and I are a couple," I said.

"Uh huh."

"Sometimes people in . . . our situation have an exaggerated view of each other. I'm not half as brave or courageous as she might lead you to believe. I'm not a hero. Not the way you might have thought she meant."

"She said if anyone could find my dad, it would be you, because you'd never give up. She said once you get your teeth in something, you were like a snapping turtle. You'd never let go until it thundered."

I read once that the true measure of a person wasn't how they behaved when people were watching them, but rather how they acted when they believed they were alone. In the same way it's hard to understand a picture if you're staring at too closely, over the years I might have developed a perspective on Merlie that was skewed by what I wanted her to be. I seldom had the opportunity to see her in circumstances that didn't include me. Audrey might not have understood it, but she had provided me with a snapshot of Merlie's true feelings about me. I was humbled and overjoyed at the same time.

I've led a reasonably itinerant life. I dropped out of seminary because of a crisis of faith. I totaled my career as a forensic psychologist by overstepping boundaries and getting too involved in a murder investigation to the point I wound up shooting a suspect to keep him from killing me. My career as a college professor was taken away when I was falsely accused of sexually harassing a coed in return for grades. My career as a gambler was so failed that I wound up thousands of dollars in debt, forced to make collections for a psychopathic loan shark. My entire adult life had descended from grace to perdition. It was only chance encounters with two people that had salvaged me and shoved me in the direction of redemption. Cabby had forced me to do my First Step at a meeting. Merlie happened to be the director of A Friend's Place when I brought someone there to get her off the streets. Two random meetings had changed my life forever.

One thing about spending your life in a perpetual failure spiral is that it plays hell on your self-esteem. Before I met Merlie, I had consigned myself to spending the rest of my life blowing a horn in a dive bar and occasionally putting my neck on the line for a desperate friend. Some days I'd skip shaving so I wouldn't have to look at myself in the bathroom mirror. My entire life was devoted to erasing my brittle karma and compensating for all the people I'd hurt because of my own weakness.

Merlie had changed everything. Before her, when I had nothing to lose, I pursued my perilous adventures with an abandon born of hopelessness. Since meeting her, I'd found something to live for. I'd always assumed I needed her a lot more than she needed me. Hearing she regarded me as some kind of tenacious, relentless hero made me realize I still had a lot to learn about how she thinks.

"I'll tell you what," I said. "Maybe she's right, and maybe she isn't. I sure never considered myself any kind of hero. But when it comes to your dad, I promise you I won't stop looking until I find him. And I haven't forgotten about your Elmo doll either. I'll get it as soon as I can."

She didn't answer. Instead, she hopped up on the sofa, threw her arms around my neck, and hugged so hard I started to see stars. Then she kissed my cheek, flushed, and ran up the stairs. As I turned to watch her, I saw Merlie standing in the doorway to her office. She crooked her finger at me. I walked to her. She pulled me into her office and closed the door.

She kissed me, not on the cheek, but full on the lips, hard and passionately. Then, as if she didn't want to let go, she rested her head on my chest.

"You *are* a hero," she said. "Don't let anyone ever tell you differently."

"Yes ma'am," I said.

CHAPTER SIXTEEN

"*I* DIDN'T TELL AUDREY everything," I said to Merlie, after we'd allowed our hearts to slow a little.

"You've learned something?"

I told her about Holbrook, and Garry Sharp disappearing from the worksite weeks earlier. Her face clouded over as I described what I'd learned from his coworkers, especially the information I'd gotten from Yancey Hines.

"I don't like the sound of this," she said. "I'm beginning to regret asking you to find him."

"It isn't a good thing that nobody's heard from him for so long. If he was all right, you'd think he'd contact Carly to check on Audrey. I think we will find Garry Sharp. My gut tells me we might not find him healthy."

She crossed the office and sat behind her desk. She steepled her fingers and stared over them at the door. She did that for quite a long time. I'd seen her contemplative state. I knew enough to wait for her.

"Promise me," she said. "If something bad has happened to Audrey's father, you'll let it go. Hand it over to Farley Nuckolls and walk away."

"Are you impounding my cape?" I asked.

"Promise me, damn it. Only two weeks ago, you were in a shootout between the cops and a pair of hired killers."

"I'm still here. Not everyone there was as lucky."

"And how long do you expect your luck to hold out? You were a gambler, Pat."

"A bad one."

"Then you should know. You've been one lucky son of a bitch for as long as I've known you. How long can you ride a streak before it self-destructs?"

It was a sobering question. I have been lucky, no doubt. Living on the expectation of good fortune is the worst sort of insurance. I'd been writing checks on my good karma account fast and furious for the last month or so. The balance was dwindling. Perhaps I had imagined, by taking on the search for Cabby and for Garry Sharp, I was building back my credit with the universe. It has been my experience that the gods of fortune watch for the fault of hubris in mankind, and they get their jollies from playing games with mortality. They must have seen me coming from a mile away.

"Let's say I'll roll with the punches. Would you like me to bring in Scat Boudreaux to watch my back?"

She shuddered. Any encounter with Scat was tantamount to arguing with Janus. You never knew which head was doing the talking. When you're dealing with the most dangerous man in Louisiana, a man who staged his own survival march across North Vietnam, after escaping from a tiger cage, by killing and eating the random Viet Cong who had the bad fortune to cross his path, you tend to tread softly. Add the fact he is almost certifiably psychotic, and even the strongest men I've known harbored a secret terror of going up against Scat. I didn't blame them.

"I'd hold off," she said. "We don't know there is real danger yet. Even if there is, let Farley take care of it. If some harm has come to

Audrey's father, it's his job anyway. Right?"

"Absolutely," I said. "I promised Audrey I'd find her dad. I didn't promise to avenge him."

"Attaboy," she said, as she stood on tiptoe to kiss me again. "Now you're getting with the program."

I still had to locate Will Truluck, the man who'd been fired from the Holbrook job after Garry Sharp had disappeared. I had the addresses I'd located in the telephone book for the two people with that name whose phones had been disconnected, but I didn't harbor a great deal of hope they'd pan out. People disconnect their landline phones all the time these days, now that cell phones are so ubiquitous in our society. Even so, it was possible the Truluck I wanted to talk with was still at one of the addresses.

One was only a mile or so from A Friend's Place, in an area north of the Super Dome. I decided to try that location first.

I picked up my tail halfway there.

I don't know whether I had been checking subconsciously ever since my conversation with Yancey Hines the night before, but as I left the Garden District I caught a glimpse in my rearview mirror of a tan Ford Crown Vic with a broken section in the radiator grill. It was staying back, five or six cars behind me. I probably wouldn't have noticed if it hadn't changed lanes at the exact time I did. I could see a single person behind the wheel, but I couldn't tell whether it was a man or a woman.

It could have been a coincidence. I hate coincidences. They bang around inside my head and create a dull thudding sensation behind my eyes, and they give me an itch that calamine can't possibly cure. Coincidences and happenstance are the things of movie fantasy. The odds of seeing a car pacing me the day after it was described by

Hines were too impossible to calculate.

I decided to put it to a test. The trip from A Friend's Place to the first Truluck address was a straight shot. Whoever was driving the tail car couldn't possibly know where I was going. I'd only decided to check that address out myself when I left Merlie. At the next cross street, I hung a quick left without hitting the turn signal. It was a short connecting street that dead-ended two blocks after my turn, so I took a right and blended in with the northbound traffic.

Two blocks later, I caught the tan Crown Vic in my rearview again. It was still possibly a coincidence, despite the burning sensation at the base of my neck that told me otherwise. After all, I was still headed north, toward the Super Dome. For all I knew the person driving the Ford was headed in the same direction.

It was time for another test. This time I took a right turn, went three blocks, turned right again, drove four blocks, and took another right, essentially making a big circle back to the street where I'd started. While two cars making the same left-right turn might be a coincidence, two cars making a circle together was beyond happenstance.

I had hoped I was only a little paranoid after Hines's description of being tailed. My hopes were dashed as I caught the tan Ford in the mirror again about ten blocks from the stadium. It was still hanging about five cars back, trying to look inconspicuous.

I hate being tailed. This wasn't my first experience with it and one thing I knew immediately was the person driving the Ford wasn't a pro. A first-class mobile surveillance requires at least two cars, sometimes three, to hand off the following chores in order to avoid being detected. Whoever was driving the Ford was working alone.

I suppose I could have found a way to lose him. I'd done it before. On the other hand, I've always subscribed to the policy that it's better to know your adversary than it is to swing at shadows.

I pulled into a local fried chicken joint and parked the car. In the mirror, I saw the Ford cruise past and turn at the next intersection. I didn't believe for a second it was about to head off its merry way. It was a cinch it would reappear shortly.

I don't carry a gun. Sure, I'm a tough guy, and I live in one of the gun-crazy states. I probably could have applied for a carry permit if I wanted. Farley Nuckolls knows I've killed a few people in my tenure in the French Quarter, so he might have put the kibosh on the application, but that wouldn't have stopped me from trying. My objection was somewhat more philosophical. I've always believed a gun makes otherwise smart people stupid. There have been more occasions in my life than I preferred to think about when not having a handgun had forced me to think faster and react better, and probably had saved my life. There had also been those circumstances in which having a gun had made the difference between living and dying, but there had been far more episodes of the former.

I don't travel completely unarmed. After turning off the car, I reached under the front seat and retrieved my "persuader"—a foot and a half of ebony dowel, gun-drilled on a lathe and filled with lead shot. It was hard and heavy. I'd broken a few hands, arms, and kneecaps with it in my time. I slipped it into the sleeve of my jacket and climbed out of the car. I reached the front door of the chicken shack when my peripheral vision caught the Ford turn off a side street two blocks down and head my way.

I waited long enough for the driver to see me before I walked into the restaurant. Instead of waiting, I walked straight past the order counter to the back door and made a quick right around the building.

There was a shed beside the restaurant that afforded me a good view of the parking lot without being too obvious about spying.

By the time I reached my hidey-hole, the Ford had pulled into the parking lot of a hardware store next door. It had parked nose out in one of the spaces there, facing my Pinto. The driver sat inside. The windows were slightly tinted, so I still couldn't get a good look or make out his features. I could see the car clearly, but the driver still couldn't see me.

I retreated to the rear of the restaurant, crossed behind the hardware store, and walked around the far side of it until I was behind the tail car. I pulled a pad from my jacket pocket and jotted down the license plate number. Then I called Farley's direct office number on my cell phone.

"What is it this time?" he asked, even before I told him who was calling. Must have had caller ID on his office phone.

"I have a tail," I said.

"I always suspected."

"Someone's following me. I have his license tag number. Can you ID him for me?"

"Why would I do that?"

"I'm about to confront the driver. It would be nice to know if he's hostile."

"Where are you?"

"Why?"

"I'll send out a squad car to harass the driver, let him know we can't have our peaceful citizens followed all over town."

"Don't do that."

"Nice talking with you, Gallegher. Gotta boogie. Real police work to do, you know."

"Wait!"

I didn't hear a click on the line. I could still hear him breathing over the din of the surrounding traffic.

"Let me give you the plate number," I said. "If anything happens to me, at least you'll have a place to start on your investigation."

"If anything happens to you, I'll take a celebratory cruise. Maybe I'll also get the city to give this guy tailing you some kind of commendation."

"Will you take the number, or what?"

There was a long silence, and then he said, "Give."

I recited the tag number. "If everything is okay, I'll call you back in five or ten minutes."

"Whatever. I don't suppose you'd like to fill me in on why you're getting followed? Does this have anything to do with Cabby Jacks or that Nigra fellow?"

"I don't think so, but it might be related to Garry Sharp."

"The little girl's father you were trying to find?"

"That's the one. I can't talk a lot about it right this second."

"Sure," Farley said. "Why involve the police in something like this?"

"Was it Mexico that made you so snarky?"

"It's all you, Gallegher. You do this to me. You're like the fuckin' albatross around my neck. Do me a favor and don't get yourself killed. I have a date tonight. I don't want to cancel it to do a new murder book on the likes of you."

This time I did hear the click on the other end. I probably couldn't have expected more. Three days back in town, and I'd already pushed my limits with Farley more than made either of us comfortable.

I stood, walked around to the driver's side of the Ford, leaned against the B pillar, and rapped on the side window glass.

For a second, there was no response. Through the tinted glass, I could see a head swivel around to look in the side mirror, but all anyone would see there was a pair of pants and a jacket. The driver had to turn all the way around to look at my face. Slowly, the window rolled down. The driver was a man. He looked about fifty, maybe older. His skin was wrinkled and his close-cropped hair was dry and wiry. He was dressed in a shopworn windbreaker jacket and jeans. He wore mirrored sunglasses.

"Nice day for a drive," I said.

"I figured you made me when you took that big circle," he said. "But it couldn't hurt one way or the other to keep an eye on you."

"Open your jacket," I said.

"Why?"

I let the dowel slip from my jacket sleeve and caught it before it could fall to the ground. I held it against the top of the driver's side door.

"Because if you don't I'm going drag you through this window and break every bone in your body. I don't have a gun. I want to make sure you don't either."

"I have one," he said. "But it's not on me. It's in a safe in the trunk."

"Prove it," I said. "I'm getting impatient."

He unzipped his jacket and showed me he wasn't wearing a shoulder rig.

"Lean forward, against the steering wheel," I said.

He'd obviously been through this drill before. He put his chest against the wheel. I reached down to reassure myself he didn't have a pistol secured in the back of his belt. He had a long wallet sticking out of his back pocket, so I yanked it before he could settle back.

"Hey!" he protested.

"Relax," I said. "I'm not ripping you off. You obviously know who I am. I'm leveling the playing field."

He had two photo ID cards in the wallet. His driver's license told me his name was Abraham Pratt. The other ID told me he was a licensed private investigator. I slapped the wallet closed and handed it back to him.

"Hold on a sec," I said.

I pulled my cell phone out and called Farley again.

"The guy's name is Abraham Pratt," he said immediately.

"Yeah, he's a PI," I said.

"Not one I've run across before. Must not be a real pro if you made him so quickly. You didn't kill him or anything?"

"He's fine. I'm fine. You didn't waste any time looking him up."

"What can I say? You whetted my curiosity. Please do me a favor and drop by today or tomorrow. My *professional* investigator warning signals are pinging off right and left. I think maybe you're into some stuff I should know about."

"Will do. First, Mr. Pratt and I are going to have a chat."

CHAPTER SEVENTEEN

I POCKETED MY CELL phone and leaned on the roof of the car to look at Pratt.

"Do I call you Abraham, or Abe?"

"What makes you think I want you to call me anything?"

"What you want doesn't matter much. I got an early start this morning. Didn't get any breakfast. You hungry?"

He had both hands on the steering wheel. The engine was still running. I could feel cool air wafting out the side window. He stared out the windshield, looking as if he might try to make a run for it, but that would have been stupid since I already knew who he was. He wouldn't be hard to find.

"I could eat," he said as he switched off the car. "You're buying."

"Fuck that," I said. "Expense it to your client."

We walked over to the chicken place. After he pulled himself from the Ford, I was surprised to find he was bigger than I had expected. Pratt would have given me some tough competition.

I stowed the dowel in my car before we walked into the restaurant. They had a nice chicken and waffles breakfast. We ordered two, with orange juice and coffee. The woman at the counter gave us a plastic marker with a number on it and said she'd bring the food to our table. I pointed to a booth near the back corner of the dining room. Pratt paid cash and pocketed the receipt.

"Boomer," he said, as we slid into the booth facing one another.

"Pardon?"

"My nickname. Everyone calls me Boomer."

"Let me guess. You were a high school quarterback."

"How'd you know?"

"You have the height. Thirty years or so ago you'd have carried about sixty pounds less, all of it suet. Boomer implies the ability to throw something a great distance. Hence, high school quarterback."

"Might have been college."

"There was that possibility. But you don't get to be a college QB unless you did it in high school."

"You have a logical mind, Gallegher."

"It gets me there."

"You got a PI license to go with it?"

"Private investigators have to follow rules. They have to color inside the lines. I prefer to make up the rules as I go. I'm a musician."

"Yeah, that much I know. I know a little more, too."

"Which puts me at a disadvantage," I said, preferring not to hear another account of my tawdry private adventures. "I suppose it would be stupid to ask who hired you?"

"Yeah. It would."

"Or why you've been following Yancey Hines around, and why now you're following me?"

"I can talk about that, a little. Not much."

"I could beat it out of you."

"You could try."

"I want you to stop."

"Guy who pays my bills says otherwise."

"See, we've already narrowed your potential list of employers down to the male half of the human race. According to Zeno's Paradox, if I can keep it up I'll never get to zero, but I will eventually learn your employer's identity."

The counter woman delivered our food. It was typical New Orleans diner fare—hot, fresh, and greasy. I poured syrup on the waffle. Pratt attacked a fried chicken thigh.

"Besides," I said. "I already know a lot about you. I'll know more in a few hours. The guy on the phone was a NOPD detective. If I know him, he's putting together a dossier on you as we sit here eating."

"What do you know already?"

"You're low-rent. Probably a one-man operation. I'm guessing you've spent most of your career playing tag with errant spouses, sitting outside seedy hotels with telephoto cameras, and testifying in divorce hearings. Once in a while you pull an insurance scam case. The gun in your trunk probably hasn't been fired in months, because you never expect to need it. You're following me around because you're too cheap to buy a GPS tracker. You're strictly a hand-to-mouth, paycheck-to-paycheck sort of guy. You aren't married, but you were once, not so long ago. And you aren't from around here. How am I doing so far?"

"Not bad."

"There's more. You've been following Yancey Hines for several weeks. No biggie. I don't owe Hines anything. Then you started following me. I never heard of Hines until yesterday, which means your client is either Bob Holbrook or Al Garlock."

"You think?"

"I suppose it could be Kellen Kenzie, but he'd more likely go for the high-priced spread. In fact, since Holbrook is also loaded, I'm betting on Garlock. We did not part on the best of terms."

Pratt didn't say anything. Instead, he focused on disassembling the chicken thigh.

"Got a question," he said.

"Shoot."

"You usually like white meat or dark meat chicken?"

"I'm a dark guy. Why?"

"Me too. Never understood why people eat the breast. It always comes out dry. So, I've always wondered. You know that little bit of organ tissue on the inside hollow of the bone in a fried chicken thigh?"

He held up the bone to show me. He didn't have to. I was familiar with it.

"Sure. What about it?"

"So, what is it? I mean, it's not the liver and it's not the gizzard. You think it's a spleen or something?"

"My grandmother called it the 'oyster,'" I said. "It's actually the kidney."

"Kidney? I thought they'd be high on the back, not in the thighs."

"What can I say? Birds are built different than us."

"Kidney. Well how about that?" He flicked it off the bone, picked it up, and tossed it in his mouth. "Sure tasty."

Having decimated his chicken, he poured some syrup over the waffle and started in on it. I had taken a more integrated approach, alternating between eating a little chicken and then a little waffle, the way the Almighty intended.

"Following me was a bad idea," I said, as I lifted my coffee cup.

"How so?"

"Before, I was simply curious. Garlock hiring a private cop to tail me makes me think he's up to something he wants to keep secret. All I wanted was a line on a guy who went missing from the pipeline project. I don't give a damn what Holbrook and the Kenzies are up to, or at least I didn't until now. I have to think there's some connection between the guy I'm looking for and the pipeline."

"Let's presume I have a clue what you're talking about," Pratt said. "My job was to keep an eye on you. That's it. Nobody told me why, or for how long. Who's this missing guy you're talking about?"

I told him about Garry Sharp and his daughter who needed surgery. I purposefully neglected to mention the notebook.

"What are you doing in the missing persons business?" he said. "They pay cops and people like me to do that sort of thing."

"It's a long story. Let's say I have a lot of bad stuff in my past to atone. Once in a while I have a chance to do some good for someone. I seem to have a particular talent for finding things others have lost or had taken from them. So, here's the deal, Pratt—"

"Please. Boomer."

"Not in a million years. I'm not interested in being your buddy, your confidante, your confessor, or anything else in your life. The only reason we're sitting here enjoying this delicious mass of calories and fat, and you're not lying in a pool of your own blood in the front seat of your car waiting for the ambulance, is because I am dead tired of violence. I am completely capable of putting you in a hospital, but I'm trying to be a more peaceful and compassionate person. I don't need you tagging along in my life. You've been made, so your usefulness to Garlock, at least as far as I'm concerned, is over. Your job is done. It's time to go find a philandering spouse or something. If I see you hovering around my space again, I'm calling my police detective friend to see if he can do something about your PI license. The same thing goes for Yancey Hines. I got no skin in his game, but I liked him, so he's off limits too. Is there anything I've said you don't understand?"

"No. I went to college, and I have a decent vocabulary. You're a big guy and for some people I suppose you can be kind of scary. The information I've compiled on you already tells me you can put some serious hurt on people. On the other hand, I was pummeled and flattened by defensive tackles and safeties for years when I was younger. I know how to take a beating. Maybe you can hurt me, and maybe you can't. I don't care, because I don't get paid enough to be a punching bag. A word of advice, if you're open to it."

"I'm listening."

"Without violating the confidentiality of my client, you may be digging for gold in quicksand. There are people out there who could squash you like a bug, flick you into a storm drain, and never think about you again. I don't know anything about this guy Garry Sharp. Never heard of him. All I'm saying is you win some and you lose some. Some games are lost before they even begin. If I were you, I'd walk away clean and never look back."

"Garlock doesn't frighten me."

"Whatever. It's been fun, man, but I have a report to write, and some new business to scare up. You're right, by the way. Getting made ended this job for me. My client probably won't give up so easily. Now you know you're being watched, the next guy might not be as—what did you call me?—'low rent' as I am. And he might not keep his gun in the trunk. As of this moment, I'm out of a job. On the other hand, I think I'd rather be me than you."

He pulled a card from his wallet and slid it across the table to me.

"In case you need someone to watch your six. Let's call it my way of thanking you for not getting physical back in the parking lot. See you in the funny papers, Gallegher."

CHAPTER EIGHTEEN

*T*WENTY MINUTES LATER I parked in front of a clapboard-covered house at the first address I had for William Truluck. I'd taken my time driving there, and I'd made a few random turns while checking my rearview mirror for any other tails. As far as I could tell, I was clean.

I walked up the dry-rotted steps to a front porch built from warped and cupped pine boards. Ancient lead paint peeled in curls on the windowsills and the front door jamb. There were a couple of mildew-covered extruded plastic Adirondack chairs on the porch. The street was quiet. Off in the distance I could hear cicadas chirping in the still heat of late morning.

I pushed the black doorbell button. Inside the house, I heard the sudden yapping of a lapdog. There were three dirty glass panes in the front door, and through them I could see a shadow moving toward me. There was a grating sound of a poorly maintained deadbolt lock, and the door opened.

A black woman wearing a loose flower print housedress and faded terrycloth slippers stared at me through the screen. She had a cigarette in one hand and her hair was in rollers. I didn't wait for her to ask who I was.

"Pardon the interruption," I said. "I'm trying to find William Truluck."

"What's your business with Billy?" she said.

"I need some information. The William Truluck I'm looking for worked until a few weeks ago on a pipeline project between Gulfport and Biloxi."

"Then you come to the wrong place, mister," she said. "My Billy has been dead for over a year. I hoped you might be from the insurance company. I've been trying to settle my claim with them for months."

"Sorry for your loss," I said. "Obviously I'm looking for someone else."

I walked back to my car and checked my notebook for the final address from the phone book. It was in Metairie. I put the address into my GPS before pulling away from the curb. When I looked over, Billy Truluck's widow still stood in the doorway, watching me. She took a long drag from the cigarette and exhaled a cloud of smoke through the screen.

* * * * *

It was nearing lunchtime, which always means clogged lanes on the I-10 and the I-90, so I avoided the freeways and instead stuck to the crosstown thoroughfares. Even so, it took me almost forty-five minutes to find my way to the third Truluck address. It was in a post-war apartment complex made from the drabbest brick I'd ever seen. The apartments had no stoops or porches. The front of the building was as flat as a dam, with front doors set flush with the asphalt parking lot. Every window I could see had an air-conditioner set into it, dripping condensation onto the ground. At the end of the parking lot was a faded metal swing set and a peeling jungle gym that was little more than an invitation to tetanus. The asphalt lot was heavily weathered, with weeds growing up through cracks.

There was nothing about the complex that indicated "home." It was a place to sleep and eat and lock the doors against the inevitable violence brought on by the night. It was a place for alcoholism and drug addiction and prostitution and desperation.

There were no doorbells I could find, so I knocked on Truluck's apartment door and stepped back, allowing the screen to wheeze shut.

The door cracked open a few inches. I could see half a face looking out at me. A smell of stale cigarette smoke and frying oil drifted through the opening.

"What do you want?" he said. The voice was raspy and a little wet, as if I'd awakened him from a nap.

"I'm looking for William Truluck," I said.

"What if he don't want to be found?"

"I need to ask a few questions of a William Truluck who worked the Holbrook pipeline job until a few weeks ago. Would that be you?"

"Depends on what you want to know."

"I'm not here to be a bother, sir. I'm trying to find another man who worked on that project, a nondestructive engineer named Garry Sharp."

"What about him?"

"He's gone missing," I said. "I've already talked with his bunkmates who worked the Holbrook job with him. I talked with Yancey Hines last night."

"What's your interest in him?"

"His daughter needs him. He's been missing for weeks and she's in a children's shelter. I'd like to get them back together if I can."

The man behind the door looked me up and down a few times.

"I got a gun," he said.

"That makes one of us. I'm not interested in trouble, Mr.

Truluck."

"What makes you so sure I'm Truluck?"

"If you weren't, you'd have slammed the door in my face by now. Mind if I come in? You could be a big help for a little girl."

He surveyed me again and finally opened the door wider.

"Reckon you better come on in," he said.

I stepped inside. He'd installed blackout shades on the windows. The room was gloomily dark, illuminated by a single low-wattage lamp on a veneered table next to a sprung-out sofa. The television was on, with the sound off. On the screen, two cartoon characters beat on each other with sledgehammers.

"Have a seat," Truluck said, pointing toward a dingy, threadbare wing chair placed diagonal to the sofa. He pulled a cigarette from a hard pack in his breast pocket and sat on the couch.

"I want to be clear," I said. "You are William Truluck, who worked for the Holbrook company on the Kenzie Oil pipeline?"

"Yeah, that's me."

"And you were fired from that job."

"Three weeks and two days ago. I'd been working with them for three months. I applied for unemployment last week. Still waiting for the response."

"So you were there when Garry Sharp left."

"I recall him being there one day and not being there the next. Figured he'd had enough, lit off in the night. Nobody ever said nothin' about him being missing. I recall they brought in another boy two or three days later to take his place. Can't for the life of me recall his name. Didn't much care for the little shit. Sharp was okay. Wouldn't give you a nickel for the guy who replaced him."

"Mind if I ask why you were fired?"

"Don't rightly know. Did you know I was a member of the Pipefitters' Association?"

"I don't know anything about you, Mr. Truluck."

"Well, I was. Up in Massachusetts. Moved down here because I started to hate snow. Louisiana is a right-to-work state. Everyone works at the pleasure of the boss. Know what that means?"

"It means they can fire you anytime they want, and they don't have to tell you why," I said.

"Sure as hell don't. One day I'm working, doing my job. Next morning boss grabs me on the way to the trench and tells me I'm gone. No warning, no reasons, just get and get quick."

"The boss. You mean Al Garlock."

"That's the sumbitch. I'm a God-fearing man, but I've had impure thoughts about caving that man's face in ever since. You met Garlock?"

"I did."

"What did you think?"

"I think the crusty S.O.B. has given me reason to dislike him," I said, playing to Truluck's emotions. Given Garlock had probably hired Boomer Pratt to follow me, there was more than a little truth in it.

Truluck chuckled. The chuckle turned into a wet cough. He wiped his mouth with the back of his hand and smiled.

"Got bronchitis," he said. "After three months as mosquito food, I'm surprised it ain't malaria."

"What can you tell me about Sharp?" I asked.

He took a drag from his cigarette and let the smoke out slowly. "Bright young man. Read a lot. He had one and only one job, to check the weld joints on the pipes. It's not a bad way to make a living. Most of the time these guys stand around waiting for labor to dig the trench, fit the new length of pipe, and weld the joint. Then they jump into the trench for five minutes, take their readings, and it's back into the air-conditioned cab of their truck for fifteen minutes.

141

Damned if I know what they do in there. Listen to the radio. Jerk off. Who knows?"

"Sharp was like that?"

"No. That's my point. He didn't look down on us trench wranglers. He got dirty. He helped out if we needed an extra hand. He hung out with us at chow and he knocked bottles with us at night when we got beer. Not a bad poker player. I'm saying that as a guy who learned not to draw to an inside straight before I could rightly walk. I liked him. Didn't like his replacement at all."

"Wayne Falkner?"

"No. You mean they already replaced Carl?"

"I haven't met anyone named Carl."

"Carl Zimmer. He's the guy they got to take Sharp's place. Zimmer was a lazy S.O.B. Never lifted a finger to help anyone. Spent all his time lounging in the truck and waiting to check the welds. Kept to himself around the bunk. Seemed a little stuck up, like he was too smart to hang out with the work gang. If he's gone, he didn't last more than two or three weeks. That's the way it is in right-to-work states. Hell, I'm probably going back to Massachusetts, work on sewer drains. It's smelly work, but by God it's more dependable, and if the boss tries to fire you, you got the union to go to bat on your behalf. Down here, it's every man for himself."

"You didn't care for Garlock, either?"

"Garlock was the worst. Harder than any drill sergeant I ever had in the Crotch. I'd bet you my first unemployment check his great great granddaddy was an overseer on a slave plantation. Some guys are tough, but they're fair. With Garlock, I have a feeling mean goes clear to the bone."

"You got into fights with him?"

"Me personally? No. I know better than to take on the boss. I saw him hit on some of the other boys once or twice. Mostly it was his mouth. He'd yell at us all day long, tell us we were behind schedule, we were lazy, he could replace us with men ten times better and faster in half an hour. Once I got sick of it and asked why he didn't go ahead and do it then. I regretted that. He sent me back to the bunk and docked me a day's pay."

"Right before he fired you?"

"No. That was first week on the job. I put up with his bullshit for another two and a half months because the pay was good."

"Tell me about the night Sharp disappeared," I said.

"All I know is he was there in the bunk trailer one night. Next morning, he was gone. I don't recall him actually leaving. I remember because we couldn't do any work without it getting inspected. It didn't pay to go ahead and lay pipe, because if a joint was bad twenty or thirty lengths back down the line, you'd have to rip it all out. Know what Garlock did?"

"No."

"Said it was cheaper to give the backhoe operator two or three days off while they got a new engineer and had us trench hogs dig with shovels. I never been in prison, but I got a real taste of it that week, I'll tell you. I remember digging away, sun beating down on us, with Garlock standing off to the side, barking orders like he enjoyed it."

"He'd had some experience running a prison road crew," I said.

"Doesn't surprise me. I think if he'd had a whip he'd have flogged us. I do hope to run into that sumbitch on the street someday, preferably with a few of my pipefitter buddies by my side."

He killed the last half inch of his cigarette in one drag and coughed out the smoke.

"I talked with Yancey Hines last night," I said.

"Sure. I know Yancey. How's he doing?"

"He quit the Holbrook job."

"Always said he was a smart man."

"He told me about a night when the bunk trailer was locked down. He said there was a diesel motor sound out in the inlet between the gulf and Lake St. Catherine."

"Sure. I remember. Wasn't the first time, either. First time was maybe a week into the job. I didn't think much about it at the time, probably because I wasn't interested in leaving the bunk."

"Did you ever see what made the engine noise?"

"No, but I know it was a boat."

"How?"

"Because I know the difference between a truck engine sound and a boat engine sound. This was definitely a boat. Maybe a dual engine job."

"And you weren't allowed to leave the trailer while it was there?"

"Didn't particularly need or want to, but I do know Garlock wouldn't have let me, because . . ."

He stopped.

"Hmmm . . ." he murmured.

"What?"

"Garry Sharp did try to leave the trailer that night. Garlock ordered him back inside, told him to stay until he was told he could go out. Sharp argued with Garlock, but that never gets anywhere. What Garlock wants, Garlock gets. So Garry turned off all the lights in the trailer and went over to a window to see what was out there."

"Did he say what it was?"

"No, but he did write something down in the notebook he always kept with him."

"I've been looking for this notebook. Everyone seems to recall him writing in it."

"Oh, he was a big one for writing. Drawing, too. Never understood what it was he was recording, but he seemed intent on it."

I reviewed what I knew and what I didn't. There was a lot more in the "didn't" column.

"Besides the night Garlock wouldn't let him out of the trailer, did Sharp and Garlock have other arguments?"

"Tons of 'em. Seems like they got into it one every other day or so. In fact, I remember they had a knock-down-drag-out shouting match at the trench site a day or so before Sharp took off. They was both red in the face, screaming at one another. I could hear them over the backhoe, and that thing makes a racket."

"What were they arguing about?"

"Something about the pipe. Sharp was pointing at the pipe and waving his hands around. Garlock tried to push him back, get him away from the other men. At one point he grabbed Sharp by the collar and tried to drag him away. Sharp twisted around and picked up a shovel. Garlock backed away after that, you bet."

"And this was right before Sharp disappeared?"

"Now that I think of it, it was his last day on the site. He left that night. Carl Zimmer was on the job three days later."

"Please bear with me," I said. "I'm not familiar with the pipeline business. I've learned lot over the last several days. You're saying Garry Sharp took his measurements of the weld joint in the trench before he got into it with Garlock?"

Truluck pulled the hard pack of cigarettes from his pocket again. "No. I'm not saying that. It wasn't the pipe in the trench he was angry about. It was the other pipe."

"Which pipe?"

"The pipe we hadn't laid yet. The pipe off to the side, waiting to be put in the trench. If you were at the worksite yesterday, I'm sure you saw it. They bring it in on pallet trucks and offload it using the backhoe as a crane. That's the pipe Sharp was upset over. Can't say why, but having worked for Holbrook and Garlock as long as I did, wouldn't surprise me a bit to find out they've been using substandard materials."

"Isn't the pipe regulated to meet specific standards?"

"Sure. It's ERW with a minimum wall thickness."

"ERW?"

"Electric Rolled Welded. It's a way you make pipe and tubing by bending steel plate around a mandrel and welding a seam down the length of it. It's the standard material for oil pipelines. Back when I was working in water and sewage lines in Massachusetts, we'd sometimes use cast pipe, but it won't contain the pressures needed in an oil pipeline."

"And there was something about the tubing that was intended to go into the trench that Garry Sharp didn't like."

"He was sure upset about it."

"How long was it after Sharp disappeared that you were fired?"

"Well, now, best as I can recall it, maybe four days. Could have been five."

I felt a tingling sensation in my chest. Something wrong was going on at Holbrook. My missing person case was rapidly turning into something wholly different. I wondered whether I was going to find Garry Sharp at all. The island where Holbrook was laying his pipeline measured perhaps two or three hundred square miles, almost all of it desolate swampland and sandy marsh. If a backhoe could dig an eighth of a mile of trench in a day, how quickly could it scoop out a hole measuring—say—three feet by six feet?

"Any idea where I might find this man Carl Zimmer?" I asked.

"Hell, Mr. Gallegher, if you'd asked me an hour ago, I'd have sent you to the Holbrook worksite. No. 'Fraid I can't help you with Zimmer."

I gave Truluck one of my cards and asked him to call me if he remembered anything else that might help in finding Sharp.

In the meantime, I decided Holbrook's operation deserved a second look.

CHAPTER NINETEEN

*B*EFORE I MADE any more enemies in the oil industry, I decided to pay a visit to an old friend. I had done about as much as I could that day to find Garry Sharp. It was time to turn my attention back to Cabby Jacks.

Quentin Wardell is a genealogist with the Church of Jesus Christ of Latter Day Saints in New Orleans. It isn't widely known, but the Mormon Church maintains one of the most extensive family history databases known to man. Their motives are simple—they believe a human being may be baptized as a Mormon even if they have been dead for decades, or even centuries. If you join the church, they make it their business to induct all of your ancestors for good measure.

Beyond being an archivist and a genealogist, Quentin is also one of the most knowledgeable persons I've ever met regarding almost any subject. What information he couldn't pluck directly from his amazing brain, he could find in short order using his online search skills. As such, he had been an invaluable source of information for me over the years since I'd embarked on my career as a "knight errant."

I found him in his office at the temple near the intersection of St.

Charles Avenue and Foucher. He had his elbows propped up on his desk, his hands interlaced into a sort of hammock on which his chin rested as he stared at his computer screen. Perhaps because of his age—he was in his middle eighties—and his profession, I always expected when I walked into his office to find a musty library of leather-covered books that would make my thousands of volumes in my apartment look puny in comparison.

Instead, his office was tidy and always perfectly clean, with only one small bookcase placed directly behind his desk. Quentin did almost all his work via computers these days.

While still spry for his advanced age, he did appear to have shrunk since I'd last seen him, almost a year earlier. His full head of shock-white hair was combed to the side. A stray lock fell across his forehead as he stared at the screen. His hearing had deteriorated further since my last visit, as he didn't react when I walked into his office, or even when I cleared my throat. I didn't want to frighten him, so I backed up and rapped sharply on his door.

He looked up from the computer and his face immediately broke into a wide grin.

"Patrick, my boy! What a wonderful surprise!" he said. "Please, come over! Have a seat. You know, I was thinking of you only the other day. And now, here you are!"

I told him not to bother getting up. I crossed around his desk and took his extended hand. His grasp was surprisingly strong. His eyes twinkled as I smiled down at him.

"I hope you've brought me a story today," he said. "It's been so long since I've been treated to one of your adventures."

I took a few minutes to fill him in on the body that had been found buried in the concrete floor of the building next to Holliday's, and how it had led me not only to solve a murder committed seventy years earlier, but also led to a modern-day shootout with minions of the Anolli crime family. When I finished, he looked as delighted as a five-year-old who had seen *The Wizard of Oz* for the first time.

"How thrilling!" he exclaimed. "Ah, if I were only thirty years younger, I think I would enjoy accompanying you on one of your cases."

"It's not as exciting as it sounds," I said. "I leave out a lot of the scut work. That's why I'm here."

"What? Already on the trail of another miscreant?"

"Not exactly. I'm trying to find someone. He's a friend of mine who's gone missing. All I know is he had an appointment on the day he disappeared, at six-thirty-four in the evening."

"You're sure it wasn't in the morning."

"Not completely. In fact, it might not be important at all, but it's most of what I have to go on."

"It's a strange time. Who makes appointments at a time like that?"

"Nobody. It's more like a transportation schedule of some kind. You know . . . trains, planes, ships, that sort of thing. I wanted to see if you could check your sources and let me know if there were any scheduled arrivals that day."

"Give me the date."

I told him the date Cabby went missing and he went to work. It didn't take long.

"To be thorough," he said, "I checked both six-thirty-four in the morning and in the evening. Interestingly, while the airport here in New Orleans is quite active, there were no arrivals or departures scheduled for either of those times that day. No busses or trains either. There *was* a scheduled arrival at the Port of New Orleans."

"A ship?"

"Indeed. Not a passenger vessel. I'm afraid it's a cargo ship."

"What's the name?"

"According to this record, she was the Rio Gaucho, a ship of Brazilian registry out of Rio de Janeiro. Now, this is unusual."

"What?" I asked.

"Well, *gaucho* isn't a Portuguese word. Portuguese is the official language of Brazil, whereas *gaucho* is Spanish, Argentinian Spanish to be exact. On the other hand, there are thousands of cargo vessels on the seas. I suppose after a while you simply name one whatever word pops into your head, like race horses. I once imagined it would be a fun thing to name race horses."

He was drifting. I needed to bring him back to the topic. "Last night I spoke with a friend of the man who disappeared," I said. "He told me he'd overheard my missing friend talk about someone he called the Brazilian."

"Aha," Quentin said. "A clue!"

"Is there any way to find out what the Rio Gaucho was carrying?"

"I don't know. I can check."

"While you're looking, it's possible Cabby was meeting a man named Nigra at the time."

"Perhaps a member of the Rio Gaucho's crew?"

"It would make sense."

"It might take me some time to find a crew manifest, if one exists at all."

"Is the Rio Gaucho still in port?"

He tapped on the keyboard and played with the computer mouse. "It appears that it is. It's scheduled to depart three days from now for a return trip to Brazil. What are you thinking, Patrick? Do you plan to visit this ship?"

"That's not a bad idea," I said. "At the very least, I'd like to lay eyes on it."

"Then please do be careful. And I expect you to come back and tell me everything that happens. I'll see if I can find out what the

Rio Gaucho was hauling, and I'll look for a crew manifest. If I find anything, I'll call you."

As I drove back to Holliday's, I tried to separate facts from supposition in my thick Irish head.

What I knew to be true wasn't much. Cabby was missing and had been for over a week. At his last Gamblers Anonymous meeting, he'd had a confrontation in the parking lot with a man who had a scarred face. He had said something about not pissing off someone called "The Brazilian." His schedule book indicated a time and the words *D. Nigra* on the day he vanished. He had been circumspect about discussing his current business when I'd last seen him face-to-face, but his history led me to believe he was involved in something illegal, or at least illicit.

Those were facts. It was possible I had conflated the information I had to build a picture badly littered with my own biases and imaginative guesses. On the other hand, I had long since learned to trust my instincts and my intuition. Having the term "Brazilian" come up twice in the course of looking for Cabby was simply too serendipitous to ignore.

It was mid-afternoon. While the Rio Gaucho wasn't scheduled to sail for several days, I decided there was no time like the present to take a look at it. I found a place to make a U-turn on St. Charles and headed toward the Henry Clay Avenue port, where Quentin had told me the Rio Gaucho was berthed.

I parked and pulled a pair of binoculars from the trunk of my car. The port is almost two miles long. It can accommodate over a dozen ships at any one time, so it took me a while to find the Rio Gaucho. Having offloaded its inbound cargo days earlier, it was now being loaded with steel shipping containers by a huge crane. On the busy deck, crewmen scrambled to secure each container as it was settled into place.

I've spent my share of time on boats, but ships of this size were a cipher to me. Even as I peered at it through the binoculars, I had no real idea what I was looking for. I was too far away to make out any of the crewmen's faces, let alone search for one with a nasty scar. Besides, I had no real reason to believe the man with the scar had any connection to this ship. After all, the confrontation between him and Cabby had taken place while the Rio Gaucho was at sea.

Nate, the fellow at the GA meeting, had said the man was about six feet tall, well-dressed, and had a foreign accent—Mexican or Cuban. On the other hand, it could also have been Portuguese. The languages were similar, at least to the untrained ear.

And Cabby had said he didn't want to piss off the Brazilian.

No.

I lowered the binoculars and tried to remember exactly what Nate had said. It wasn't "piss off the Brazilian." He'd said he didn't want to "piss in the Brazilians' grits." Cabby had a long tradition of finding niche positions with larger crime families. He'd already insinuated he had been working on something not completely legal, which suggested he'd again discovered a way he might contribute— however slightly—to a larger criminal enterprise.

In my time in New Orleans, I'd dealt with old-line Sicilian mobsters, a new crop of younger crime families with no clear roots to the old country, fresh-off-the-boat Vietnamese gang members, and had even had a run-in or two with some crazy Russian syndicates. About Brazilians, I knew absolutely nothing.

I had a feeling I knew someone who would.

I pulled out my cell phone and found Chester Boulware's number in the directory.

"You change your mind, Gallegher?" he said as soon as he

answered.

"What, Gary Tate didn't pan out?"

"Oh, we found him. Got him as he hopped off the plane from Cancun. He was tanned, fit, and ready to squeal on the Anolli family. He's going to be a real asset in putting Claude and Angie away for a long time. I hate saying things like this, but I owe you one."

"Maybe we can get square right away."

"What'cha' got?"

"You know anything about Brazilian organized crime here in New Orleans?" I asked.

"Don't tell me you're in trouble with those guys."

"No, but a friend of mine may be mixed up with them."

"The guy who disappeared? The one who asked you to find him if he did?"

"The same. One of the people I talked to said he overheard Cabby talking with some fellow who had a foreign accent and a huge facial scar. Said Cabby declared that he didn't want to anger the Brazilian, or maybe it was the Brazilians. Hard to say, given the way it was phrased. I've been working so far on the assumption he was into some small-time stuff. I've discovered a couple of things along the way that suggest he might be hooked up with a larger operation. That indicates gangs."

"Man, you do not want to mess with the Brazilians, Gallegher. I think I might know this guy you describe, the one with the scar. He's trouble, the kind you might not have encountered before. Most of these gangs are related in one way or another with the PCC, a group in Rio that got its start as a bunch of unrelated neighborhood drug dealers."

"PCC?"

"Primeiro Comando da Capital, or First Capital Command. They got tired of killing one another and decided to band together. They run the *favelas*, or slums, all over Rio. These days, about every gram of heroin, weed, or meth that circulates in Rio has been stomped on by the PCC."

"What about here in New Orleans?"

"Some of the bigger players decided to diversify and extend their markets. At first, they got involved in gambling and extortion, the usual mob stuff. A few managed to get work visas for cover jobs here. Over time they developed a core group of players in the city who funnel drugs and money back and forth between here and Rio. If I'm right, the guy you want is named Rodrigo Torres Villar."

"What do you know about him?"

"Enough to advise you to give him a wide berth. This is one nasty player. He was inducted into the PCC while he was in prison in Brazil. Reports indicate he's bright and highly resourceful. He rose through the PCC prison ranks, and his PCC connections greased the local courts and got him an early release."

"How does a guy with a prison record get a work visa to come to the US?"

"What can I say? Money talks and bullshit walks. His people got to the right connections here. He was on the next plane out of Rio."

"What's he into here?"

"Everything. Drugs, whores, gambling, a little extortion here and there. He even oversees a few legitimate operations like coin laundries, parking lots and the like, anything that takes mostly cash because it's easy to cook the books and there's no paper trail. You ever eat at one of those Brazilian *churrasco* joints where they run around with meat on skewers and slide it off onto your plate? He probably has his fingers in it. The PCC hides their dirty money in their legitimate cash businesses. After a while it's hard to figure where anything came from. Like I said, he's bright."

"And dangerous."

"Dangerous ain't the word. From what I hear, this guy is always thinking of new ways to extend his business interests. One thing he's been into recently is importing fake archeological relics from South America. There are collectors who go batshit over pre-Columbian artifacts. Villar has a couple of crews in places like Ecuador and Chile cranking out replicas around the clock. I mean, this shit is museum-quality. Indiana Jones would have a hard time telling it from the genuine article."

"Smuggling, then?"

"Sure. Smuggling would be his kind of thing. Why?"

"My friend Cabby had an appointment book with what looked like a meeting scheduled for the day he disappeared. There weren't any trains or airplanes scheduled to arrive at that time, but there was a cargo ship called the Rio Gaucho. I'm scoping it out right now. It's Brazilian registry, out of Rio de Janeiro."

"Too much coincidence for my tastes, old son."

"I had the same thought. How big is the Brazilian crime contingent in New Orleans? How many people?"

"Hard to say. They aren't hardcore yet. For the moment, everything is peaceful between the different national gangs. I figure there's a core group of fifteen or twenty neighborhood bosses repping the PCC. Villar is one of them."

"I can't figure what a guy like Cabby Jacks would be doing for the Brazilian mob."

"Beats me, but I don't know the guy. One thing I can say. These Brazilian boys are clannish and nationalistic to a fault. They don't let a lot of people into the club. If your friend was doing some work for them, it wouldn't have been high-level stuff. They don't trust Americans much."

"Could be good or bad," I said.

"How so?"

"If he wasn't key to their operations, then he wouldn't have been a valuable asset, which would make him expendable. He might have disappeared because he got taken off the game board permanently."

"Or," Boulware said, "if you want to put a positive spin on it, maybe he found himself a hidey-hole and is riding out some bad times until it's safe to show his face again. Tell you what. Since I owe you one, I'll check out this Rio Gaucho cargo ship, see what it was carrying. My advice to you is to lay off the Brazilians until we have more information. You go stumbling around in their territory, and Shorty's likely to be looking for a new horn player. I know a guy, works for I.C.E. He recently transferred here from San Francisco after some dust-up with the Chinese Triads there. I'll consult with him. He might want to talk to you."

CHAPTER TWENTY

I GOT BACK TO Holliday's a half hour later. Even though we were scheduled to open in a few hours, the place was empty. I figured Shorty must be out running some errands.

I hiked up the stairs to my apartment, took a quick shower, and changed clothes. With any luck, I could steal a couple of hours with Merlie before I had to go on at ten. We hadn't seen a lot of each other since returning from San Francisco, because of all the time I'd spent trying to juggle two searches. I missed her face.

When I got back downstairs, the bar was still empty, so I was careful to lock the door as I left and headed for my car.

I hadn't made it ten feet before two men fell into lockstep with me, one on either side.

"Good afternoon, Mr. Gallegher," the one on my right said. He extended a card. I took it. It said *Borglund Security and Investigations*.

"Which one of you is Borglund?" I asked.

"Neither," he said. "I'm Dickens. He's Fenster."

I paused on the sidewalk to get a better look at them. They were stereotypes. My first guess pegged them as retired federal agents. They walked with the same *fuck you* swagger I'd seen many times with Chester Boulware, the kind of pseudo-psychopathic saunter that conveyed their complete lack of fear of anyone or anything. They either worked out relentlessly or were wearing body armor—probably the latter.

Dickens was about six feet tall. His hair had probably been jet-black at one point but was now gray at the temples and pewter elsewhere. He kept it cut half an inch long and loaded down with some kind of goo to keep it in place. I couldn't see his eyes because of his impenetrably dark sunglasses. As his head turned in my direction, I saw they were bifocals, which probably meant he was in his late forties or early fifties. He wore a conservative, black, wool summer suit with a hint of pinstripes—probably his concession to individuality, since Fenster's suit was solid black. As we walked, he held his head forward, breaking the wind with his chin. He kept his hands at his side, never scratching or touching his face. I'd seen the discipline before in federal agents and pro baseball outfielders. The hands were always free and ready to go for a weapon, which I felt certain both of these characters carried under their carefully-tailored haberdashery.

Fenster was a little shorter than Dickens, but otherwise they might have been cast in the same mold. His hair was a little longer than Dickens's, but still shorter than my typically unruly inch and a half or so. When I stopped, he stopped, almost without any hesitation or lag time, which indicated excellent reflexes. Compared to the kind of guys I ran into who thought they were tough, these fellows were the real deal. While my first impulse was to tell them to get lost, I already knew they wouldn't, and they might be offended enough to do something nasty to me. My better option was to play along and see what they wanted.

"So, what's the special tonight?" I said. "Waterboarding or battery clamps on the nipples?"

I was a little surprised when Dickens laughed. Up to that point, he hadn't seemed capable of it.

"Nothing so sinister," he said. "Mr. Fenster and I have been dispatched to invite you to a meeting with one of our clients."

"And, by invite, you mean intimidate."

"Not at all. If you don't want to go, we are not instructed to force you or detain you further. You'll be perfectly safe. You might even enjoy it. After the meeting, we'll return you to your club. If you want to walk away, please do so."

"Well, that's a relief. I was beginning to wonder whether I could take both of you at the same time."

This time Fenster chuckled, but he didn't say anything. Dickens was the one empowered to speak for their client. From his reaction, he also didn't believe I could take either of them separately, let along both together.

He was probably right. I'm not half bad at the intimidation game myself. It's sort of the stock in trade when you become a leg breaker for a loan shark. I've been in my share of fights over the years. I usually win. On the other hand, most of the guys I'd beaten hadn't been pros. Dickens and Fenster had probably been in the violence game a lot longer than I had.

"I'm sure you needn't worry," Dickens said. "I think you could benefit greatly from taking this meeting. In fact, it's possible your whole life could change. This could be your lucky day, Mr. Gallegher."

"Sure," I said. "Lucky me."

As if on cue, a Lincoln Town Car limousine pulled alongside us. Fenster opened the back door and held it.

"If you please," Dickens said.

I sure as hell wasn't going to learn anything by running or telling them to ram their invitation. My alternative was to accept their offer and hop into the car.

It was a cushy limousine, though I couldn't claim to have enough experience with the type in order to make an expert comparison. The seats were plush leather. The windows were darkened to an extent that defied the state laws regulating them, but if you could afford a ride like this, you weren't troubled much by breaking such regulations. A small flat screen television, set into a panel behind the driver's seat, showed a baseball game. Braves were playing the Astros. Astros were up by two.

I took the forward-facing seat. There were two bucket seats on each side of the console housing the TV. Fenster sat in one. Dickens took the other.

"Is this the part where you toss a bag over my head so I can't see where we're going?" I asked.

"Too melodramatic," Dickens said. "Not our style. Would you like something to drink? We have a fully stocked bar."

He slid open a panel beneath the TV, revealing dozens of two-ounce minibottles of various high-priced liquors. Above the screen, he opened a door to a small refrigerator containing several bottles of beer and some soft drinks.

I was in the mood for a beer, but I also wanted to keep my wits about me.

"Got a Diet Coke in there?"

Fenster raised an eyebrow.

"Diet?" Dickens said.

"What can I say? I'm trying to maintain my girlish figure."

Fenster chuckled again as Dickens fished an eight-ounce plastic bottle of soda from the refrigerator and handed it to me.

We'd turned right onto Decatur, then right again several streets farther on, so we were headed north, toward Lake Pontchartrain. I twisted the cap off the bottle and took a swig. It was ice-cold. There are few pleasures quite as sublime as the first slug from an icy bottle of pop. In most cases, I'd have taken the time to savor it, but my mind was working overtime as I tried to figure out what was happening.

"Let me guess," I said. I pointed at Fenster. "You were Secret Service. Your buddy Dickens here was FBI."

"Wrong on both counts," Dickens said. "*I* was Secret Service. Mr. Fenster was with the State Department in Consular Operations. Not bad, Mr. Gallegher. Good observational skills for an amateur."

"Ouch," I said, and took another swig from the bottle. I pulled their card from my pocket and read it again. Borglund Security and Investigations was headquartered in Atlanta.

"You boys aren't from around here," I said.

"No," Dickens said.

I pointed at Fenster. "Does he talk?"

"When I have something to say," Fenster said. His voice, given his muscular build and general tough demeanor, was surprisingly high and a little raspy.

I pointed at the television screen.

"Your Braves are taking a beating."

"I'm a Boston fan," Dickens said.

I smiled as if he had imparted the missing piece to the puzzle of existence. I pointed at Fenster.

"Dodgers," he said.

I'd gotten seven words out of the Sphinx. I felt as if I'd accomplished something. "So," I said, "About this Borglund Security and Investigations outfit. Can anyone join, or is it an ex-spooks only sort of operation?"

"We're almost all former government operatives of one type or another," Dickens said. "The government spends a lot of money to train its covert and law enforcement operatives, but they don't spend a lot on salaries. It isn't unusual for agents to put in their twenty, muster out with a small but dependable pension, and go to work for more . . . shall we say *generous* employers."

"That explains the snappy suits," I said. "I know a guy with the Justice Department who would fit right in with your operation."

"Agent Boulware," Dickens said.

I pointed at him. "You're good. You're *very* good."

"Before the evening is over, I'm sure you'll discover that we know a great deal about you, Mr. Gallegher."

We arrived twenty minutes or so later at a gated community on the shores of Lake Pontchartrain. I'd been there once before, several years earlier, when I'd been hired by a wayward wife to find her lover, whom she believed had been killed by her jealous husband. That enterprise had ended badly. The wayward wife and I hadn't stayed in touch, despite the fact I had a little over a million dollars of her late husband's money in an offshore bank account.

The limo pulled into the shell and gravel parking lot of a marina and parked at the gate to a personal dock. Dickens held the door for me as I slid out and felt the crunch of shells under my size fifteen Reeboks. Fenster punched several buttons on a keyboard next to the gate, hiding them with his other hand in case I might try to memorize them. The gate lock opened with a metallic clank.

I followed Dickens and Fenster onto the dock, which extended some fifty or sixty feet out into the lake. At the end floated a seventy-foot yacht. The name *Sweet Crude* was stenciled on the bow with gold leaf. The deck sat about fifteen feet above the waterline. Portholes set at eye level as we approached on the dock were lit up. Through them I could see the boat was handsomely decorated with fine hardwoods in the cabins.

Dickens and Fenster stopped at the base of a steel gangway

placed between the deck of the Sweet Crude and the timbers on the dock.

"After you," Dickens said.

I took a deep breath and strode up the incline. Dickens followed me, but Fenster stayed behind.

"He's not invited?" I asked, pointing back at him.

"Different detail," Dickens said. "He's making sure you and our client aren't interrupted."

"And what are you doing?"

"Seeing to it your conversation with our client is as pleasant as possible."

"You're here to make sure I don't take your client off at the neck."

He smiled, more or less the way a shark does the instant before it bites off your leg.

"Something like that," he said. He pointed toward a sliding door amidships. "If you please."

I walked past him into a salon only slightly smaller than my apartment, but infinitely better appointed. My feet sank an inch into plush cable cut pile carpet as I took in the room. The walls were paneled with rich dark teak, with vertical strips of tiger-striped maple every five feet. Two sofas had been installed, one port and one starboard, against the outside walls. I estimated the beam of the yacht to be about fifteen feet, which left plenty of dancing room between the sofas, if it hadn't already been filled with two oval coffee tables also made of teak with tiger maple inlay. A loveseat sat perpendicular to the sofas. Beyond the loveseat was a cherry dining table, on which some enterprising soul had laid a feast. I saw cracked king crab legs, various satays and tapas, crudités, and several items I couldn't recognize. On a bar behind the dining table were three heated serving trays with the lids closed. Behind the bar was a complete selection of liquors.

I looked up and discovered a tray ceiling bordered in more deeply polished teak. The second level of the tray was a mirrored ceiling. Made me wonder what kind of parties the owner of this yacht threw.

"Please," Dickens said, "Have a seat. I'll inform our host that you've arrived. Can I get you a drink?"

"Nothing for me. I haven't finished burping up the Diet Coke."

Dickens opened a door and stepped into a hallway that led toward the bow of the boat. He left the door open. Not long after, I heard people coming toward me along the hallway. I couldn't make out what they were saying, which might have been their intent. Seconds later, two people stepped into the salon, a man and a woman. Dickens followed them into the salon and took a position in a far corner, close enough to keep an eye on things but far enough away not to be intrusive.

The man was tall, tanned, and fit. His azure eyes seemed to flit constantly around the room, as if he was terrified of missing a single detail. He wore a short-sleeved solid-royal-blue button-down shirt and expensive black twill slacks. His shoes might have cost as much as my car. He didn't wear socks. His hair was silver except for a persistent strand of jet at a front cowlick. He wore it long and swept back.

The woman was probably in her fifties and stunning. She had icy Nordic blonde hair you can't get from a bottle, no matter how hard you try. Her eyes, unlike the man's, focused on my face with laser precision and stayed there. She seemed to be studying my features. She stood in the middle five-foot range, a lot of it legs and the rest like some sort of Greek statue. She appeared a little top-heavy, in a way only modern surgery can achieve, which forced me to consider that her porcelain features might also have been enhanced along the way. If so, her surgeon was to be commended. After Merlie, she was the second most beautiful woman I'd seen all week. As if to accent her pallor, she wore a white oxford cloth shirt unbuttoned halfway up and cinched under her bosom, leaving her midriff bare, and a pair of white Capri pants. She also wore gold sandals. She stood off to one side, arms folded under her breasts and surveyed me as the man walked around the dinner table and held out his hand.

"Mr. Gallegher," he said. "What a pleasure it is to have you visit. My name is Kellen Kenzie."

CHAPTER TWENTY-ONE

"AND THIS IS my lovely wife Claudine," Kenzie said, gesturing toward the blonde. Claudine Kenzie didn't budge from her watch. She preferred to observe me from a distance.

I had that effect on a number of women.

"We were about to have a bite when you arrived," Kenzie continued. "We have some other guests arriving in about an hour. You're welcome to stay and meet them, but I expect our business will be concluded by then. Please, will you join us in a little snack?"

Claudine, as if on cue, did a half-pirouette and her arm snagged Kenzie's. It was precise and only seemed a little rehearsed—or perhaps they did this dance all the time with strangers.

I hadn't had a bite since my chicken and waffles that morning, which is a long time for a guy my size. I joined them at the table.

"Nice little putt-putt you have here," I said, as I picked up a plate.

"Yes," Kenzie said. "Thank you. The big one is in Galveston."

"How many gallons per mile do you burn in it?"

Kenzie looked up at me. For a second he seemed confused.

"Silly me," I said. "Doesn't matter to you, does it? After all, if you have all the petroleum in the world, who cares about filling the tank on the family ocean liner? How does it work with guys like you? Do you ever stop at a gas station, or do you have underground tanks installed under your servants' quarters?"

For the first time, I saw a smile creep onto Claudine Kenzie's frosty features. Perhaps she wasn't used to hearing her husband spoken to that way. Perhaps the impolite jolly Irish giant amused her. Perhaps I missed her meaning entirely, and she was actually imagining feeding me like chum to the sharks in the Gulf of Mexico. There were a lot of possibilities.

"I'd imagine I fill up the tanks about as often you do your quaint little Pinto," Kenzie said, without looking at me as he scooped a dollop of caviar onto his plate.

"Okay, you've done your homework."

"Oh, I know a great deal about you," Kenzie said. He put down his plate and reached behind the bar to retrieve a file folder. "According to Abraham Pratt, you detected he was following you only five minutes after he started."

"Boomer? *You* hired him?"

"Yes."

"Weird. I figured he was hired by Al Garlock."

"I have no idea who this Al Garlock is."

"He's the foreman building your pipeline."

"Ah. I see. No, I asked Mr. Pratt to find out what he could about you."

"I suppose I should be insulted you didn't hire the high-priced spread, like your boys from Borglund Security here." I jerked my thumb toward Dickens, who acknowledged it with a blank stare.

"We tend to reserve Borglund's services for our more important investigations."

"And your less subtle abductions," I added.

"I'm sorry. Did you feel taken against your will?"

170

"Only slightly less than the Lindbergh baby. They didn't rough me up or anything. I appreciated that."

"So why did you come?"

"If a door opens, go through it. They promised I wouldn't be hurt. I took that at face value. If I hadn't come with them, I wouldn't have learned anything."

"And what have you learned?"

"First of all, I made your son-in-law nervous by visiting the pipeline project. He thinks I know something that, clearly, I don't. Or maybe I do know, but I don't know I know it. That's the way things work out sometimes."

"I did originally hire Mr. Pratt to follow you because of Robert's alert. He said you were snooping around the site looking for a man named Sharp. After you uncovered Mr. Pratt this morning, I asked Mr. Dickens here to assemble some more information on you. I have to say, I'm impressed. You come with a surprising history."

"Things happen," I said. "Sometimes life is a river and you're only a stick of flotsam it carries along."

"Ah, yes. The internal versus external locus of control theory," Claudine said from her vantage near the sofa.

I raised an eyebrow.

"We aren't completely dissimilar," she said. "I studied psychology before I met Kellen. Dartmouth undergrad, master's at Texas Tech."

"Nothing," Kellen said, "to match your doctorate."

"Zounds," I said. "What else do you have in that folder? Any tips on this year's Super Bowl?"

Kenzie opened the folder and scanned it.

"Not that it's pertinent," he said, "but I'd be interested in hearing why you dropped out of the seminary."

"Crisis of faith. I discovered I didn't have any."

"Then why did you enroll?'"

"I was misinformed. I heard all the hot chicks went there."

"To a Catholic seminary?"

"Maybe I should have hired Borglund to research them first."

Dickens actually snickered but worked hard to suppress it. Despite the fact he'd essentially strong-armed me, I was beginning to like him. Still didn't trust him as far as I could kick him, but he was agreeable enough. Kenzie ignored him. I had a feeling he did that a lot with the help.

"And you worked for the Nashua Police Department in New Hampshire."

"With," I said.

"Pardon?"

"I wasn't exactly on the payroll. I consulted with them as a forensic psychologist. I got a per diem and expenses."

"Until you killed a murder suspect."

I paused to pop a boiled shrimp in my mouth after dredging it in a first-class cocktail sauce. Kenzie waited patiently while I chewed.

"Look," I said, after swallowing. "I already lived this story. I'm not in the mood to recap it. It wasn't that great the first time around. The perp was a stone psycho serial killer who deserved to have his breathing license revoked. He killed the detective investigating the case and was seconds away from doing the same for me when I punched his ticket. I've lost a little sleep over it since, but I don't regret it. It was him or me.

"This conversation is killing my appetite, so let me condense it for you. The police know about six men I've killed in the last fifteen years. There might be others, but that's none of your business. I haven't done more than a full day in jail for any of them, because the DA always ruled them justifiable under the circumstances. I don't wake up each morning with the urge to cut some asshole's wires. Regardless of how the movies make it look, taking some poor schnook's everything is a tough deal. It eats at your soul like boiling lye. I don't die easily, Mr. Kenzie. Neither did the men I killed, but they did die in the end. I'm still here, and I feel fine. Mostly."

I punctuated my speech by skewering another shrimp and picking up a crab leg.

Kenzie glanced at a Claudine.

"Sounds like we've found the right man," she said.

I had extracted the meat from the crab leg and had it halfway to my mouth. I placed it back on the plate.

"Hold on," I said. "I think I skipped ahead here. Did I miss something?"

"I have an idea," Kenzie said. "Let's eat for a few minutes, settle down a bit. After a little nosh, we'll start over. I've found negotiations always go better on a full stomach."

I didn't necessarily agree, but my stomach chose that second to growl. Loudly.

"Okay," I said. "But only because I'm hungry."

As I might have noted before, I'm a big guy. Big guys need a lot of calories to keep the furnace stoked. I loaded up my plate. Kenzie and his wife also made their own plates. We retreated to separate sides of the salon to nibble.

I had to hand it to Kenzie. He understood people. He had recognized that the discussion had reached a dangerous level and had diffused the heat with a break. Not giving a damn about other people's feelings in an argument, I was not in the habit of conducting them in rounds, like a prize fight. Once I got revved up, it was typically full speed ahead until I ran out of steam or the other guy was out cold on the floor. That's the way we thugs roll.

While we ate, Kenzie made small talk, mostly about New Orleans. He talked about the restaurant on Bourbon Street where he stole the chef who now ran the galley on the *Sweet Crude*. Claudine, who seemingly spoke only when absolutely necessary, nibbled on a meatball and a couple of shrimp as her head moved back and forth like a spectator at a tennis match, following the conversation between Kenzie and me.

As the food on our plates began to dwindle, our topic began to shift to oil, which led to the pipeline. I'm no fool. Kenzie was working his way back to whatever reason he had summoned me. I knew it. He knew I knew it.

"You met Robert Holbrook," he said, as he placed his plate on the coffee table.

"Your son-in-law," I said.

"Yes." There a twinge of regret in his voice. It might have been distaste.

"What about him?"

"Do you have children, Mr. Gallegher?"

"There might be one or two running around New England I haven't been told about, but to the best of my knowledge I am childless."

"You may be fortunate. Claudine and I have two children. Our son, Charles, was never interested in the oil business. He and I disagreed, strongly, about this when he was in college. I didn't handle things as diplomatically as I could. We didn't speak for several years. I'm happy to say we reconciled, eventually, but it was difficult."

"You and he were too much alike," Claudine noted.

"As you have said many times, dear. I think every man wants a son, at least until he has one. Daughters are different. Seconds after they are born, they wrap their fathers around their little fingers and the bond is permanent. You've met Robert. Have you met our daughter, Astrid?"

"Haven't had the pleasure," I said.

"She was a beautiful girl who grew to be a breathtaking woman," Kenzie said.

"And spoiled," Claudine added.

"Undoubtedly," Kenzie said. "Fathers and daughters. It's a time-worn calculus. I indulged her shamelessly. And why not? I could certainly afford to. In the process, I may have missed instilling certain important values. I adore her, sure. I'm also realistic enough to recognize that she is petulant and headstrong. She met Robert in college. Nobody else would do."

He paused and stared off into space.

"My son-in-law is a wastrel," he said, finally. "He's lazy, careless, and not particularly faithful. This Mr. Garlock you mentioned must be doing a creditable job, because the pipeline is more or less on schedule. This can't be attributed to Robert. He's seldom on the site."

"As president of Holbrook Transport Systems, I'd imagine that's not uncommon."

"President," Kenzie said. "Yes. A self-appointed title. For all intents and purposes, I own Holbrook Transport Systems in every way except legally. I wrote a check to Robert for the startup money. Running an important contractor for Kenzie Oil would put a little starch in his spine. It seems I misjudged the boy."

"Is this meeting tonight about Robert?" I asked.

"Yes. I'm afraid my son-in-law is in trouble, the sort that could reflect badly on my daughter. It could have an adverse effect on Kenzie Oil."

I glanced over at Dickens, who stood golem-like in the corner. He didn't fidget. He didn't pick at his nails. His arms stayed relaxed at his side. For all anyone could tell, he was a mannequin.

I entertained the notion of getting up and leaving. It was obvious our conversation to this point had been the setup. Kenzie was about to flip his hole card. I wasn't sure I wanted to hear any more. My other-people's-problems plate was overflowing already. I shifted my gaze from Dickens to the salon door and back. Dickens shrugged a little. Then he almost imperceptibly shook his head. I couldn't tell whether he was advising me or warning me. In either case, it didn't look like I was going anywhere. I was now strapped in for the entire ride.

Again. Story of my life.

"Okay," I said, trying to make myself sound as disinterested as possible. If he caught it, Kenzie didn't let on. "What kind of trouble?"

"I have reason to believe he has been cutting corners on materials. Are you at all familiar with metallurgy?"

"As you noted, my PhD was in psychology. We didn't analyze a lot of metals in that discipline. I did have an interesting conversation in the last day or so with a gentleman who currently works on your pipeline, fellow named Wayne Falkner. He told me a little bit about the pipe that's used. I didn't follow a lot of it, but I got the impression it's a fairly specialized material."

"Mr. Falkner works for me."

"Did Carl Zimmer work for you also?"

"No. I found him a better position elsewhere in order to get Falkner onto the jobsite. My son-in-law, as I mentioned, is lazy. He's also greedy. He makes far more from my contract with his company, which, in effect, is actually *my* company, than he deserves based on his effort. Despite the fact that when Claudine and I eventually die his wife will inherit a king's ransom, Robert seems determined to cheat his way to independent prosperity."

"The pipes," I said. "Garry Sharp's notebook."

Kenzie looked at his wife. She bobbed her head, almost imperceptibly.

"What about this notebook?" Kenzie asked.

"Sharp was keeping a notebook before he disappeared. According to the other men living in his trailer, he was also making drawings of the pipes that were going into the trenches. From what I was told, he was highly industrious about it. When he skipped the job site, he left some expensive equipment, but the notebook is missing. It must have been important."

Kenzie stood and retreated to the bar, where he poured two fingers of single malt into a wide glass. He held up the bottle and looked at me.

"Sure," I said.

He poured another and brought it to me before returning to his seat. He didn't offer one to Claudine. Maybe she didn't drink. She didn't seem to mind.

"I have reason to believe," Kenzie said, "that Robert has been using counterfeit pipe in this pipeline project. The contract with Kenzie Oil stipulates the alloy and the pipe thickness to be used and that the pipe must be American made. I'm a bit of a stickler about this. There is evidence that Robert has been importing cheap Chinese steel pipe made of a less durable alloy. It carries the same markings as the correct stock from the plant in Pittsburgh from which he is supposed to be buying his materials."

"I think I get it. Garry Sharp's bunkmates told me about a fight Sharp had with Al Garlock before Sharp disappeared. They said it was about the pipe, but they didn't know any more. Sharp did the nondestructive examination of the pipe after it was welded in the trenches. He knows steel inside and out. I'm betting he discovered not long after arriving on the job that he was dealing with substandard materials."

"No doubt," Kenzie said.

"There's more. According to Sharp's coworkers, every once

in a while, they'd be locked in their trailer and the lights on the worksite would be turned out. One of the men reported hearing heavy equipment outside and a large diesel engine, like on a boat or a large truck."

Kenzie took a sip of the whisky. He set the glass down on the coffee table. "You know a lot more than I imagined," he said. "I'm impressed."

"How risky is it to use this counterfeit pipe?" I asked. "After all, steel is steel, right?"

"To a point, yes. Pumping oil from Gulfport to Biloxi requires a significant amount of pressure. To accommodate that pressure, the pipe must be of sufficient thickness to prevent bursting. In order to make the pipe more cheaply, the Chinese don't pay quite as much attention to occasional variances in thickness. You see, the pipe starts life as long sheets of steel, about two feet wide. These sheets are formed gradually into tubes and the seams of the tubes are welded closed."

"ERW . . . Electric Rolled Welded steel," I said.

"Again, you know more than I expected. These tubes are cut to length and a slightly larger diameter flange is welded to one end. In essence, that's the pipe we use. The materials specified to be ordered from Pittsburgh are rigorously inspected before leaving the factory. I can't say as much for the Chinese knockoffs. In the cheap pipe, there are more inconsistencies in wall thickness, which leads to weak spots. The welds on the flanges aren't checked as thoroughly."

"I get it," I said. "Using the cheap counterfeit pipe could lead to a rupture under pressure."

"And an oil spill. Can you imagine the damage to my company, not to mention my reputation, as a result of an environmental disaster related to my pipeline?"

"It would be substantial. You might have to lay off a senator or two. Maybe a governor."

I might have imagined it, but Kenzie appeared to flinch ever so slightly. I'd hit a sore point. I didn't care. I hadn't asked to be brought aboard his boat.

"It wouldn't put me out of business," he continued. "No company the size of Kenzie Oil is ever destroyed by scandal. We'd take a huge financial hit, but it would be temporary. Everyone in the petroleum industry runs the risk of a spill. It's part of the business. On the other hand, if it came to light that a Kenzie spill was due to the use of flimsy cheap materials, there would be investigations. Someone might have to go to prison."

"Not you," I said.

"No. Robert, perhaps."

"Which would be terrible for your daughter."

"She adores Robert, for reasons I don't completely understand. Despite his spendthrift lifestyle, his drinking, and his whoring, Astrid dotes on Robert. I would hate to see her devastated by his downfall, even if it were the result of his own weakness."

"I don't get the scam," I said. "Your contract with Holbrook stipulates that he buy his pipe from this company in Pittsburgh. Presumably, someone at his company is keeping records. Wouldn't those records look a little hinky if there weren't any receipts for the pipe?"

"Oh, he's buying the pipe from Pittsburgh," Kenzie said. "I checked on that, first thing. He takes Kenzie Oil money and orders the Pittsburgh pipe. The pipe is delivered to the worksite. At some point, he sells it to his counterfeit suppliers. They pay him in cash and fake pipe. He pockets the cash and puts the pipe in the trenches."

"The diesel engines," I said. "They could be a boat delivering the Chinese pipe and hauling off the good stuff."

"An excellent possibility," Kenzie said.

"The solution is obvious," I said. "Fire Holbrook, replace him with a reputable contractor, and replace the defective pipe."

"Simple to say. Not so easy to do. My information indicates he only started using the Chinese pipe a few weeks ago, around the time the project forded the Saint Catherine Pass. It's all confined to the island between Alligator Bend and Lake Saint Catherine. So, maybe, six or seven miles of pipeline. Physically, replacing it would put us only a few months behind deadline. On the other hand, if I fire my son-in-law, who on earth would ever issue him another contract?"

"This is about saving face."

"His. Mine. The company's. Yes."

I sat back and took a sip of the single malt, my first since Kenzie had handed me the glass. It was smooth and smoky, and it felt like a tepid fog as I let it slide down my throat. For a guy who drinks mostly beer and iced tea, it was a sublime experience. It also gave me a few seconds to think through what I'd heard.

"I don't see where I fit in," I said.

"You scared Robert the other day. You showed up looking for a man nobody cared about. You talked with people who knew things he didn't want divulged. That's why he called me, and why I hired Mr. Pratt to follow you. I didn't know who you were. You were a wild card. For all I knew, you were part of the conspiracy. After I received Mr. Pratt's report, I asked Mr. Dickens from Borglund to run a proper check on you. You're something of an adventurer. You seem to find yourself frequently in danger, but you always survive."

"So far, so good. People tell me I'm a lucky son of a bitch," I said.

"Yes. I can understand. Here is my problem. If I confront Robert directly, I could shame him. It wouldn't bother me, since I don't like the man. My daughter, however, would be traumatized. It could harm our relationship. I don't know who is buying my good pipe and providing Robert with the fake stuff. Robert knows all the people I work with from Borglund. He'd recognize them, or their type, immediately. I can't chance sending in a man like Pratt. He's a bungler. You found him out after only five minutes. My best chance of ending this catastrophe without destroying my family is to find out who Robert is dealing with and get them out of the picture. I need an intermediary who can do that for me."

"And you think this intermediary would be me."

"It's why I invited you here tonight. When Mr. Dickens brought me the dossier on you this afternoon, I saw an opportunity to resolve this entire mess. I sent Mr. Dickens and Mr. Fenster to invite you here so I could ask whether you might be able to help."

For the first time, I saw a crack in Kenzie's demeanor. He was worried. He'd been painted into a corner and he wanted me to be his escape hatch.

I took another sip of the single malt and mulled my options.

"Why should I?" I said.

Kenzie looked as if I'd taken a swipe at him. He was obviously accustomed to people doing whatever he asked. He wasn't prepared for resistance.

"I beg your pardon?"

"You have a nice boat," I said. "Your food is delicious and your liquor is top shelf. You have a beautiful wife. Your life is right out of a Horatio Alger novel. If you've read the information in that folder completely, you probably already know I live a relatively impoverished existence."

"Surprising, considering how much money you have in your Cayman bank account," Kenzie said, his face almost blank.

That rocked me. As far as I knew, nobody but Merlie and Scat Boudreaux knew about my retirement fund in the Caymans. I must

181

have looked as shocked as I felt, because Kenzie grinned as if he had captured my king on the third move of a chess match.

"Okay, you know stuff," I said. "I guess tons of money can buy almost anything, including information. That's one of the things I don't like about you, Kenzie. I don't like your politics. I don't like your conspicuous consumption. I don't like the fact you're trying to shape this country to fit your warped idea of a plutocratic paradise by systematically stuffing politicians and judges in your pocket. Why should I give a damn whether your family gets blown to pieces because your daughter married the wrong guy, and that guy tried to out-asshole his father-in-law? And, more than anything else, why should I put my neck on the line to help you?"

Judging by his reaction, my opinion of him meant next to nothing. That he knew about my supposedly secret Cayman account had knocked me back on my heels, but my tirade barely ruffled him. Advantage Kenzie. He brushed a little lint from the razor crease in his trousers. The symbolism was obvious. My opinion of him was about as important as the lint.

"I won't apologize for my beliefs or my tactics," he said. "I can provide incentives. For instance, there's this."

He pulled a couple of keys from his pocket and tossed them to me.

"The next time you visit the parking lot behind Irene's Cuisine, don't be surprised to find your Pinto missing. I took the liberty of having it hauled off. Those are the keys to a BMW Three Series, seven miles on the odometer."

I stared at the keys in my hand.

"You . . . you took my *car*?" I almost bellowed.

"It was a mercy crushing. Believe me, you'll enjoy the Beemer. It's already registered in your name. I transferred your old tags to it. The title is free and clear. It's in the glove compartment. All your belongings from the Pinto have been moved to the new car's trunk. No strings attached. You can get up and walk away right now. Even if we never speak to one another again, the car is still yours."

For once I was almost at a loss for words.

"I liked my car," I said.

"You'll like the new one better."

"If you think you can buy me with a car . . ." I started.

"I don't. The car is a good faith gesture. There's more where that came from. If you decide to help me, and you're successful, I'll deposit one hundred thousand dollars in your Grand Cayman account. In addition, I'll donate an additional hundred thousand to . . ." His face clouded for a second. He looked over at Dickens and snapped his fingers.

"A Friend's Place," Dickens said.

"Yes. The shelter you purport to represent. I would imagine that amount of money could be put to good use there."

I stood and walked toward the hatch to the deck. Part of me wanted to walk away, leave Kenzie stewing in his private hell. I almost walked out. Then my anger got the best of me. I turned and crossed the salon to where Kenzie sat. Out of the corner of my eye, I saw Dickens stiffen. Without looking at him directly, I held up my hand. Even so, I saw an expression of concern cross Kenzie's face. It was, perhaps, the first genuine emotion he had demonstrated during our discussion. I lowered my voice and addressed him in the growl which had turned many a gambler's knees to rubber and their bowels to water.

"What kind of man are you?" I asked. "You walk all over people's lives. You act as if every person you meet should kiss your ring and acquiesce to your every whim. You think you can wave huge checks in front of my face and I'll forget everything you stand for and all the evil you and your type commit in this world? Trying to buy me is one thing. I don't need your money. I have enough to live on for the rest of my life if I choose. Trying to manipulate my emotions by bringing the shelter into the negotiations is a low blow. Tell you what. I'll give the shelter a hundred grand myself not to have to deal with you."

I have to give Kenzie credit. Maybe he felt secure because Dickens was there to protect him, or maybe he had lived so far above the rest of us for so many years, he no longer experienced true fear. When Big Bad Pat made the scene, most sane men crumbled, with good reason.

Kenzie shrugged, and put forward a grin so fake I almost admired him for it.

"I tried," he said. "In a way, I'm glad to see you turn me down. It helps to know what kind of person I'm dealing with. You are obviously a man of integrity."

"So now you want to ingratiate yourself with me?" I said.

"Not at all. It would have been easier if you had agreed to do this for the money. Like a good gambler, something about which I hear you know a thing or two, I don't like to play my entire hand at once. I have one more incentive for you. It may resolve one of your current problems."

He signaled Dickens, who opened the door to the hallway and disappeared. He returned with a man in his late thirties, dressed in jeans and a knit pullover shirt. The man crossed the salon and held out his hand.

"Mr. Gallegher," he said, "I'm Garry Sharp. I understand you've been looking for me."

CHAPTER TWENTY-TWO

I HAD RECOGNIZED SHARP the instant he walked in the door. I think I might have been shocked to see him. As he walked toward me, his hand extended, I was angry at how well and truly I had been played.

I took his hand, braced myself, and put my entire body into a punch that caught him under the right eye and propelled him over the love seat and almost into the buffet table.

It was one of those times I was happy to be left-handed.

Dickens didn't budge. Kenzie and his wife Claudine both watched in open-mouthed surprise.

From behind the love seat, I heard, "What the *fuck*!"

I resisted the urge to walk over, grab Sharp, drag him to the deck, and toss him overboard. Instead, I waited for him to get to his feet.

"Why'd you do that?" he asked. He held a napkin to the small gash on his cheek. "What'd I ever do to you?"

"Nothing," I said. "Do you know where your daughter is, Sharp?"

"Sure," he said. "She's at that shelter. Mr. Kenzie told me this afternoon."

"And you don't care?"

"I care. As far as I knew, she was with Carly, my girlfriend."

"Ex-girlfriend," I said. "Carly doesn't like you much. You also owe her a couple hundred dollars."

"And she'll get it. Geez, can I get some ice for this?" he said. He looked over at Dickens, who only shrugged. Finally, Sharp walked behind the bar and put some ice cubes in a napkin.

"Your daughter needs medical attention," I said. "The director at A Friend's Place asked me to find you so you could give permission for an operation."

"I have that covered," Kenzie said. "This afternoon, when I found out about young Audrey, I had a Medical Power of Attorney form drafted and signed by Mr. Sharp. It gives you the authority to authorize the girl's medical treatment."

"Me!"

"For reasons I can't completely divulge at the moment, Mr. Sharp needs to remain missing for the time being."

"I don't understand," I said.

"It's a little complicated," Sharp said, holding the makeshift ice pack to his cheek. "Getting the job on the Holbrook pipeline project wasn't an accident. I was hired by Mr. Kenzie here when he began to suspect Robert Holbrook was substituting substandard pipe for the specified materials. My job was to determine whether the right pipe was being used on the job."

"Your notebook," I said.

"Safe and sound, in Mr. Kenzie's care. Besides my training as a nondestructive examiner, I have enough college training in metallurgy to discriminate between the correct pipe and the counterfeit stuff. While I was supposedly examining the welds, I was also taking small samples of the pipe to be examined by a real metallurgist. I delivered the samples to him one week before I left the job site. After he confirmed my samples weren't from the Pittsburgh foundry, I had to find a way to get away from the job."

"The fight with Al Garlock," I said.

"Exactly. I got in his face and told him there was something wrong with the pipe. I expected he'd fire me on the spot. He didn't. I had to find another way to get out. I didn't know whether Garlock was involved in the pipe switch, but it was a sure thing he'd go to Holbrook. It was a matter of time before they'd find some way to shut me up, perhaps permanently. A couple of nights later, we were locked in the trailer. I think that's when the transfer was made. I hoped I could get a look at the switch, but it was too dark. It was too dangerous to wait for another shipment, so I took off a few nights later while everyone was sleeping."

"You left all your equipment," I said.

"It's been replaced," Sharp said, looking at Kenzie.

"The least I could do," Kenzie said. "I found out after Garry walked off the site that someone was following the two men who had shared his trailer."

"Truluck and Hines," I said.

"Yes."

"You had Pratt following Hines."

"Once again, you impress me," Kenzie said. "My intent was for Mr. Pratt to keep an eye on Hines in case someone tried to harm him. I wasn't able to determine who that might be. Abraham Pratt, as you discovered, may not be the most competent private investigator in town."

"What about Carl Zimmer?" I asked.

Sharp looked confused.

"He replaced you on the job but was fired two weeks later."

"That was my doing," Kenzie said. "I needed my own person onsite. I found a better position for Zimmer, out of state. It gave me an opportunity to get Wayne Falkner on the site. Unfortunately, he hasn't had any more luck than Garry did in finding out who's bringing in the fake pipe. That's why I need you."

"I don't see how I can help," I said. "You have a guy on the site and he can't find anything."

"You're resourceful," Kenzie said. "You find ways when others can't. You've already rattled my son-in-law. The more we can keep him off-balance, the more likely it is he'll make a mistake. As soon as we find out who's supplying the pipe, we'll take them out of the picture and he'll be forced to complete the project with the right materials. Face saved, family left intact, everything is back to normal."

"What about Audrey?" I said to Sharp.

"I want her taken care of," he said. "How much longer can she stay at the shelter?"

"Maybe a week."

"That may be all we need," Kenzie said.

"I have other obligations," I said. "Another missing person, an old friend. I've been looking for him at the same time I've been searching for Sharp here. I can't let that go."

"You'll find a way," Kenzie said. "I have faith in you. In fact, perhaps I can help you with that problem also. If you'd like, I can get Borglund Security and Investigations to help out."

"I want him," I said, pointing at Dickens. For once, the golem moved. He pointed toward his chest and mimed *me?*

"I can't spare Mr. Dickens," Kenzie said.

"I get him or the deal's off."

"Why, for Pete's sake?"

"A hunch. I think I can trust him. He reminds me of a cop friend of mine here in town. If things get nasty, I have a feeling Dickens won't fold."

"Anything else?" Kenzie said.

"I'll let you know. Give me the Power of Attorney papers. I want Audrey to get her surgery as soon as possible."

CHAPTER TWENTY-THREE

*K*ENZIE WAS TWO steps ahead of me. He had already had the power of attorney papers drawn and signed by Sharp, and had notarized them, giving me authority to approve Audrey's surgery and any other care she might need. I had a feeling Kenzie enjoyed staying two steps ahead of people. I was careful to give Sharp one more baleful glare before leaving. I didn't want him to think we were parting as friends.

Dickens walked me down the gangplank to the dock and the parking lot.

"Back to your club?" he asked.

"Not yet. We have a stop to make on the way." I gave him the address. I saw his eyebrows raise a bit.

"This should be fun," he said.

We piled into the back of the limo. I cadged another Diet Coke. Beating up on Garry Sharp had built up a thirst.

"He's not as evil as most people think," Dickens said as we turned out of the parking lot and headed back toward the city.

"Kenzie?"

"Yeah."

"Saying he isn't as evil as most people think leaves the door open for a whole lot of bad."

"You're a psychologist."

"Right."

"A forensic psychologist, as I understand it."

"Right again."

"Then you know a thing or two about psychopaths."

"I've bumped up against my share over the years."

"No doubt. I already told you I was Secret Service before joining Borglund Security. I didn't tell you my detail."

"Let me guess. White House."

He shook his head. "Naval Observatory. In Georgetown."

"Like playing Triple A baseball."

"I watched over the Second Lady."

"Double A, then. So you didn't even get the Veep."

"I didn't mind. The guy was an asshole. They're all assholes, when you get right down to it. You don't reach that level of power without slipping a little on the blood of the people you put down on the way up. The entire government is run by high-functioning psychopaths. So are most of your Fortune 500 corporations. We can't imprint our values on people like that. It's like trying to order a pizza over the phone in Sanskrit. Kenzie's no different than most CEOs. He's vain and cocksure and he's used to getting what he wants. The values and problems of the average working Joe would completely confound him."

"You're kind of loose with the talk about your boss."

"I work for Borglund Security. Kenzie is my client, nothing more. If he asked to replace me tomorrow, it wouldn't hurt my career a speck. He won't, though, because he knows I get the job done. You surprised me. You actually rattled Kenzie once or twice. His wife liked you."

"Lady Macbeth? She's cute."

"She's also the one you want to watch. Kenzie is smart and greedy, which I suppose is bad enough. She made him rich and powerful. There was all kinds of communication passing between them this evening, some of which you might have missed."

"Like a magic trick," I said.

"How so?"

"Kenzie is slick and ingratiating. He does the patter and the razzmatazz while Blondie is picking your pocket. Or, in this case, sizing me up and giving Kenzie the high sign that I'd do. It didn't get past me, Dickens. You got a first name?"

"Chuck."

"Chuck? That makes you . . ."

"Please. Don't. Heard it all before."

"We'll keep it Dickens. I have a partner named Chick already. I don't need to juggle Chick and Chuck all day long."

We turned onto Bourbon Street and followed it through the French Quarter to almost where it ends at the Esplanade. The driver pulled to the curb in front of an olive-drab industrial building. Hanging from a pole, jutting out over the front door, was a sign that read *Semper Fi.*

"So, this is the place," Dickens said.

"You might want to stay in the car," I said. "The guy inside isn't fond of Feds."

"Then it's a good thing I'm retired. I wouldn't miss this for the world."

"It's your skin."

Dickens followed me through the door of Semper Fi. As I expected, Sonny sat behind the front desk. He held an old Sergeant Rock comic book in the one hand he had left and was reading it with his one remaining eye. His German shepherd/wolf mix, Howitzer, jumped to his feet and growled. Sonny yapped at him in German and

191

Howitzer folded back down onto the floor. Howitzer's eyes didn't leave me for a second.

"Told you to bring him treats," Sonny said, his voice turned to gravel from years of smoking and cheap Kentucky whiskey. "He's nice to folks who bring him treats."

"Is he in?" I said, gesturing toward the back.

"He was last time I looked. You know him. Here one minute, gone the next. Like a ghost. Feel free to check. You can leave your Fed here. Scat don't take kindly to Feds."

"Am I that obvious?" Dickens asked.

"Either you're a Fed or you're an insurance salesman. Scat don't take kindly to insurance salesmen, either. Whichever way, it's healthier for you to stay up here and keep me and Howitzer company."

"I need to introduce them," I said. "I have a job for Scat. It's going to involve Mr. Dickens."

"Boss ain't gonna like it," Sonny said, but he pushed the button to unlock the door to the back storeroom.

"Follow my lead," I told Dickens. "And don't look around too much. There's a lot of stuff back here that probably should stay Scat's secret. He doesn't like people to get nosey."

We found Scat Boudreaux sitting in a recliner toward the back of the warehouse. He had his feet up, and he was watching an old movie on a brand new sixty-inch flat screen he had mounted to the wall. In his lap was an AR-15 rifle which I had no doubt had been modified for full-fire. Scat didn't look away from the screen, but the barrel of the rifle followed each step we took.

"Got out of bed this morning feeling purty good," Scat said. "First decent night's sleep I've had since you got me shot in the back three weeks ago. Shoulda known it wouldn't last. Shoulda known, soon's I started to feel proper, you'd show up and try to get me to do some dirty work for you. You got some balls, trackin' Feds into my place."

"He's not a Fed anymore," I said. "He's with a private security firm.

"Once a Fed. So, Mr. Private Security Firm, s'pose you slowly remove your ordnance and place it on the table next to you. And remember I don't ask twice."

Dickens turned to me.

"Is he serious?"

"Do it. Like he said. Slowly and carefully. You obviously know who he is, which means you know what he can do."

Dickens shrugged. "Hell, how can I refuse the most dangerous man in Louisiana?"

He unbuttoned his jacket and removed his pistol from its shoulder holster, holding it gingerly by the butt, between his thumb and index finger."

"Both of 'em," Scat said. His eyes were still riveted on the TV screen.

Dickens pointed toward a faded and peeling chair next to the table. "May I sit?" he said.

"Sure," Scat told him. "Take a load off, especially off your left ankle where you got that Bernardelli throw-down popgun strapped."

Dickens sat and pulled up his pants leg. He dropped the tiny automatic on the table alongside his other pistol. I raised my eyebrows at him.

"Old habits," Dickens said. "Believe it or not, Mr. Boudreaux, I'm actually happy to meet you. I'm a bit of a fan. You have quite a reputation." He glanced around the warehouse. "Well-deserved, it seems. How the ATF allows this place to keep standing beats me."

"Professional courtesy. Plus, I got the building booby-trapped eight ways from Sunday. Feds would much rather have this end of

Bourbon Street not become a crater. Truth be told, once in a while they have need of my services. What'cha' got, Gallegher?"

I left Dickens sitting in the ratty chair next to the table and crossed the floor to an equally disheveled sofa on the other side of Scat's TV.

"I need help. I'm stretched, commitment-wise. I can't cover everything that needs doing. Mr. Dickens here is former Secret Service, but he works for a private security firm. Specifically, at the moment, he works for Kellen Kenzie."

"Weeeeelllll, why di'nt you say so?" Scat said, with sort of cackle. "I mean, who wouldn't want to throw in with a snake like Kenzie? Why, his name done come up in an article I was reading on the computer the other day. You recall back when them ragheads took out the Twin Towers up in New York and punched a big hole in the Pentagon a few years back? Sure you do. It was in all the papers. As it happens, one of our former presidents was shacked up in a hotel down in Florida with half the family of the old boy who masterminded the attack. Two hours after the towers fell, not a plane in the country was in the air. They'd all put down at whatever airstrip would accommodate them. All but one, that is. Seems some high-up muckety-mucks wanted the family out of the country, so one plane, one solitary airplane, was allowed to take off and leave American airspace. It took the whole lot of them off to Abu Dhabi, where they were sequestered in an estate while the world sorted out who was the good guys and who was the bad guys. Wanna guess who owned that estate?"

"Kellen Kenzie?" I ventured.

"God, no. What in hell would Kenzie need with a palace in Saudi Arabia? But he did broker the arrangements with the guy who *does* own it, a Russian Jewish feller named Bronkovich. Now, I have it on good and reputable authority that Bronkovich is hip deep in

Illuminati and Bund activities in Europe and the Middle East. Fact is, he's basically a one-worlder Commie gangster who'd toss his mother into a blast furnace if there was a buck in it, but he's also tight with a super-secret society made of the descendants of the Knights of Malta, who have basically run European politics since the early Renaissance. In other words, Kellen Kenzie is part of the plot. He's a cog in the multinational conspiracy. Guilt by association, old son. If this ex-Fed works for Kenzie, he must part of the conspiracy also."

I stole a glance at Dickens. Most people, the first time they're subjected to one of Scat's paranoid rants, start to sweat around the hairline and look around for the nearest exit. They'd be right to do so, since Dickens was absolutely right when he referred to Scat as the most dangerous man in Louisiana. That might have been an understatement. Scat Boudreaux, even as he had reached his sixties, was quite possibly the most dangerous man in the country.

Dickens wasn't intimidated. He looked fascinated, the way an entomologist might upon running across a new species of caterpillar.

"We might have a problem," I said. "As of an hour ago, I'm also working for Kenzie."

"So, you finally done gone and sold out," Scat said. I could hear a tinge of disappointment in his voice.

"It's a means to an end," I said. "I was doing a job for Merlie."

Scat relaxed a little. Here was a man who spent almost a year in a Viet Cong tiger cage, who had single-handedly wiped out the entire camp of his captors before cannibalizing his way across 'Nam to friendly lines. I'd seen him shoot a man in the lung with a fifty-caliber automatic, and the only remorse he expressed was that he'd missed by half an inch. Yet, for reasons that defied explanation, he had a soft spot in his heart—or maybe it was in his head—for the auburn-haired, violet-eyed love of my life.

"Well, I reckon that's differ'nt," he said.

"One of her kids needs knee surgery. Her father was missing. She asked me to find him."

"How's that workin' out for you?"

"I found him. He's working for Kenzie. He's been in hiding for the last several weeks. Kenzie's son-in-law owns a pipe-laying company over in Algiers. He's caught up in some kind of scheme to substitute sub-quality pipe for the good stuff and pocket the difference. Kenzie's daughter has the old man wrapped around her little finger, so he doesn't want to simply squash the son-in-law like a bug. He wants to know who's supplying the bogus pipe, and what's happening with the good stuff. I suspect he plans to take his son-in-law's business partners off the map and force him to use the right pipe for the rest of the project, but that's someone else's problem. In any case, in return for me helping to find them, he's going to donate a hundred grand to Merlie's shelter."

I judiciously skipped the part where I got a hundred large and a Beemer out of the deal.

"Miz Merlie could do a lot of good for her kids with money like that."

"She sure could. At first, I told Kenzie to go jump, but it's possible some good can come out of working for him, if only for a few days."

"I'm a little unclear about something," Scat said. "You only come to me when you or someone you care about is in danger and you need someone to cover your six. Beyond the damage to your soul, I'm not sure I see where you need a lot of protecting in this gig."

"You remember Cabby Jacks?"

"Cain't say as I do."

"He was a runner for Mookie over at the Hilton."

"Short, skinny feller?"

"That would describe him. I owe him a huge favor. Now he's collecting. He's gone missing. His friend approached me and asked me to find him."

"Lotta' lost people in your life lately."

"I can't be in two places at once. Thought you might want to make some easy money."

"What'cha' need?" he asked.

"The pipeline company is laying pipe near Lake Saint Catherine. It's a lousy place, mostly sand and mosquitoes and snakes and swamps, with a lot of evergreen forests. It's a place not fit for man or beast, but somehow I think you'd feel right at home there."

"Not following you, Streak."

"The bogus pipe is brought in at night, probably onboard a boat of some kind. Holbrook, Kenzie's son-in-law, keeps all the workers locked in their trailers during the offloading and exchange, and they douse all the lights in the camp to keep the workers from seeing the boat. I'd like you to do surveillance from the woods surrounding the worksite. I want to know when the boat makes its deliveries and who's on it when it does. Ideally, you'd get a name off the boat and maybe a registry number so we can trace the folks behind the scam."

"What happens when you have that info?"

I stole a quick glance at Dickens. He didn't look back.

"Not my problem," I said. "I hand the information over to Kenzie and hope I never see him again."

During the entire conversation, the AR-15 barrel had remained pointed straight at Dickens' heart. If it bothered him, he didn't show it. He did appear to relax a bit when Scat placed the weapon on the coffee table in front of him.

"Not too hot this time of year, so I could wear a gillie suit if I needed to. Not that it matters, you unnerstand. Hell, I once't lay naked covered with sand for three days waiting for a target to show up in Ong Thanh, over in the Binh Duong province in-country. Like having my own private cat box. Got the bastard, too. One shot, right here." He poked the middle of his sternum. "Cost you a thousand a day. If'n you want me to do Kenzie's wet work for him, put an end to his whole mess, price goes to five grand a day."

"Not necessary," Dickens said. "If you get us the information we need, Borglund Security will take care of the rest. Won't be any need for . . . um, wet work."

Scat looked a little disappointed. "Well, then, it's a thousand a day."

"Dickens here will see to it you're paid," I said.

That took Dickens off guard. "What?" he said.

"Hell, you'll just charge it back to Kenzie. Cost of doing business, or, more appropriately, cost of having someone else do your business. It's a contract fee. I'm sure you've paid those before."

"No doubt," Dickens said. "A thousand a day. We'll cover it."

"I'll start tonight," Scat said. "Have to pack a few things first. Give me the current coordinates. I'll be in place before the sun rises tomorrow."

Dickens made a quick telephone call, wrote some numbers down on a small spiral pad he'd taken from his jacket pocket, tore the sheet out, and handed it to Scat.

"I presumed an ex-military guy like you would want map coordinates, latitude-longitude, that sort of thing," he said.

"That's right," Scat said, as he pocketed the sheet. "No offense, Mr. Secret Service, but it'd suit me proper if we didn't meet again. From here on in, I'll communicate with Gallegher, and he'll act as a conduit between me and you, or me and Kenzie. I'll tell Gallegher here how much to pay me. You can forward it through him. Y'all scoot, now. I got stuff to do."

CHAPTER TWENTY-FOUR

*D*ICKENS OFFERED TO drop me off at Holliday's, but I told him I'd rather walk. I needed some time to sort stuff out in my head, and I also wanted to make a short stop at Irene's Cuisine. He gave me his number and I keyed it into my cell phone. The last thing he told me before I got out of the car was to stay in touch. I had a feeling it wouldn't be hard. Kellen Kenzie was into me for two hundred grand and a car. Probably didn't mean much to him, but he didn't strike me as the sort of guy who worked a lot on trust. I had a feeling I might not see him, but Dickens was sure to keep a tight rein on me until the whole business with Kenzie's son-in-law was put in the rearview mirror.

I found the Beemer in the parking spot behind Irene's where I had left my Pinto earlier that afternoon. I felt a tugging sensation in my chest at the thought of my car being crushed into scrap. It had been a piece of garbage, but it had never stalled when I needed it. When I mashed the button on the new key fob in my pocket, I heard the crisp metallic sound of the door locks raising automatically. Within seconds, I found myself sitting on the leather bucket seat, getting a feel for the steering wheel.

It felt good—thick, solid, and tight in my hands. A guy my size tends to have hands to match. The Pinto—being built over forty years ago—had a skinny, hard plastic wheel. This wheel felt substantial and reassuring. I felt a little guilty enjoying the prospect of using it, almost as if I were somehow disrespecting my old ride, but I had to admit it: the Beemer was a first-class piece of machinery.

I had a feeling it would take me weeks to figure out the fighter-jet console and what all the various switches and buttons did. A road trip with Merlie seemed to be in order.

First things first. I still needed to find Cabby, and get Kenzie's information for him. Finding Garry Sharpe hadn't cut my caseload in half. It had only compounded it.

As if on cue, my cell phone rang.

"Gallegher," I said.

"Hi. This is Ross Duncan."

Another twinge of guilt. I'd been so busy over the last several days, I'd forgotten to touch base with my client. I had a brief mental image of Duncan sitting by the telephone, waiting impatiently for some sort of news from the Jolly Irish Giant.

"Mr. Duncan."

"I wanted to check in, to see if you've . . . you know, had any success locating Cabby."

"You haven't heard from him, I take it."

"If I had, I'd have called you right away."

I locked the car and started walking the three blocks to Toulouse Street and Holliday's. As I walked, I filled him in on what little information I'd gathered so far, leaving out some of the more private information some of Cabby's fellow GA members might not have wanted me to share openly.

"I have a few questions for you," I said.

"Shoot."

"Do you recall Cabby ever referring to someone named Nigra? First name might have begun with a 'D'."

"It doesn't ring a bell. Why?"

"I found a reference to what might have been a meeting on the evening Cabby disappeared. It included the name D. Nigra. I figured it was a person Cabby was meeting."

"If he was, he didn't tell me about it."

"What exactly did he tell you about his business dealings?"

"Not a lot, I'm afraid. Whenever I'd ask him about his work, he'd get quiet. Once I pressed him. He told me the less I knew, the better for everyone."

"That didn't bother you?"

"At first it did. On the other hand, it made him seem more mysterious. Every once in a while, he'll show up with a fist full of cash, and we'll party on that for a few days. Once he took me to Cabo. Another time we flew first class to Vegas."

"Did he gamble in either place?"

"Hell, no, Mr. Gallegher. Cabby was proud of his five-year medallion in the program."

"So there's no chance this money he flashed around came from betting or cards or the ponies? Anything like that?"

"I'd have to say no. Cabby does like to take risks. Sometimes it's a little scary to ride with him when he's driving. The risks he takes these days don't involve wagers. He's sworn off gambling for life. If he relapsed, I think he'd tell me."

"Has he ever mentioned a man named Rodrigo Torres Villar?"

There was a brief silence on the other end.

"Now, that sounds familiar," Duncan said. "Not like a name he used all the time, but I think I've heard him mention Villar. Wait! Yes. It was on a telephone call. I had stayed over at Cabby's apartment one night. We'd done a lot of bar-hopping on Bourbon Street the night before and I wasn't fit to drive. Anyway, the telephone at his apartment rang around seven the next morning. I remember because *nobody* is up at that time in the French Quarter on a Sunday morning. Cabby answered it and then left the room, closing the door. He did that from time to time when he wanted his privacy. I could hear part of the muffled conversation through the door. At one point, he raised his voice and said something like, 'I heard you the first time, Villar! I told you. I'll get it.' He sounded angry and maybe a little scared. Is this Villar a bad person?"

One of the worst, I wanted to say, but I held back. No point in getting Duncan frightened, at least not yet.

"His name came up. Cabby had a heated conversation with a man fitting Villar's description outside a GA meeting a couple of weeks ago. Did Cabby mention anything about Brazilians?"

"Not as I can recall."

"One other thing. Did he ever mention meeting a ship, or discuss a ship arriving at the Port of New Orleans? Specifically, a ship called the Rio Gaucho?"

"That one I'm sure of. No. I've never heard of a ship called the Rio Gaucho. Does any of this help?"

"Everything helps, kid. Sometimes it takes a while to figure out how, but everything helps."

"Should I file a missing person report with the police?"

"I'm already ahead of you. I have a guy in the police department. We work together from time to time. I've informed him about Cabby going missing and he's aware of my investigation. Like I told you before, I can give this a lot more time than he can. He'll know what I know, though. Between us, we'll find Cabby for you."

Duncan thanked me and we hung up as I turned the corner to walk into Holliday's.

The door was locked. I unlocked it. The place was empty and

silent. I checked my watch. It was a quarter past seven. By now, Shorty should have been prepping the place for the evening music crowd. I crossed behind the bar and checked the ice bin for beer. There were beers stacked inside of it, but they hadn't been iced down. Holliday's had gone dark only once in the eight years I'd played there, on the night a couple of years earlier when Shorty had been arrested on suspicion of killing his girlfriend.

I pulled the cell phone from my pocket and thumbed Shorty's home number as I started up the stairs toward my apartment. I stopped on the third step. The door to my place was open. Merlie stood in the doorway.

"I found Garry Sharp," I said, as I headed toward her. "Why's the club dark?"

She stayed in the doorway until I reached the landing and then reached out to hug me. I could see streaks in her makeup where they'd been carved by tears.

"What is it?" I said, as I held her close. "What's happened?"

"Oh, Pat," she said, a short sob between the words. "I didn't want to call you. I didn't want to tell you over the phone."

"What?" I said again.

She laid her head against my chest and started weeping again.

"Sam died," she said.

CHAPTER TWENTY-FIVE

*D*ON'T GIVE ME this 'cycle of life' shit. Don't try to comfort me with reminders that a guy lived a good long time on this earth and now has a chance to rest. There's no rest in the grave, no sense of accomplishment, no looking back on a life well-spent. It's mold and decay and corruption and eventually you're forgotten completely by the world you once walked. It's the same for any of us, but it's worse when you lose a friend.

Sockeye Sam and I had spent eight years on the stage at Holliday's together. We had learned how to play off of one another. We had a musical understanding. I knew when he was in the mood to run off on forty-eight bars of pure improvisation and he knew when I felt like cutting loose and expurgating my soul with a little invention of my own. We had our rhythms synched to one another on stage. I was aware he had somehow kept track of my little adventures, probably through conversations with Shorty. In fact, it was Sam who had come to me the last time Holliday's had gone dark—on the night Shorty had been arrested by Farley Nuckolls in the death of Lucy Nivens—and had pressed a sweat-stained, smoky, inch-thick stack of ten-dollar bills in my hand to hire me and try to get Shorty cleared.

And I did go to work for him, and I did clear Shorty, and I eventually caught the real killer, even if nobody on earth except for Farley, Shorty, and Merlie knows it.

It seemed Sam knew me so much better than I had known him. I was ashamed to admit as much to Merlie at the funeral home the next day, as we watched a long line of family members and friends assemble to remember him.

"I didn't know he was in the Navy," I said. "I never knew he had such a large family. I never knew he had so many friends. He showed up at nine each night to get ready for his shift, and he disappeared between one and two each morning while Shorty and I cleared the bar and mopped up for the night. I think I knew him, musically, as well as any man can know another, but I didn't know the man."

Sam was entitled to a military funeral, but there was business to attend to first. In New Orleans, a funeral is equal parts somber reflection and opportunity to party. The day after Sam died, his coffin was paraded down Bourbon Street in a small parade made up of some of the French Quarter's finest musicians. I was invited to join them. At first, I felt unworthy, but they insisted, and I took up a place in their midst and played the usual dirges, my ability to see where we were going occasionally blurred behind tears.

That night we held the wake at Holliday's. For the first time in decades, Preservation Hall—where Sam had played so many years before I arrived in town—went dark. Its players congregated in Holliday's, instead. Merlie and I sat in the crowd, tossing back Abitas and reflecting. Chick Kasay arrived around ten o'clock, even though he and I were off duty. He grabbed a beer and joined us at the table. He didn't talk a lot. Seems he never did, except when he was needling me for some war story about my dangerous dalliances. This evening, he was content to sit and tap his feet to the syncopated rhythms and allow Merlie and me to grieve our lost friend.

"Let's get out of here," I said to Merlie after the second set. "I have something to show you."

I took her hand and led her downstairs and out to the sidewalk. We strolled up Toulouse to Charles and swung around the back side of Irene's Cuisine. I pulled the BMW key fob from my pocket to press the unlock button. There was a chirp from my parking space, which drew Merlie's attention.

"Where's your car?" she asked.

"You're looking at it. Let's take a drive."

I held the passenger door open as she slid across the leather bucket seat, then took my place beside her, behind the wheel. When I pressed the start button, the display on the dashboard showed the car had exactly seven miles on it.

"Bitchin' wheels," she said. "Want to tell me where you got it? Did you break into your piggy bank in the Caymans?"

"It's part of the deal on Audrey. It's what I wanted to discuss with you. Very shortly, you are going to receive a hefty donation for A Friend's Place from an unlikely source. Also part of the deal."

I pulled out of the parking lot and drove north, toward Lake Pontchartrain.

"As I said last night, I found Garry Sharp. I didn't tell you where or how. I guess you could say he found me, or someone else found him for me, or . . . well, I don't know exactly how to put it. Let's say we were brought together, and he needs to stay in hiding for a while. That's why I was given medical power of attorney for Audrey. This car, the power of attorney, the donation to the shelter are compensation for me helping out a man I detest."

"Who?"

"Kellen Kenzie."

"Bullshit!"

I didn't say anything. Instead, I drove on through the dark, the concern on my face illuminated by the soft orange glow from the dash instruments and the muted radio. As we neared the lake, I had my thoughts better arranged.

"When I started nosing around Holbrook Engineering, looking for Sharp, I landed on Kenzie's radar screen. Holbrook is Kenzie's son-in-law. He's also in trouble—mostly of his own making. Kenzie considers the guy to be a complete waste of skin, but his daughter loves him, so Kenzie is trying to find a way to fix things without his daughter finding out what a dipshit she married. Part of fixing things involved Garry Sharp—the reason Sharp has to stay out of sight. Kenzie recruited me to help fix Holbrook's circumstances. I'd like to say he twisted my arm, because then I wouldn't sound like a complete sellout. I know who he is and what he represents. I don't like being beholden to a fascist like Kenzie. On the other hand, a lot of good can come out of this deal. Audrey gets her knee fixed. She and her father will be reunited. You can do a shit ton of good work with the money he's donating to the shelter. And I got this car and a chunk of cash for my retirement fund."

"He bought you."

"Yeah. I could argue the point, but in the end . . . yeah. He found my price."

"Wait. How much?"

"How much what?"

"I was so focused on Kellen Kenzie that I missed the amount. How much is he giving the shelter?"

"A hundred thousand."

"A hundred fucking thousand *dollars*?"

"Why, Miss Scarlett, how you do talk," I said, feigning a magnolia drawl.

She fell silent. Eventually, we found ourselves driving the lake shore road. I pulled into the parking lot of a closed restaurant. Lights on anchored sailboats and cabin cruisers bobbed up and down out on the brackish water. We stared at them for a while.

"You're putting me in a hell of a spot," Merlie said, finally. She placed her hand on mine and squeezed a bit, to demonstrate she wasn't taking it personally. "Taking Kenzie's money. I don't know whether I can."

"Rationalize it. It's worked so far for me."

"And it's a nice car. I know you'll miss your little yellow Pinto."

"Not so much," I said. "I mean, I was angry at first that Kenzie replaced it without asking. I have a feeling asking is something he isn't accustomed to doing. On the other hand, it was a forty-year-old piece of junk, and this car is new and paid for."

"It's a hell of a lot safer, too," she said. "I was always worried you'd get rear-ended in the Pinto by a Mack truck and go out in a blaze of glory. Shit, Pat. Listen to us. We're actually trying to sell ourselves on Kellen Kenzie's largesse, when in fact he simply bought us."

"Adulting is hard," I said.

"It's a solid gold bitch," she said.

"Ain't it the truth?" I said. I put the car in drive to head back to Holliday's.

We were halfway back to the Quarter when I remembered.

"Aw, hell," I said.

"What?" Merlie asked.

"I told Audrey I'd pick up her Elmo doll at Carly McKee's place. She said she stuffed it under the bed. Mind if we take a detour?"

"In this car? I don't mind a thing, long as I don't have to talk to her. Woman who comes on to my man the way she did is begging for a beat-down. How in hell does this radio work?"

She fiddled with the knobs while I hopped off the highway and headed back in the other direction toward Metairie. It was after nine o'clock, and the roads were relatively clear, so we made great time. I pulled up in front of Carly McKee's shitbox house after only twenty minutes or so.

"Place looks dark," Merlie said.

"She might be out for the evening. I got the impression she likes to party."

"Doesn't explain the 'For Rent' sign in the front window."

She pointed, and I saw it too.

"Strange," I said. "Let me check it out."

Kenzie had told me he'd had all my stuff from the Pinto put into the Beemer trunk. It took me a couple of minutes to figure out how to open the latch, but when I did I saw he was right. I grabbed my flashlight and stepped up the walk to Carly's front door. I rang the doorbell, and could hear the sound from inside, but nothing else.

I shined the flashlight into the picture window. The ratty carpet was still there, and I could see the indentations where furniture had sat. As far as I could tell, the house was empty.

I walked around to the back door, off the carport, and tried it. Locked. I sprayed the inside with light, and still came up with nothing. It looked as if Carly McKee had bugged out, and from the looks of things she'd done it in a rush. I walked back to the car.

"Looks like she's moved," I said.

"Maybe she was planning to all along."

"I was here only three or four days ago. I didn't see any packing boxes or signs that she was planning to leave. Strange. Wait here."

I left the car again and walked around to the back of the house. There was a rolling trash bin sitting at an angle to the carport. It was overflowing with the detritus of Carly's life. I rolled it into the carport and dumped the contents onto the concrete floor, examining the trash with my flashlight. It took a little effort, fishing through the garbage, but I finally found it.

A minute later, I was back in the Beemer. I handed a scruffy object to Merlie.

"Looks like Elmo," she said.

"I had a feeling Carly wasn't the sentimental type, and I was pretty sure she wouldn't lift a finger for Audrey, so it stood to reason she'd dump the toy."

"You waded through this woman's trash to find Audrey's doll?"

"Man's gotta do what a man's gotta do."

She leaned over and kissed me on the cheek like she meant it.

"You are a hero," she said. "Let's go. This place depresses me."

CHAPTER TWENTY-SIX

*C*HESTER BOULWARE WAS waiting for me at the bar when we returned. He was accompanied by a huge Asian man who had a shaved head and wore a summer wool suit that strained to contain his muscles.

"Boulware," Merlie said as soon as we walked in the door. "That can't be good."

"He's helping me with this Cabby Jacks search."

"Who's the wrestler?"

"Haven't a clue."

I left her at a chair near the stage, grabbed a beer from the cooler behind the bar, and headed for Boulware's table.

"Take a load off," Boulware said. "Want you to meet a buddy of mine."

The Asian man held out a meaty paw, the size of a small ham.

"The name's Hong. James Hong."

"I imagine you love saying that," I said.

"Bet your ass."

"James is with I.C.E.," Boulware said.

"I don't know what that is," I said.

"Pardon my friend Gallegher here," Boulware said to Hong.

"He's been living in a cave since the turn of the century. I.C.E. used to be I.N.S. Immigration and Naturalization. Nine-Eleven changed that."

"Okay," I said. "I get the connection. Agent Hong is here because we've been talking about Brazilians."

"Sort of," Hong said. "Agent Boulware sent out some feelers on Rodrigo Torres Villar. I was intrigued. I'm working a different sort of case, but Villar's name has popped up from time to time in association with it."

"What sort of case?"

"Nothing to do with the Brazilians, at least on the surface. Their involvement is tangential. I was transferred to Baton Rouge from San Francisco not long ago."

"I was there last week. Lovely city."

"Tell me about it. Miss it a lot, especially when I discovered the air down here is mostly soup. I didn't come here voluntarily. There was a nasty triad war in Chinatown that reflected badly on me. I gave a private investigator a little too much leeway. It blew up in my face. Sending me to Baton Rouge was a sort of demotion."

"Sorry to hear it."

"I'm working my way back. I specialize in Chinese gang activity."

"Don't see a lot of that here in New Orleans. We have some tough guys in the Vietnamese gangs."

"Part of why they sent me here. By dumping me in some backwater without a lot of tong and triad activity, they wanted to marginalize me. I'm making do."

"What's this have to do with Villar?" I asked.

"A confluence of interests. First, tell me what you know about him."

"Not much more than Boulware here told me. He's a major

badass in Rio, and not a lot better here. Chester probably already told you I'm looking for a friend of mine who's disappeared. This friend met with a man matching Villar's description a week or so before he vanished. They had an altercation in a church parking lot a few blocks from here. Villar made some threats. My buddy said something to the effect of 'I know better than to piss in the Brazilians' grits.' At first, I presumed he was talking about a specific person. Now I think he meant an entire group."

"Villar and his crew have been making some inroads here in the States," Boulware said. "Can't figure out how your friend fits in."

"Cabby is a gopher. He knows how to acquire things. You need a Sherman tank a week from Tuesday? He knows how to get it. A criminal organization trying to muscle into a new territory must have logistical problems. Maybe that was Cabby's role. When we last talked, about six months ago, he implied he was making a good living, but it wasn't one hundred percent legit. I don't see what any of this has to do with Chinese mob activity, though."

"Boulware told you I work for ICE. My last assignment in San Francisco had to do with smuggling people from the PRC into the United States. Once here, they were forced to work for the triads. It wasn't exactly slave labor. Most of them worked for legitimate money-laundering operations. They made okay money, but they were never going to pile up enough to pay off the guys who brought them here. The Hong Kong triads see this country as an untapped gold mine of opportunity. They smuggle in people, electronics, housewares, bogus baby formula, you name it."

I had a momentary rare flash of inspiration. "Subgrade oil pipe?"

"One of China's biggest industries is steel. It's not great steel, but yeah."

"How do they smuggle all this stuff into the country?"

"The same way as anyone," Hong said. "In dribs and drabs.

You can't bring in entire container ships of contraband and offload it at the nearest seaport. Sometimes they use smaller ships, mix in the illegal booty with the legal stuff. Sometimes they offload the contraband onto another boat, or a lot of boats, out beyond the twelve-mile limit. Think your missing buddy might be able to scare up a flotilla of smuggling vessels?"

I sat back in my chair and took a long drag from the bottle. "This can't be happening," I said. "Not twice in one month."

"What?" Boulware said.

"I've been looking for two people," I said. "Found one of them last night. It's complicated, but the case involves a guy illegally trading in substandard oil pipeline materials from China. I was hired to help find out the source of the bad pipe. I have a . . . partner staked out in the woods near the pipeline site waiting for another transfer."

"Not the nutcase," Boulware said.

"Yeah," I said. "The area around the pipeline project is full of snakes, mosquitoes, nutria rats, and quicksand. It's like old home week for Scat."

"Who is this guy, Scat?" Hong asked Boulware.

"I'll fill you in later. It's a good story. You'll like it. So, how long has Boudreaux been stationed there?"

"I contracted with him last night. Based on my inquiries so far, every several days a diesel boat makes its way to a point near the worksite. All the workers are locked in their bunk trailers during the transfer. The good pipe is loaded onto the boat, the bad stuff is offloaded, and Holbrook pockets the money from the smugglers. The bogus pipe comes from China."

Hong leaned forward and cupped his chin in one palm.

"This *is* interesting," he said.

"Tell me something," I said. "Does the name Nigra mean anything to either of you?"

They looked at one another. Neither showed any sign of recognition.

"My friend, the one who's missing, might have had an appointment on the night he disappeared with a fellow named Nigra, first initial 'D.' I've been trying to find this guy for almost a week without success. The police have no record of him. Nobody I've asked has ever heard of him. I checked with another friend a few days ago, a guy who has a world of information at his fingertips. The appointment with this Nigra guy was supposed to take place at 6:34 pm on the night Cabby vanished."

"Pretty precise time," Hong said.

"A Brazilian cargo ship called the Rio Gaucho was scheduled to dock at the Port of New Orleans at 6:34 that evening," I said. "I scoped it out two days ago. It's still there. I have no idea whether Villar is involved with it in any way, but the only solid clues I've found while looking for Cabby are Villar and the ship. He's Brazilian, the ship is Brazilian. If his business is smuggling, maybe he had some cheap Chinese oil pipe on his manifest."

"Tell me," Hong said, after mulling it over and taking a swig of his beer, "do you think your pal Cabby could scare up a few trawlers if he needed to?"

"He sure could," I said. "Procuring stuff is his thing. But this is absurd. It's unrealistic for me to head off on two completely unrelated searches and then have them intersect."

"It's happened before," Boulware said

"It happened again a few weeks ago, too," I said. "I can't get that lucky."

"Well, you know what they say about you," Boulware said. "You are one lucky son of a bitch."

I excused myself to grab another beer from behind the bar. As I did, I caught Merlie's eye from across the room. She looked worried.

I blew her a kiss to reassure her and headed back to Boulware and Hong.

Between us, we probably weighed the better part of a half-ton. We probably looked like we were part of a convention of football fullbacks.

"Something I don't get," I said to Hong. "You said the bells and whistles went off when Boulware here sent out an inquiry on Rodrigo Villar. What's the connection? I don't see how the Brazilians might get mixed up in Chinese smuggling."

"It's a small world," Boulware said.

"And getting smaller," Hong added. "Most of my work in San Francisco had to do with human trafficking between China and the U.S. Been to Cuba lately?"

"It's embargoed."

"But you could go there if you wanted," Boulware said. "First, you'd have to go to Mexico, or Venezuela, or any of dozens of other countries who have trade and travel agreements with Havana. Then you simply book a trip from that country to Cuba, which recognizes US passports for entry. In fact, they like Americans a lot down there, because the *Yanquis* bring all this lovely *dinero* with them."

"It's the same with human trafficking and smuggling," Hong said. "Since Nine-Eleven, it's gotten harder and harder to sneak illegals into the country, at least by sea or air. Any ship or flight originating in eastern Asia is watched very carefully."

"Our relations with Brazil and many other South American countries, however, are relaxed and copacetic," Boulware said. "So, if a PRC national wants to enter the US without doing the paperwork first, one way is to enter from a friendly country."

"Like Brazil," I said.

"Like Brazil. If Villar is using Brazilian-registered ships to freight in Chinese steel and other contraband, what's to stop him from bringing in a few people at the same time? Getting them off the ship would be a piece of cake, whether he waited until it was docked, or offloaded them onto a trawler or a fishing boat or some other kind of vessel out in international waters."

"So you don't care if Villar is bringing in materials."

"Professionally? No. Not my bailiwick. I deal in human contraband. However, if we can link Villar to smuggling . . . well, damned near anything . . . we can take him off the board. One less headache I have to deal with."

"I need to put someone else in on this conversation," I said

I pulled out my cell phone and keyed in Dickens' number.

"You've heard from Boudreaux?" he said, even before I could say hello.

"No. But I have some new information. Can you get to the club in the next fifteen minutes?"

"I can be there in ten."

"Good. I have some people you want to meet."

Boulware's face assumed a look of disgust the second Dickens walked through the door.

"This is your guy?" he asked.

"What about it?"

By then, Dickens had seen me and made his way through the tables to where we were sitting. He stopped when he saw Boulware.

"Chester," he said.

"Chuck. I should have guessed. Gallegher here is like some kind of grease trap for people like you."

"So, you've met," I said.

"Son, you are looking at Charles Dickens, late of the United States Secret Service," Boulware said. "They were probably as happy to muster him out as he was to get away. He's a sellout, trading on the skills Uncle Sugar taught him, to make some big bucks before he pulls the ripcord and lives the life cushy for the next thirty years. Found the dog yet, Chuckles?"

Dickens waved at the air, as if trying to dispel a rotten odor. I raised my eyebrows.

"It's an old story. Some people can't let go. These are the people you want me to meet? I could have saved myself the trip. Yes, Agent Boulware and I have crossed paths. I don't know you," he said, pointing at Hong.

Hong offered his gargantuan hand. "Hong. James Hong. ICE."

"Bet you love saying that."

"Everyone seems to think so."

Dickens turned to me. "So, what's the deal?"

"I contacted Boulware a couple of days ago to ask about the Brazilian mob, specifically about one member of it."

"Brazilians? What in hell do Brazilians have to do with . . ." he stopped. Then he said, "How much have you told them?"

"Not much. No names so far. I don't think it would take them long to put the pieces together if they were so inclined. The other job I told you about? It might be linked to the problems I'm helping your client resolve."

I laid it all out again, from the beginning. When I told him about the Rio Gaucho, Dickens dropped his cavalier act and showed extreme interest.

"You've scouted this ship?" he said.

"The other day. Anyone have any idea how we might get a look onboard?"

"Too late," Hong said. "If you've ever been around a shipping yard, you'd know. It's amazing how quickly they can offload and reload a cargo freighter. No, if we tried to raid the Rio Gaucho right now, we'd only find outgoing stuff. Everything they brought in with them should be long gone."

"Let's say they did bring in this counterfeit oil pipe," Dickens said. "And let's assume it's the same stuff that's been substituted for my client's pipe. That means there should be a delivery to the Holbrook worksite soon."

"All they'd need is a boat to load it on," I said. "A trawler or maybe some kind of diesel barge, something with a crane or a cherry picker and a light draft. The water in Lake Saint Catherine near the worksite is only a few meters deep."

"That narrows the options," Hong said. "How many vessels like that can there be in the area?"

"This is the Mississippi Delta," Boulware said. "The kind of boats we're talking about are the workhorses all up and down the river. There might be hundreds within a thousand square miles of here."

"Can you contact your guy in the field readily?" Hong asked me.

"I can try. He's going to let me know when the transfer takes place."

"How?"

"He probably has a telephone with him, but it will be turned off. Scat Boudreaux prides himself on being invisible on the job. He wouldn't take a chance on his phone going off and giving away his position. I have his number. I can send him a message."

"Good," Hong said.

"What do you want me to tell him?" I said.

"Nothing yet. We need to think this through. First thing in the morning, I'll toss out a dragnet on every shred of information about the Rio Gaucho. If there is any connection to Rodrigo Torres Villar or any of his PCC compatriots, I'll find it. I'll also try to find out what was actually on the ship's cargo manifest, see if there are any gaps that don't make sense."

"What do you mean?" Dickens asked.

"The manifest should list every bit of cargo the Rio Gaucho brought in. There is video surveillance of the shipyard. The manifest will list every cargo container by number, and what was in it. If some of the containers offloaded on video aren't accounted for on the manifest, that's a gap. If your guy ... Boudreaux? ... contacts you before then, have him get as much information as he can on the boat doing the transfer. The more intel we have, the better."

We made a few more plans before Boulware and Hong took off. As soon as they cleared the door, Dickens turned to me. He didn't look happy.

"If Mr. Kenzie wanted help from the Feds, he could have gone to them directly," he said.

"I didn't go to them. They came to me. I contacted Boulware about this other matter I've been handling while I was looking for Garry Sharp. He's the one who told me about Villar and the PCC. I had no idea they might be linked to my other deal until about five minutes before I called you. As we were talking, I saw a possible connection, and it was off to the races."

"Mr. Kenzie will not be happy if his name is publicly associated with this matter."

"Well, we'd hate for Mr. Kenzie to be unhappy. What's all this stuff about a dog?"

"An old story, like I said. Drop it. So, what's next?"

"Next, I plan to have one more brew, enjoy the Preservation Hall Band's last set, and then I'm going to take my gorgeous redhead over there upstairs. I've exhausted all my investigatory options for one night. I need some rest. I'd suggest you do the same. The minute Scat calls, I have a feeling things are going to happen quickly."

CHAPTER TWENTY-SEVEN

"*I*DON'T KNOW WHICH I like least," Merlie told me as the Preservation Hall guys prepared for their last set of the night. "You working for Kellen Kenzie, or you hanging out with Boulware. And who were those two other men?"

"One's with immigration and the other's a private security operative working for Kenzie. I never met the immigration guy before. The private guy is named Dickens. He's running interference for me. He may not be completely aware of it yet."

"What do you mean?"

"He works for a company called Borglund Security. Kenzie offered me some of Borglund's resources in return for helping him with his hammerhead son-in-law. I demanded he give me Dickens."

"Why?"

"A hunch. I get a good feeling about him. I think he'd stand up in a crisis. Something still bothers me. It seems as if my Garry Sharp case and my Cabby Jacks case are related to one another. It's possible Cabby is working for the guy Sharp was trying to identify for Kenzie."

"Hmmm . . ." Merlie sipped at her drink. "A brilliant man I know once said 'I don't like coincidences.'"

"I was right then. It's still good advice now. One thing still puzzles me. Who in hell is—"

"Hey guys!" Chick Kasay said as he pulled a chair up to our table. "Mind if I join you?"

"Sure, kid. Have a seat," I said, turning back to Merlie. "So, like I was saying, who in hell is this guy D. Nigra, and what's his relation to Cabby Jacks?"

"Did you say Nigra?" Chick said.

"What about it?" I asked.

"*D.* Nigra?"

"That's right."

"I might be able to help you, if you let me in on what it's about."

"It's personal business, Chick," I said.

"Oh, well, if you don't want to know . . ." he grabbed his beer and started to walk away.

"Wait!" I said. He turned to face me. "Okay, but it doesn't go beyond this table. A friend of mine is missing. He's been missing for almost two weeks. I searched his apartment a few days back and found a notation in his calendar for a meeting on the night he disappeared with someone named D. Nigra."

"So it's one of your . . . what in hell do you call what you do, anyway?" he asked.

"Favors. Yeah. It's a favor I'm doing for my missing friend, but it's more than that. I owe him big."

"Repaying a debt," Chick said. "I dig it. I owe a lot of people stuff myself. Someday I'll make good on it. Sit tight."

He walked up to the stage, grabbed one of his guitar cases, and brought it back to the table. Gingerly, he opened the case and pulled out an acoustic guitar. The spruce top was darkened with age. The lacquer finish was crazed with craquelure, like a fine piece of ancient

Chinese porcelain.

"Martin HD-28," he said. "Pre-war."

"Which war?"

"World War II. This puppy was built in 1934."

"Museum piece," I said.

"Well, sure, but so is a Stradivarius and people still play them."

He turned the guitar around to show me the back. The wood was beautiful. It was chocolate brown streaked with yellow and gold and black, all flowing like oil on water through the grain.

"*D. Nigra*," Chick said. "At least that's the Latin name for it. The full name is Dalbergia Nigra."

"I've been looking for *wood*?"

"Not any ordinary wood. This is the Holy Grail of tonewoods. This wood resonates like no other. There are players out there who'd kill their grandmothers for an axe made from this stuff. The English name is Brazilian Rosewood."

"Brazilian?"

"The very best. The major builders don't use this stuff anymore. They've had to find alternatives."

"Why?" Merlie asked.

"It's endangered. All the clear-cutting you've heard about in the Amazon Basin in South America? A lot of Dalbergia got destroyed, burned like trash by people whose souls wouldn't fill a mosquito's thimble. A lot of it was over-harvested in the first half of the twentieth century for everything from flooring to furniture to musical instruments. You can't get this stuff anymore. It's protected by CITES."

"What's that?" I asked.

"The Convention on International Trade in Endangered Species. The demand for Brazilian rosewood became so extreme, it was almost harvested to extinction by 1973. Rosewood is gorgeous, but it doesn't like to grow anywhere except South America and it takes a long time to mature. So, CITES put it on the embargoed list in 1992. The only Dalbergia Nigra you can use legally has to have been harvested before 1992 and stored. You have to provide certification the wood is CITES-compliant before you sell it for any purpose. Most of the known old-growth stock is owned by the major guitar making companies like Martin and Breedlove and Gibson. You can bet they guard it like the gold in Fort Knox, because when it's gone, it's gone for good."

I pulled out my cell phone and dialed Boulware's number.

"Miss me already, Gallegher?" he asked.

"Is Hong still with you?"

"Natch. It's a long drive to Baton Rouge."

"Put him on."

I heard the phone being jostled. Hong came on the line.

"What do you know about CITES and Brazilian rosewood?" I said.

"Next to nothing. Educate me."

"This guy I've been looking for? The one who went missing and had a connection with Rodrigo Villar? I told you he wrote the name D. Nigra and a time on his datebook. I found out, at least I think I found out, what it means."

"Okay."

"It's not a person. It's a type of wood. The letter 'D' stands for . . ." I glanced at Chick and rolled a finger in the air.

"Dalbergia," he said.

"Dalbergia," I told Hong. "Dalbergia Nigra is the Latin name for Brazilian rosewood. The Rio Gaucho was scheduled to arrive from Rio de Janeiro at 6:34 pm on the night Cabby vanished. I'm guessing it was carrying a shipment of Brazilian rosewood."

"What about it?"

226

"You're into smuggling. My guy here says this rosewood is the hardwood equivalent of unobtainium. You can't harvest it and you can't export it, because it's protected as an endangered species. You can only sell stuff that was harvested before 1992. Even then you have to provide documentation it meets the qualifications as old cut lumber."

"I get it," Hong said. "Limited availability makes it valuable, which means it's worth smuggling."

"If Villar is involved in this, I'm betting he's also falsifying CITES certifications. The end users probably don't know they're buying fresh-cut rosewood. Or maybe they don't care, as long as they have the documentation in hand. They can always plead ignorance if the paper looks good."

"You're probably right. What do they use this wood for, anyway?"

"Mostly furniture and musical instruments these days. According to my guy, a lot of guitar companies are hoarding the stuff. They charge top-shelf prices for instruments made of it. But I don't think they would touch new stock unless it had unquestionable provenance. So, we'd have to figure how Villar might distribute the stuff once he offloads it from the ship."

"Let me talk to him," Chick said. I handed him the phone.

"My name's Chick Kasay," he said. "I told Mr. Gallegher about the Brazilian rosewood. Listen, he's right. The major manufacturers wouldn't be interested in this new rosewood. It's too risky for them to handle it. I'm a guitarist. I know a lot of small guitar builders, the kind of guys who make five or ten instruments a year, all hand-crafted. It's a cottage industry for most of them, and they might make enough to eke out a living. If they can build an axe out of Brazilian, they can charge two, three times as much for it, maybe more, with the same man-hours put into it. These guys can't afford to buy large amounts of rosewood, but they can afford one or two sets at a time."

I had a feeling Hong and I had the same question: *Where would they buy it?*

I must have been right, because Chick said, "Mostly online, like on auction websites, eBay, Craigslist. These sites are a huge underground economy. There are people making tens of thousands of dollars a year from online sales, none of it reported to the IRS. So, say I'm a small-time builder in East Bumfuck, Alabama, and I want to craft an instrument out of Brazilian. I search online for someone who's unloading a back-and-sides set with proper CITES documentation. Hell, the builder probably wouldn't know real documentation from bogus. Probably wouldn't even care. He can always plead ignorance if the FDA asks any questions."

I gestured for Kasay to hand the phone back.

"We're in my wheelhouse now," I said. "This is what I do, find lost people and lost things. The kid's right. If we find the end users, we can track back to their suppliers, and from them to *their* suppliers, and we'll eventually get to Cabby Jacks."

"How do you figure?"

"He didn't write *Chinese steel* on his datebook. He wrote Brazilian rosewood, or the Latin equivalent. Maybe he was in charge of offloading and handling it. I can help with this. We find Cabby—"

"And he can put the finger on Villar for smuggling this stuff into the country."

"It's as good to put Villar away for smuggling endangered species of wood as it is for smuggling people, right?"

"Might be better. We might be able to flip him. Hold on."

He covered the phone with his hand, but I could still hear his muffled conversation with Boulware.

"Is this guy the real thing? Can he do what he says?"

"Gallegher's a pain in the ass. He doesn't recognize any authority anywhere and he has a bad habit of going cowboy. But, yeah. He isn't given to bragging. If he says he can do it, he likely can."

"Can you control him?"

"Not a chance. He has one thing going for him. He's lucky. Luckiest damned son of a bitch I ever met. Smart, too. I'll tell you his story on the way back to Baton Rouge. What's he suggesting?"

"He wants in."

"You could do worse."

"That's what I thought in San Francisco and look what happened."

"It's your play, James. I just brought you two together. Whether you dance is up to you."

Hong came back on the phone. "Okay, Gallegher, let's run with this. You start checking stuff from your end. I'll work on mine. I'm going to give you my phone number. Put it in your phone and call me the minute you have something. Got it?"

"We're going to keep this communication a two-way street, right?"

"Sure. I find something, I let you know. You find something, you let me know. And call me the minute you hear anything from this guy Scat Whatsisname. We're working on two different ends of this smuggling business, but between them I think we have a shot at Villar."

And, I thought, *a chance at finding Cabby Jacks*.

CHAPTER TWENTY-EIGHT

*T*HE TELEPHONE JANGLED me awake around eight the next morning. For most people it would be a minor annoyance, but I work in a night club that doesn't announce last call until well after midnight. Part of my paycheck covers helping to close the joint up, so it's rare for me to see my pillow before three or four in the morning. I need ringing telephones right after cock's crow like I need testicular torsion.

Merlie had stayed with me the night before, but she'd risen at six-thirty, showered, and headed to work shortly after kissing me goodbye, which broke my slumber for about a minute and a half.

"Yeah?" I mumbled into the receiver.

"Patrick?"

It was Quentin Wardell, my font of information from the Mormon Church.

"You found something?" I asked, suddenly wide awake.

"Perhaps. You wanted me to find out what I could about this ship, the Rio Gaucho. It took a while. Do you still need the information?"

"Absolutely."

"The Rio Gaucho is a relatively small container ship, roughly ninety meters long by thirteen meters wide, weighing in at roughly three thousand metric tons dry—"

"I've seen the ship, Q."

"Sorry. It was built in 1970 at a shipyard in Telemark, Norway. It was bought by the A.C. Frundgren Company that year. It was in service with them until about 1982, when it was refitted, again in Telemark."

I tried to stifle a yawn. Quentin is a great source of information, but sometimes it takes him a while to get to the point. He enjoys demonstrating the fruits of his own investigative labors. I like to stay in his good graces, so it's best to let him get to the important stuff at his own pace.

"Who owns it now?" I asked.

"Well, that is the question, isn't it? After it was sold in 1985, to a Panamanian company, it plied a route around the Gulf of Mexico. Its cargo consisted mostly of fruits and vegetables, sometimes some grains. It is able to carry over a hundred thousand cubic feet of cargo in its hold, along with a fair number of containers on its deck."

"This Panamanian outfit still owns it?"

"Dear me, no. This is where the story gets interesting. While it was owned by them, its name was the Juanita de Fundo. Probably a relative or girlfriend of someone in the company. In 1992, the ship was taken out of service and sat in a shipyard in Cartagena for almost two years, before being purchased again by a company named F.I.S.B. Limited."

"At which time they changed the name to the Rio Gaucho," I said.

"Exactly. Here's where the story gets interesting. F.I.S.B. Limited appears to exist for one purpose . . . to own a fleet of ships."

"That isn't unusual, is it?"

"It is if the company doesn't manufacture anything, import or export any goods, or hire the ship out to other companies who do.

This Rio Gaucho does not appear to have ever been hired by any third-party company to haul anything."

I was still a little groggy, so it took a moment for the last bit to sink in.

"How could they make any money?"

"The only way I could think of was if it was purchased by a company to transport that own company's goods. But, as I noted, F.I.S.B Limited doesn't make or export anything. All they do is own this ship, along with others. So, I began investigating who owns F.I.S.B. Limited. That's when the trail became ... convoluted."

"Convoluted how?"

"Well, it appears F.I.S.B. Limited is some sort of holding company, a subsidiary of another corporation. You must understand, Patrick, laws regarding incorporation vary from country to country. Some require strict articles of incorporation. Others tend to be laxer in their regulations. In the case of the owners of the Rio Gaucho, I discovered a labyrinth of dummy corporations with twists and turns like a giant rollercoaster. Trying to pull all the intertwined companies apart took quite a lot of doing. In the end, I discovered something disturbing."

"What?"

"All of the holding companies and dummy corporations ultimately led to one name, a corporation headquartered in Rio de Janeiro, Brazil. That company, called Lazzarro Limited, appears to be a front for a particularly dangerous band of Brazilian gangsters."

"The Primeiro Comando da Capital?"

"Why, yes. Is that helpful?"

"Absolutely. Your information and mine appear to be dovetailing. We already knew the Rio Gaucho was of Brazilian registry, but now it appears its owners are actually the Brazilian mob."

"You do seem to have a penchant for getting involved with

underworld types, don't you?"

"Not by choice. Were you able to find anything on the Rio Gaucho's current cargo? That is, what it was hauling when it arrived in New Orleans?"

"Not much. The information I was able to obtain simply indicated textiles and manufacturing equipment. The manifest wasn't terribly explicit, I'm afraid. I do have a list of the primary crew. In all, the ship carries a crew of about thirty men. Does this help?"

"Everything helps if I didn't know it before. When is the Rio Gaucho scheduled to leave New Orleans?"

"They appear to be here for another several days. According to my information, they should sail next Thursday."

"So, six days," I said.

"So it would seem."

"Quentin, I owe you big. If things turn out, I may be by in a week or so with a story that will rock your socks off."

"Oh, I do look forward to it."

An idea occurred to me. "Can you do another search for me?"

"Certainly."

"I need to know everything you can assemble about a man named Kellen Kenzie."

"The fascist?"

"A little extreme, don't you think?"

"Most fascists are."

"I want to know anything you can find. Family history, business holdings, the whole enchilada. And I need it quickly."

"Would tomorrow be all right?"

"Tomorrow would be perfect," I said. "And, something else. Might be nothing, but it gnawed at me all last night. I spoke with a woman a few days ago, at her home. I went back last night and it looked as if she had moved out. I'd like to know where she landed."

I gave him Carly McKee's information, what little I had, and left him to do his magic. As I had told him, maybe it was nothing. We live in a transient society. People pick up and go all the time. This particular disappearance seemed too convenient for my tastes and handing it over to Quentin took it off my plate for a while. I had other stuff to do, including one huge obligation that had nothing to do with Kellen Kenzie, Garry Sharp, or Cabby Jacks.

I had to say goodbye to a friend.

CHAPTER TWENTY-NINE

SOCKEYE SAM'S FUNERAL was scheduled for noon. He had served in the Navy in World War II, probably seeing action that made my worst fight seem like a barroom scuffle. He was entitled to burial with full military honors—flag-draped coffin, twenty-one-gun salute, and a military honor guard. The one exception, which it turns out he had included in his will, was that I was to play Taps at his gravesite, instead of a bugler. When his daughter called and informed me of Sam's request, I barely held it together long enough to accept.

I showered and dressed in my best suit—which, as it happens, was also my only suit—and ran through the piece three or four times again, as I had done the day before. It was so simple, compared to the complex melodies and inventions I meandered through on stage at Holliday's every evening. Four lonely notes, almost like a child's first piece of music, and yet they were so poignant and so gut-wrenching because they symbolized the memorialization of the life of a man who had given so much, asked for so little, and had been my sole partner on stage for eight years.

I picked Merlie up at A Friend's Place around eleven to make the drive out to the Lower Ninth Ward, where Sam had lived for almost fifty years. Strangely, I had never asked him where he rested his head at night. He showed up at ten, played until two, and then always seemed to vanish sometime between our last set and when I mopped the floor of the bar before heading up to my own humble lodgings. He never asked for a ride home and he never asked for a ride to work, so he simply appeared, did his job better than any other pianist in the French Quarter, and dissipated like smoke when he was done.

His home was small, but well-kept. It had a fresh coat of robin's-egg blue paint on its aging cypress siding and a pleasant covered gallery out front with three pristine white-enameled wicker chairs. A single door graced the middle of the gallery. I knew without opening it that it led to a hallway stretching the length of the building. In the old days, they called it a shotgun house because, it was said, if you opened the front and back doors you could shoot a shotgun straight through the house without hitting a single wall.

Every gallery on the street was populated by residents sitting in rockers or plush wicker chairs, swiping funeral parlor fans back and forth to keep cool. As Merlie and I stepped from the car, I didn't see another single white face in either direction.

Sam's daughter, Odetta, opened the front door before I had a chance to ring the bell. She was the antithesis of her gaunt, wizened father—a short, plump woman with flashing eyes and a warm, inviting smile.

"Mr. Gallegher," she said. "I am so happy to welcome you to our home."

"Please," I said. "Call me Pat. It's an honor to be invited."

She led us inside. There was a small living room to the left of the hallway and an identical dining room to the right. Both rooms were packed with mourners, well-wishers, and maybe one or two hangers-on who had shown up mostly because an enormous spread of food always appears at wakes in southern funerals. I heard more voices echo down the hall from the kitchen at the back of the house.

Odetta tried to introduce me to some of the people, but my preoccupied mind was incapable of remembering their names. I smiled and shook hands and even accepted a hug or two from family members who knew of me from Sam's stories. It seemed he had regarded me as some sort of tarnished hero. My legend—meager as it was in real life—had grown to comic book proportions with the retelling among his buddies. A couple of men tried to ply a war story or two from my random dangerous adventures over the years, but I deferred, suggesting we should probably better spend our time recalling the man Sam had been.

Shorty showed up about ten minutes after we arrived, looking stiff and uncomfortable in a pinstriped summer wool suit which had probably hung on a store rack the day before. He wore it well and reluctantly at the same time. He looked at me sheepishly when I gave him the thumbs-up. I was surprised when Chick Kasay walked in the door. He had replaced his cutoff sweats and cargo pants with a crisp dark suit and tie. His spiky hair had been slicked back over his scalp. He'd deep-sixed the facial hardware. For the first time since I had met him, he appeared respectable.

A few minutes later, we all piled into our respective cars and drove the half mile to the local A.M.E. Zion Church. The minister there, who called himself a bishop, hovered in his pulpit over the flag-draped coffin and delivered a short but illuminating eulogy for my lost friend. The choir, on cue, launched into a raucous hymn, accented by trills and hand-clapping. After a brief prayer of intercession to ask the Almighty to accept Sam with open arms, it was time to move to the graveyard behind the church for the interment.

Like most cemeteries in New Orleans, it wasn't practical to actually bury the dead. Instead, caskets were placed inside above-ground tombs—marble for those who could afford them, and concrete and brick for common men like Sam. Three Navy seamen stood near the crypt, their rifles at port arms. Two more sailors, clad in brilliant dress whites, waited patiently for the coffin to be delivered to a bench in front of the crypt. The bishop offered another prayer and, on a signal from one of the officers, it was time for me to play.

A lot of things went through my mind as I played the mournful twenty-four notes, the saddest eight bar blues I'd ever blown in my life. I recalled my first night at Holliday's, only a week after arriving in New Orleans trying to escape the shame of my dismissal from my university in New England. Sam—then a spry young man only in his eighties—had frowned after our first set and opined it would take quite a while for us to find our common musical ground. I recalled how he slowly taught me the New Orleans sound, which he had learned at the side of some of the greatest names in the business, now long-dead. I remembered how he had trusted only me to save Shorty's hide when he was accused of murder. Mostly, I remembered the thousands of nights we stepped into the soft spotlights of the sorry platform we called our stage, and for four hours at a stretch lost ourselves in the genius of Monk and Nestico and Basie and Gershwin and a hundred other composers. We had been a team.

I hit the last note. The armed seamen raised their rifles and ripped off seven shots each in perfect unison. Some of the people in the crowd—including Merlie—flinched with each volley. I didn't. I had been exposed to too much gunfire in my life to be surprised by it anymore. Curiously, I noticed Chick also stood stock-still through the salute, but I dismissed it.

The honor guard folded the flag and presented it to Odetta. She hugged it to her bosom as if she might be embracing her father one last time. Then, the bishop said another prayer, the pallbearers placed

Sam's coffin inside the crypt, and my friend was gone forever.

A funeral is a strange thing, when all is said and done. The deceased is finally at permanent rest and suddenly nobody seems at all certain what to do next. Some hovered near the crypt. Others wandered amongst the graves and visited long-lost loved ones. Others seemed to drift away singly or in pairs toward the church. Odetta thanked me for playing Taps and for being such a good friend to her father, before she was spirited away by other mourners.

Merlie stood at my side, her arm entwined in mine. "It was beautiful," she said. "You never played better."

"I was flying blind," I said. "I had things on my mind."

Chick Kasay stepped up to us. "This isn't the time," he said. "But when you get back to the club we need to talk. I think I've found your Brazilian rosewood."

CHAPTER THIRTY

*A*FTER DROPPING MERLIE off at the shelter, I threaded my way through traffic to the French Quarter, carefully parked the Beemer in the lot behind Irene's, and made my way through throngs of early-afternoon Bourbon Street revelers to Holliday's.

I needn't have rushed. The bar was empty when I arrived, the front door locked. I let myself in, changed clothes in my apartment, and waited in the bar for Chick to arrive.

He showed up about a half hour later. He'd changed into his usual deadly casual attire, but left his hair slicked back. Maybe he saw it as his next look. I offered him a beer from the cooler behind the bar and we settled at one of the tables.

"So," he said, "after we talked last night, I went home and couldn't sleep. I pulled out my computer and started doing searches for online sales of Brazilian rosewood. I found a few listings here and there, mostly out-of-state, which didn't help us much."

I did not miss his use of the word "us," instead of "you." It appeared Chick was trying to deal himself in on Cabby's disappearance. I considered correcting him, but the information he was providing was good and I didn't want to break him off when he was on a roll.

"Then, I thought it might help to locate someone who might be building guitars and stuff with Brazilian rosewood. This morning, before I headed out for the funeral, I called the Guild of American Luthiers in California. "The guild of what?" I asked.

"Luthiers. People who make stringed musical instruments. I told them I was a hotshot Juilliard grad, which I am, and I was interested in finding someone to build me a Brazilian rosewood Martin HD-28 knockoff. I told the lady on the phone I was living in New Orleans, but I could travel a hundred miles or so for the right craftsman. She gave me a list of names."

"Whom you called," I said.

"How'd you guess? Yeah, I phoned them from my car on the way to the funeral. The first two cut me off as soon as I mentioned Brazilian, said they didn't have it in stock. One said he might be able to find a back and sides set for six hundred or so on an online auction site, but that didn't help me. Then I called the third guy."

"And he had some."

"Boy howdy did he. The guy's name is Trey Houser. He said he obtained three primo sets of Brazilian a few weeks back. He quoted me a price on a new guitar. Want to hear the best part?"

"Sure."

"He's local. Has his shop a couple dozen blocks from here, south on Decatur. I told him I might drop by sometime this afternoon. So, what happens next?"

I drained my beer and tossed the empty into the bin next to the bar.

"What happens next," I said, "is I thank you vociferously and go visit this whatchamacallit."

"Luthier, and I have a list of reasons why you want to reconsider."

"Starting with?"

"Starting with you don't know jack shit about guitars. You don't even know what they call the guy who builds one. Also, you don't know where he works. You wouldn't know Brazilian if it whacked you on the butt. Take me along. I'll fill in all the blanks."

I considered it. Chick was right. I was treading on foreign territory here, a place where I didn't speak the lingo. On the other hand, I was used to working alone. I had my own style, my own way of drawing the truth out of people. On occasion my methods tended to lean toward the heavy-handed. I probably wouldn't need to scare information out of Houser, but it would be a lot harder if he suspected he had an ally in Chick, who might intervene on his behalf.

Holding him off was a losing battle.

"First things first," I said. "We need to let Agent Hong in on our plans. I've had a lot of experience running afoul of the authorities. It doesn't usually turn out well."

I pulled out my cell phone and hit Hong's number. He answered on the third ring.

"What'cha' got, Gallegher?" he said.

"With the help of my music partner, we may have located a lead on the Brazilian rosewood we discussed last night. Are you in Baton Rouge?"

"No."

He didn't elaborate. The tone of his voice indicated he didn't plan to.

"All right. Chick and I are going to pay the guy a visit. You have a problem with that?"

"Not as long as you keep me in the loop. You don't act on anything you learn before you run it past me. You got it?"

"Perfectly. This guy we're visiting isn't the source of the rosewood. He's an end user, but he knows where he purchased his goods. One step leads to the next."

"Until someone chops you off at the ankles. Be careful, dude.

If your questioning leads to Villar, he can be a dangerously-nasty character."

Trey Houser's guitar building shop was in the rear of a musical instrument store, near the point where Decatur Street dead-ends into St. Ferdinand Street. Chick and I walked in, told the clerk at the front we wanted to see Houser. He directed us through a curtained doorway in the back of the store.

We found Houser making tiny curls of wood shavings on the back of a guitar project with a metal scraper. He'd make a couple of passes, examine the result through magnifying goggles he wore, feel the wood with the palm of his hand, and scrape it again.

Houser looked to be in his middle thirties. He wore a Grateful Dead shirt under a pair of faded and tattered Oshkosh overalls. His hair fell to the middle of his back and was tied into a ponytail. When he removed the magnifying goggles, his eyes were the color of dark chocolate. He had huge hands, the palms thickened with calluses that could probably stop a knife attack. Chick cleared his throat to get Houser's attention.

"Help you?" Houser asked, barely looking up at us.

"I called you this morning about a Brazilian rosewood HD-28 copy," Chick said.

Suddenly, Houser became Mr. Friendly.

"Well, you should have said something earlier. Welcome." He strode toward us, his had extended. "Trey Houser. Nice to meet you."

We all exchanged handshakes.

"This your dad?" Houser said to Chick, pointing toward me.

"Hell, no. This is Gallegher. We play together in a club over on Toulouse. You said you have some new Brazilian sets in stock?"

"Sure do."

"If we can come to an agreement on price, could I choose which set I'd like to use?"

"You got the cash, you're the boss. The sets are over here."

We followed him across the shop to a set of shelves, where dozens of thin-sliced pieces of wood were layered with one-inch thick wooden blocks.

"I take good care of my tonewood," Houser said. "Every set is air-dried and stickered." He pointed to the blocks, which I guessed were the 'stickers.' The point was obvious. By separating the guitar sets, air was able to get to all four sides, which kept the sets dry. In a city where you can wring fresh water out of the air with a towel, it was a good idea. I also noted Houser had the air conditioning running full blast, which kept the humidity down in the shop.

Being a brass player, I didn't know one kind of wood from another. My primary exposure to the stuff was when I grabbed a toothpick after a nice meal at Irene's. Houser hoisted three sets of guitar wood from the shelf, as if he were lifting a newborn from a bassinette, and carried them over to a large, square workbench in the middle of the shop. Each set was composed of four pieces. Two were short and wide. I supposed they were used for the guitar back. The other two were long and narrow, for the guitar sides. Compared to the guitar Chick had shown me the night before, it was relatively unimpressive stuff. The browns and blacks and yellows were all mudded and dull. There were visible saw marks running in horizontal rows all the way down the length of each piece. A guitar in the raw, I guessed.

"You are in such luck," Houser said to Chick. "I almost never have Brazilian in the shop, for obvious reasons. Most of my guitars these days are built from either East Indian rosewood, or walnut, or mahogany. Even mahogany's getting scarce lately."

"Because of the CITES injunctions?" I asked, trying to sound knowledgeable.

"Naw. Honduras mahogany isn't on the CITES list yet. I expect it will be in the near future. It's still available, but it's running out. There are about a dozen or so species of mahogany and a few close genetic relatives that work as well and sound as good, but everyone wants the good old close-grained Honduras stuff. You can still trade in the new-cut stuff as long as you can provide an export certificate. Not like this Brazilian. The tree this stuff came from was felled almost forty years ago. It's been sitting and drying, waiting for me to turn it into an instrument since before I was born. Something to think about."

"Sure is," Chick said. "Speaking of CITES, you have the certification papers, right?"

"Wouldn't have bought it without them. Illegal, you know. Don't want to get in trouble with the Feds. I have them in the file cabinet over here."

He rummaged through the top drawer in a metal file cabinet in the corner of his shop and pulled out a folder which he brought back over to the workbench.

"Each set is numbered," he said. "And the three sets of certifications I have here match the numbers."

"Mind if I take a look?" Chick said.

"No problem."

I looked over Chick's shoulder as he examined the papers. He put a studious look on his face, nodded a couple of times, and said "Uh-huh," once.

"All in order," Houser said.

"Um, not exactly," Chick said.

Houser's face took on a look of concern. "What? There's a problem?"

"Can't say for sure," Chick told him. "You've bought CITES-enjoined tonewood before?"

"Sure, a few times. Like I said, I don't usually have sets in stock."

"Then it might be a lucky thing I came along today. You said the tree was felled forty years ago?"

"Well. You know, more or less."

"And the paperwork seems to support it, except look here. The name of the authority in Brazil who certified the harvest dates. Alberto Culombo? His signature is dated August of 1994."

"Yeah?"

"Alberto Culombo *was* a Brazilian minister of export, but he died in 1992. By 1994, the minister of export was a fellow named Diego Morales."

"What are you saying?" Houser asked.

"These papers aren't in order. Where did you buy this rosewood?"

"What are you, some kind of cop?"

Chick walked over to the wall of Houser's shop and picked up an archtop guitar hanging there. "May I?" he said.

Houser handed him a pick and he ripped off a complicated rendition of Chick Corea's "Spain."

"You know any cops can play like that?" he asked, as he placed the guitar gently back on its hanger. "I'm a musician. I don't make enough money in a year to pay for the legal trouble I could get into owning an axe that isn't legal. Most luthiers I've met don't get rich, either. Maybe this rosewood is righteous, maybe it isn't. Where'd you get it again?"

"A buddy of mine called me the other night, said he saw some for sale online here in town. Turns out I knew the guy who placed the ad. I've bought East Indian from him before. His prices have always been good. I drove over to the guy's house, bought it directly from him on the spot. Hell, this shit cost me almost two thousand dollars. If it's not legitimate—"

"Maybe it's a misunderstanding," Chick said. "Hell, for all I know, I got the date of Culombo's death all wrong. I can check it later. In the meantime, maybe Gallegher and I should pay this guy a visit, let him know he might want to pull his advertisement until he can straighten this out."

Houser looked back and forth at us.

"I'd better go with you," he said.

CHAPTER THIRTY-ONE

*T*HE GUY WAS named Fred Altschuler. He lived about a mile and a half north of Houser's shop. Houser had to put his tools and projects away. Chick and I waited for him out front, beside the Beemer.

"Nice catch on the Alberto Culombo thing. How'd you know he died in 1992?" I said.

"Hell, for all I know, Alberto Culombo is sitting by a pool in Bahia, bouncing his granddaughter on his knee," Chick said. "I never heard of the guy before. I needed an excuse to turn the conversation away from buying a guitar and back toward the rosewood itself."

"Sharp," I said. "Almost like you've done this sort of thing before."

"Lying? Sure. Do it all the time. Here comes Houser."

We all piled into the Beemer. Houser directed us to Fred Altschuler's place. It turned out to be a squat cinderblock affair with a wrought-iron security screen door on the front. The roof was made of fading ceramic terra cotta tiles, a couple of which were missing. The front yard was fenced. A large, muscular bull terrier lounged on the concrete front stoop until we stepped up to the gate. As Houser reached for an intercom mounted to the post, the dog jumped to its feet and began to growl, as if daring us to come one step closer.

"Don't mind him," Houser said. "He's basically a big fluffy asshole."

He punched the intercom button. A few seconds later, the speaker crackled and a high-pitched male voice said, "What?"

"It's Houser. I need to talk to you about the Brazilian you sold me."

"All sales are final," Altschuler said.

"If you don't mean 'final' as in 'the last sales I ever make to Trey Houser,' then we need to talk. I've given you a lot of business over the years."

"Whatever," the voice said. The connection broke off with a metallic click.

The front door opened. A skinny, balding man in cargo shorts and a stained tee shirt stepped out on the stoop.

"Who's with you?" he asked, when he saw us with Houser.

"A couple of customers. This one," he pointed to Chick, "wanted me to build a guitar out of your Brazilian stock."

Altschuler whistled and said something in a language I didn't know. The dog settled down by the side of the front steps.

"Y'all come on in," Altschuler said, gesturing us through the gate. "I ain't payin' the power company to keep the skeeters cool."

The inside of Altschuler's house was dingy and dusty. Venetian blinds in the front windows were cracked enough to allow narrow streams of sunlight through. They illuminated thousands of dust motes suspended in the chilly air. The couch was old and sprung out, with the pillows becoming threadbare in spots. I could see from the living room into the kitchen, where dishes were piled in the sink. In an earlier time, they probably would have been joined by pots and pans, but microwave ovens had long since taken the place of real cooking. I couldn't imagine Altschuler engaging in anything resembling *haute cuisine*.

"Here's the thing," Houser said. "We were examining the rosewood you sold me. There's something wrong with the CITES certifications."

"Wrong how?" Altschuler asked.

"The dates are wrong. The guy who signed these certificates died two years before they were processed."

"No shit," Altschuler said. "Lemme see."

Houser handed the folder over. Altschuler looked through them. He handed the folder back.

"That changes things. I don't know whether this is good paper or not. I'd have to check it out. If you're right, I'll gladly refund your money. I don't need a reputation for passing bogus goods. I *sure* don't need the kind of heat selling illegal lumber might bring down on me. If it's not legit, I'm as surprised as you. I'll make it right."

"What can you tell us about how you bought it?" I asked.

"Why do you want to know?"

"We haven't been completely up front with you. We are musicians, just as Chick told Mr. Houser here. We play at a bar over on Toulouse, called Holliday's. I have a friend who may be mixed up in some kind of scheme to sell bootleg Brazilian rosewood. He's gone missing. We're trying to find him."

"I see."

"So," I said. "Anything you could tell us about where you got this rosewood would be a huge help."

"No problem," Altschuler said. "Well, actually, it is a problem for me. I'm out almost three grand for those sets I bought. I wouldn't mind getting my hands on the guy myself, for taking me like that. I should have known it was too good to be true. A sweet deal on primo Brazilian guitar sets doesn't come along every day."

"How did you come across them?" I asked.

"Fella called me, said he'd seen my ads online for tonewoods. I used to build guitars myself, until rheumatoid arthritis caught up with me. Had dozens of sets stacked and stickered in my shop out back, but I couldn't use a plane or a scraper anymore without paying for it with a night of no sleep and achy hands. Finally had to give it up. I've been parceling out my stock ever since. After a while, I figured it was a good way to shore up my Social Security, so I started buying sets cheap where I could find them, selling them for the best price I could get. You have any idea how many guys take up guitar building each year?"

"No idea," I said, trying hard to hide my lack of interest.

"Hundreds all across the country. Most build one disappointingly bad instrument and decide it's too difficult, or they don't want to invest the time to work on their craft. They quit, usually after they let their early enthusiasm get the best of them and bought five or six expensive sets of tonewood. These guys, they never start out with something cheap like walnut or sapele. They go for the good stuff right off the bat. Waste of good wood, it would be, except I'm happy to take it off their hands if we can arrive at the right price. They always wind up taking a bath on it, but at least they don't lose everything. So, I get this call a few weeks back from a guy who said he had a bunch of Brazilian sets with the CITES certs. I figure he's another hobbyist who got in way over his head. We arrange to meet, and he shows up looking like some sort of banker. Dressed real nice, y'know? I reckon, maybe he's taking time off of work to show me what he has. Then it becomes clear he don't know much at all about building guitars. Seems he's some sort of middleman. The paper looks good to me, so far as I can tell, since I don't trade in a lot of CITES-listed woods, and his price per set is almost too good, so I decided to take it off his hands. 'This stuff is fresh off the boat,' he told me. We haggled a little and then we made a deal. I got five more sets out in the shop right now. Paid a little over three-fifty a set for all eight. Sold three of them to Mr. Houser here for six-fifty each."

"This guy who sold you the tonewood," I said. "He told you it was fresh off a boat?"

"The exact words he used. Guess it should have been a red flag, now I look back on it. Most of the Brazilian I've run across, and there ain't a lot, has been seconds from the guitar factories, stuff with blemishes and shit. Factories want clear wood. Independent builders sometimes like to get a set of slightly-blemmed stock. Some of them think it gives their guitars character. This stuff was clearly not factory seconds. It was the real deal. I figured I got a steal on it. Turns out I was the one got robbed."

"Do you have any information on the man who sold you the wood?" I asked. "A telephone number, address, anything?"

"Naw. Wish I could help you. We did the deal in a McDonalds up the road a bit. Haggled over a cup of coffee inside and made the transaction, all cash, out in the parking lot. I drove off with the Brazilian. He drove off with my money. If I could help you guys, I surely would. I wouldn't mind getting my hands on the fella myself for five minutes."

"How about a name?" I asked.

"Well, lemme think on it. It does seem that he had a funny sort of name. Happy. Slappy. Something like that. I figured it was a nickname."

"Cabby?" I suggested.

"Yeah!" Altschuler said, breaking into a grin that displayed browning, deteriorating teeth. "Cabby! Cabby Jacks. That was the guy's name. How'd you know?"

CHAPTER THIRTY-TWO

I CONSIDERED ASKING ALTSCHULER if he was completely certain, but what was the point? There was probably only one Cabby Jacks in the world and no way for Altschuler to know the name unless he had actually done the transaction with him.

"Did he leave you any contact information? A telephone number?"

"Well, lemme see here. I do seem to recall he gave me a number. You gotta remember, this was weeks ago. For all I know, I scribbled it on a scrap of paper and tossed it after the sale. I coulda stashed it away. A sweet deal on Brazilian doesn't come along every day. Gimme a sec."

He crossed behind his workbench to a chest of drawers that appeared to serve as his filing system.

Ross Duncan had given me Cabby's cell phone number on the night he came to me at the club asking for help. One of the first things I had done was call it, only to get a "number not in service" message and a direct link to voicemail. I'd left a message, naturally, but I figured the phone and Cabby were no longer together, so I hadn't tried it again.

"Here it is!" Altschuler cried, after rummaging through the top drawer. "I recall it, because I wrote it on the back of a Popeye's receipt I had the night he called."

He handed me the slip. I didn't recognize the number. I pulled out my cell phone and dialed it. There was a connection, but it simply rang five or six times and then went to a generic voicemail. I was certain it wasn't the number Ross Duncan had given me.

"Burner phone?" Chick asked.

"What in hell do you know about burner phones?" I said.

"Me? Nothing. Something I saw on TV once."

"Well, you might be right. Smugglers like Villar probably have barrels of prepaid phones lying around for one or two uses before they get tossed. This might be one of them."

"If it's got GPS, you might be able to trace its location."

I stared at him, as if I were seeing him for the first time. "TV again?"

"I guess."

"You guess. Well, maybe it's a good guess. I think Agent Hong might be able to help us with this later." I recorded the number in my cell phone directory and handed the slip of paper back to Altschuler.

"You find this guy Jacks, you tell him I have a score to settle with him. If this rosewood isn't legitimate, he owes me a buttload of money," Altschuler said.

"You'll be the first person I call," I said. Then I turned to Chick. "Let's get Mr. Houser here back to his place. I think it might be a long night."

"Wait a minute," Altschuler said. "I may have another idea how you could locate Jacks."

He had my immediate total attention.

"Take a look at these rosewood sets." Altschuler pointed to the workbench. "Look at the saw marks on them."

I took a long look at them, but had no idea what he was trying to say.

"It's not economical to transport guitar sets all the way from South America pre-sawn. Takes up way too much space, because you have to sticker them and package them individually to keep the humidity at sea from warping them or hydrating them. To be useful as guitar sets, this wood has to have a moisture content of less than ten percent. Hell, some violin makers store their wood to air dry for decades before they put a gouge to it. Guitar makers aren't quite so particular, but pre-sawn sets traveling by ocean would take a long time to dry again once they hit land. A billet could probably weather a voyage easy without taking on a lot of moisture. In fact, there's several companies up in Canada building guitar tops from spruce billets that sat at the bottom of Lake Superior for years."

"What's a billet?" I asked.

"Well, it's basically a log, with the bark removed and cut to maybe four or five feet in length."

"So you're saying this wood came here as logs and was sawn to size and thickness after they arrived."

"It's a good guess," Altschuler said. "It's called resawing. Taking a thick piece of wood and sawing it along the grain to produce thin sheets. These sets are about a quarter inch thick, but they still need to be worked down to about a tenth of an inch before you can even think of building a guitar with them. They also have to be quarter sawn."

"You are talking way above my head," I said.

"Quarter sawing is a process that allows you to cut lots of thin sheets from a board, with all of them having the grain, you know, the growth rings, all perpendicular to the flat face of the board."

"Still in the dark," I said.

"Here. Look." He held up one of the guitar back pieces and showed it to me on edge. There were a series of precisely vertical stripes running across the thin edge of the wood. "Those are growth rings, one for each growing season. To get this pattern, you first have to saw the billet into quarters, like you'd cut a pie into four wedges. Then you carefully re-saw thin strips from each quarter, to get the vertical grain. It's the most stable way to cut wood. Almost every guitar builder in the country wants quartersawn stock. Now, any craftsman worth his salt has a bandsaw in his shop with the oomph to saw a three- or four-foot-long piece of rosewood into plates like this, but this wasn't done by any home shop bandsaw. The saw marks are too rough, even for a three-quarter inch blade with three teeth per inch. No, this was cut using a circular saw, and not a particularly sharp one from the looks of it."

"Could you do it here?" I asked.

"Shit, no. Ain't no way I could do this. See the width of this plate? Must be eight inches easy. Even if it was the first cut off the wide end of the quarter, the original log must have been seventeen, eighteen inches thick. Ain't a home shop bandsaw in the world powerful enough to slice through a billet that wide. What you got here was done by a professional sawyer."

"And where would I find one of those?"

"Any sawmill, I reckon."

"How many sawmills do you suppose there are in New Orleans?"

"Not a whole lot. If you take into account all the parishes around there, there might be ten or twelve in a fifty-mile radius."

"What about in the city itself? Let's say this log came in on a ship docked at the port of New Orleans and you wanted to get it sawn right away?"

"Well, I only know of four sawmills in the area, if you don't count Claymore's."

"Why wouldn't I consider Claymore's?"

"On account of it's closed. Been closed for a coupla years."

Chick tapped me on the shoulder. "We could check four sawmills in two hours or so."

"Yeah, we could," I said.

"I can give you a list," Altschuler said.

CHAPTER THIRTY-THREE

CHICK WAS WRONG. It took about three hours to clear the four sawmills Altschuler gave us. The first two told us outright they were too busy handling bulk pine dimensioning, for two-by-fours and such, to take on any specialty work. At the third sawmill we were told they hadn't seen any rosewood in years. That left Bianchi and Brothers, an outfit in Slidell. They didn't answer their phones, so Chick and I set out across Lake Pontchartrain on I-10 to see if anyone was home.

Jake Bianchi was in the front office when we arrived, eating a muffaletta sandwich. He was a powerful-looking man wearing faded jeans and a Saints tee shirt, which showed off the kind of biceps you don't get jerking iron in a gym. In contrast, he had a moon-like baby face with pudgy cheeks, a dimple in his chin you could dip guacamole from, and deep-set dark brown eyes. He was balding badly and hiding it worse. He didn't look at all happy to have his meal interrupted. Outside, we could hear the constant whine of a huge circular saw blade as it sliced two-foot-thick logs into boards.

"Brazilian rosewood?" he asked. "Must be some kinda glut on that shit lately."

"You've had some come through?"

"Naw. I did get a call from a fella about six months ago, though. Said he had access to some logs and wanted to know if I could quartersaw them. Turned him down flat."

"Why?" Chick asked, beating me to the punch.

"You ever try to resaw Brazilian? Shit's harder than a two-dollar whore's heart." He paused to laugh at his own joke. "Only shit that'll wear out a blade faster is ironwood, or maybe jatoba, what they call Brazilian cherry. Don't know what's in the water down South America way, but it sure makes for some hard as shit lumber. This guy said he had fifteen billets. Said he wanted them all quartersawn. Nertz to that, I said to him. I'd have to tack on an extra thousand to have my blades sharpened every third billet."

"Did he come to you personally, or call you on the phone?"

"He dropped by himself. Strange little fella. Dressed to the nines, with an expensive haircut. Looked like some kind of riverboat gambler. Had eyes were always darting left or right, never seemed to like the idea of making eye contact."

I turned to Chick. "Cabby," I said.

"Yeah, that was his name," Bianchi said. "Cabby something or other. Can't recall for certain what his last name was, but even if I had a dozen blades to waste I wouldn't have taken his business. Brazilian is risky, on account of that international trade in endangered species bullshit. Someone shows up at your door with a shit-ton of it, it looks strange. I don't need no trouble here."

"Did he leave you with any contact information?" I asked.

"Soon's I turned him down, he was out the door. I guess he's real good at takin' no for an answer. What's up with him? Is he some kind of criminal?"

"Not one you'd have to worry about," I said. "Fact is, he's missing. We're trying to find him. We know he's been peddling Brazilian rosewood around the area for a few months and he's probably getting his lumber resawn somewhere around here. There are only four sawmills in easy access of the port. Yours was last on our list."

"You check out Claymore's?" Bianchi asked.

"Heard it was closed."

"It was. Jim Claymore come down with the ALS. You know, Lou Gehrig's disease. Got diagnosed about a year ago. His oldest boy, Josh, got killed in Afghanistan. His younger boy, Samuel, don't have the sense God give a billy goat, so there was nobody to turn the mill over to. Jim figured he needed money more than he needed a business to wear him down to the hubs, so he closed his sawmill and put it up for sale."

"Did someone buy it?"

"Word is they did, but they haven't reopened it yet. On the other hand, he put it on the market about six months ago, right around the time your boy Cabby dropped by my shop. I heard it sold quick, but I never heard who bought it."

"You have an address for Claymore's?" I asked.

Claymore's Sawmill was a low-rent affair, compared to an operation like Bianchi and Brothers. It was located on a bend in the Mississippi River. An oiled dirt road led to a lot surrounded by a chain-link fence, but the mechanical gate was open, which in Louisiana was about as legal as a welcome mat. We drove through and found ourselves in a field with two structures. One was a double-wide industrial trailer that likely served as the sawmill's office. The other was an open covered shed containing two large belt-driven circular saws hooked up to a couple of Cummins diesel truck engines.

Nobody answered at the trailer when we knocked. As I waited,

Chick wandered down to the sawing shed and started poking around. I started to reel him in, but decided it made him feel useful.

I knocked one more time for certainty. As I waited to see if anyone would answer—not so much because I expected them to, but because it gave me an excuse to be there—Chick called to me from the shed.

"Gallegher! Come look at this!"

I gave up on the trailer and joined him in the shed.

"Sniff," he said. "Tell me what you smell."

I took a long whiff. "Roses," I said. I looked around, but there weren't any bushes in the area.

"They call it rosewood for a reason," Chick told me. "When you cut it, it smells like roses. And look here."

He pointed to a pile of sawdust at the end of the carriage that held the logs steady while being sawn lengthwise. He picked up a handful of the dust and held it up to my face.

"I think we found where they've been milling your friend's lumber," he said, softly.

I was torn between the impact and meaning of our discovery and my own adrenaline rush as two large black SUVs turned into the lumberyard. One pulled in front of my new BMW. The other drove directly toward the milling shed.

"Who do you suppose those people are?" Chick asked.

"Best guess? The guys who aren't going to be happy we're here. You hang loose. Let me do the talking."

The doors to the front car opened. Three men piled out. Each one carried a sidearm, un-holstered and ready for business. They were obviously muscle, long on bravado and short of brains. They quickly formed a small semicircle around us. Only then did the back door of the second car open.

The man who stepped out was swarthy, with coal-black hair that

266

swept down over his ears on both sides of a part high over his left cheek. He wore dark glasses and had a beard trimmed short and neat. A wicked scar traversed one side of his face like a riparian canyon. He was dressed in expensive summer wool slacks, a pima cotton shirt with barely perceptible pinstripes, and a tie the color of dried blood. He didn't wear a jacket. He passed through the men surrounding us and walked straight up to me.

"You are on private property," he said. He had a strange accent. It was something like Spanish, but with a lilt I didn't recognize. I knew from the descriptions I'd gotten that he was Rodrigo Torres Villar, so I supposed his original language must have been Portuguese.

"You're Mr. Claymore?" I said.

"Mr. Claymore no longer owns this sawmill. I would appreciate it if you would explain what you are doing here."

"I'd be happy to, but guns make me tongue-tied. You can see neither of us is armed. You think you can ask your friends to put away their weapons?"

Villar looked around at the other men. He said something softly and they holstered their pistols. They didn't move an inch away from us.

"Now," he said. "An explanation."

"I'm looking for a friend," I said. "He's been missing for a couple of weeks. I heard a rumor he might be here."

"This friend. He has a name?"

"Brian," I said, using Cabby's birth name. "Brian Jacks. Don't suppose you've run across him in the area?"

Villar pulled a card from his shirt pocket and held it up so I could see it.

"By chance, does this belong to you?" he asked.

I could see, even from a few feet away, that it was one of my cards from A Friend's Place.

"You're carrying it," I said. "Seems to me it belongs to you."

Villar pulled a cell phone from his pocket, fiddled with it, and held it up to me.

"And this telephone number. Does it also belong to me?"

I saw my own cell phone number on the screen.

"A person called this telephone almost an hour ago, but he did not leave a message. Is it possible you are that person?"

He gestured to one of the guys in the semicircle, who crossed to me and rummaged through my pockets until he found my cell phone. Villar compared my phone to the number on the one he was carrying.

"You have been asking around about things that are not your business, Mr. Gallegher," he said. "You should be careful. Not everyone you meet is trustworthy. This card was given to me by a young man named Nate MacDonnell. He says you gave it to him a few nights ago, when you showed up at a meeting at his church. He told you things. Perhaps he should have kept them to himself. He contacted me because he thought I might pay him for information that you were asking about me. He was right. I appreciated the information. May I suggest you are treading on dangerous ground?"

"I thought it felt familiar," I said.

Villar chuckled and waggled a finger at me. "After Nate gave me your card, I checked you out. You have quite a reputation among men who do not impress easily. They also told me you could be trusted, unlike Mr. MacDonnell. They told me you keep your promises. Perhaps I could exact a promise from you here, today. I believe we could come to an agreement which would be beneficial to both of us."

"Keep talking," I said. "I used to be a psychologist. Listening is one of the things I do best."

"I am a busy man. I have a great number of obligations. I do not

268

have time to deal with distractions. You have become a distraction. An intriguing distraction, to be certain, but a distraction nonetheless. I would like you to go away, forget you ever saw me, and not meddle further in my business. I would consider that a great favor. As I understand it, you do a lot of favors, do you not?"

"My share," I said, trying not to sound like my mouth was bone-dry. "Let's say I do this favor for you. What do I get in return? Can you help me find my friend?"

His face appeared to turn to stone in an instant. His eyes went dark with menace. His voice dropped half an octave as he said, "If you do this favor, you get to leave this place, and you get to live. I think that is a bargain."

I looked around at the men in the sawmill yard and tried to do the calculus on getting out of the situation with my skin. They had holstered their weapons but had kept their hands close to their waists. Villar didn't appear to be armed, which was something, but there were at least two other men in the cars. I could probably take one of the guys in the circle, maybe two, and it was possible Chick might be able to take one himself. No matter how I did the figures, I kept coming up short in the equation.

On the other hand, I felt a great deal like a mouse cornered by a feral cat. I didn't believe for a second Villar expected me to back down and give up the search for Cabby Jacks.

Then there was Chick to consider. He had dealt himself in on my brittle karma. I hadn't been obligated to bring him along. I still wasn't certain why I had. I wasn't particularly keen on carrying the weight of his fate should we take on the Brazilians and I lived but he didn't. By allowing him to do a ride-along on my perilous endeavors, I had taken partial responsibility for what might happen to him.

"A question?" I said.

"You have an unending supply of them," Villar replied.

"The phone you're carrying. My friend Brian Jacks used it a few weeks ago to contact a possible business partner. That's why I called it a while ago. May I ask how it came into your possession?"

"An easy question," Villar said. "I gave it to him."

"I made a promise to Jacks a few months back. I call him Cabby."

"I am familiar with his nickname."

"I told him if he went missing, I'd find him. I don't care about your business. If you've made inquiries, you know I've been trusted by people on both sides of the legal tracks, because I not only keep promises, I can also keep a secret. Cabby is important to me. I owe him a debt I can never completely repay. If you know where he is, perhaps we can sweeten this deal. You hand him over to me, we'll all walk away, and nothing will be said about this again."

Villar tugged at one ear and smirked.

"I apologize, Mr. Gallegher," he said. "I believe I have mistakenly given you the impression we are in a negotiation. Now I see my offer is of little interest to you."

He turned to the three men. "Take them into the bayous. Kill them and leave them for the alligators."

CHAPTER THIRTY-FOUR

*T*HE THREE MEN had their pistols in their hands before he finished giving the order. They were well-trained. One stood back, well outside our reach, ready to finish the job here if we resisted, while the other two grabbed Chick and me and began to push us toward the front car.

Villar turned and walked back toward his own car, ignoring the struggle behind him.

It was easy to see our all too brief future. A short ride in the inky-black trunk far beyond the western borders of the city, a brief instant of light as we would be pulled from the car, and then—what? For some reason I recalled a lecture from graduate school in my neuroscience class. The professor had been asked what the likely experience was for someone who was killed instantly—say, by a high caliber bullet to the back of the head.

'Probably nothing," he had said. "The damage to the neural circuits would be so fast, there would likely be no time for the higher cortex to process what is happening. It would be like flipping a light switch. There would be no conscious experience at all. One instant conscious, the next, nothing."

Nothing. By which he meant the big nothing. The forever

nothing. The nothing that keeps on coming.

While it came as some small comfort to know we probably wouldn't suffer, I was much more inclined to skip the entire trip.

"Bob Holbrook is planning to sell you out!" I shouted.

I glanced over at Chick and found him staring back at me.

What the fuck? he mouthed.

Villar was about to step into the car, but he stopped, his hand flat against the roof. He slowly turned back to me. For a second, I saw a glimmer of apprehension in his eyes, but that might have been wishful thinking. He reached into the car and pulled out a .45 automatic. Then he walked toward me.

"You have my attention," he said. "And my curiosity."

He stopped a foot or two in front of me and pointed the pistol at the point above the bridge of my nose.

"The oil pipe," I said. "It's good, but not good enough. People have asked questions. The Feds are involved now. Holbrook is gutless. He'd sell his own mother to get out of a jam. He's going to roll over on you."

"This is intriguing," Villar said. "And I do appreciate you telling me, but, for the sake of clarity, just how the fuck do you know about this pipe?"

"It's a long story. I can help you. I've met Holbrook. He's a waste of skin and a liability to you. I'm willing to trade what I know for our lives."

Villar seemed to examine my eyes, as if he could divine through them whether I was telling the truth. The .45 didn't waver as it jammed into the skin of my forehead.

"You do not know as much as you think," he said. "Holbrook has nothing to tell the Feds. Someone has given you bad information. Bad information is worthless to me."

For a second, I expected him to pull the trigger, and I'd find out—or not—whether my old professor had been correct. Then I detected the sound of a police siren. Everyone in the circle froze.

One of the men who had been dragging us toward the car looked worried.

"*O que é isto, chefe?*" he asked.

"*Ser calmo, tolo!*" Villar barked back at him.

The siren grew louder as two patrol cars pulled over the hill about a half mile from the sawmill, their flashers blazing.

"*Coloque as armas. Temos de deixar!*" he called out. All the other men holstered their weapons and headed for the cars. Slowly, Villar pulled the pistol from my head.

"It would appear that, besides being trustworthy, you are also lucky, Mr. Gallegher," he said. "Please do not misunderstand. I expect we will meet again."

He climbed into the back of the second car. Both cars peeled out of the sawmill lot, pitching up rooster tails of dust that hung in dull-brown clouds as they headed away from the patrol cars.

"I think I shit my pants," Chick said.

I looked over at him. He was grinning, like he'd had a great night out with the boys.

"Good. It would be embarrassing if it were only me," I said. "I've dealt with the cops before. We stand next to the car and don't move. Speak only when spoken to and only answer whatever questions they ask."

"You mean, like why we were hanging around a sawmill with a bunch of armed Brazilian thugs?"

"It won't come to that. We tell them the truth. We're looking for a friend."

The patrol cars lurched into the sawmill yard and skidded to a stop several yards from the BMW.

"Stay still and keep your hands where we can see them!" boomed a voice from the loudspeaker on the roof of one of the cars. Both Chick and I reflexively held up our hands as a patrolman jumped from each cruiser. I was a little relieved to see they didn't have their weapons drawn. One of the patrolmen was tall and lanky. The other looked like a college middleweight wrestler, a solid fireplug of a man with shoulders two feet across.

"Identification!" the wrestler barked. "Slowly!"

Cautiously, I pulled my wallet from my pocket as Chick did the same. We handed them over. The wrestler glanced at my driver's license.

"Gallegher?" he said, sounding a little surprised. Then I recognized him. A year earlier I was called to a murder scene near the Superdome. The squat patrolman had been in charge of keeping the scene clear. Farley Nuckolls and I had chatted with him. I had endured a short period of relative renown in the press during the investigation, but fame is fleeting, so I was a little surprised that he recognized me. I took a furtive glance at his nametag.

"Officer Cawley," I said.

"What in hell are you doing hanging around this sawmill?" he asked. "We got a call about some kind of knock-down, drag-out fight here, but you two don't look scuffed up at all. Y'all know this is private property, don'cha'?"

"I'm looking for a friend. He deals in exotic woods and we heard he might be using this sawmill to process them. There's a missing person report out on him. Name's Cabby Jacks, but you'll probably find him listed as Brian. You can call Detective Nuckolls at the Rampart Street station. He'll confirm the report."

"All y'all stand still for a sec," Cawley said. He took our wallets with him to his squad car.

The lanky policeman kept an eye on us, but he didn't look entirely suspicious. In fact, he seemed a little shy. After a couple of minutes on the phone, Cawley returned. He handed our wallets back to us.

"Detective Nuckolls confirms your missing person report on this Jacks fellow. He's not happy you're out conducting an unapproved investigation on your own."

"He never is. Pardon me for asking, but who called you?"

"Beats me. I just take the calls from the dispatcher. Detective Nuckolls told me to let you get on your way. He told me to advise you to do it quickly."

"Yes sir," I said. "Clearly we were misinformed. Cabby Jacks is obviously not here. Guess it's a dry hole, right?"

"I reckon," he said. "The detective also says he'd like you to call him. He wants to have a word with you himself."

"Thanks. I will."

"Y'all be on your way, y'hear?"

"Yes sir."

The patrol cars left the sawmill in a substantially quieter manner than they had entered it. Chick opened the passenger door of the BMW and collapsed into the seat. I slid into the driver's seat and expected to find him hyperventilating. Instead, he was collected and even smiling a little.

"That was fun," he said. "What's next? We gonna knock over a liquor store? I could use a drink."

His question was answered almost immediately, as another car crested the hill and drove toward the sawmill. It pulled alongside the Beemer. Chuck Dickens climbed out.

"You called the cops?" I asked.

"Yeah. Looked like you needed the cavalry, like really bad."

"You've been following us."

"From a distance. You've made a lot of stops today."

"Funny I didn't see you. I'm not too shabby at making a tail."

He shrugged and tried to look awkwardly bashful. I wasn't fooled for a second.

"You have something on the car, right?" I said, pointing to the Beemer. "Some kind of GPS tracker."

"Mr. Kenzie likes to keep track of his assets."

"I suppose I should thank you. For a second there I thought I'd run out of luck."

"Good thing I was around then."

I pulled my cell phone from my pocket and hit the speed dial for Scat Boudreaux. He answered on the first ring, his voice a raspy whisper.

"What is it, Gallegher?"

"Head for the barn," I said. "I have a feeling there isn't going to be any boat showing up at the Holbrook camp."

"Finest kind. Gettin' a little bored out here anyway. Laying pipe is about as interesting as croquet."

"I'll see you at Semper Fi. We need a new plan."

"I have good news and bad news," I told Dickens.

"Yeah?"

"Actually, it's bad news and worse news. First, I think I burned your boss's son-in-law."

"Speaking for Mr. Kenzie, that's not such bad news. What's the worse news?"

"Looks like we're going to have to save him from Villar."

Dickens put his hands on his hips, took a quick look around the sawmill yard, and spat in the dust. "Well," he said, "That sucks."

CHAPTER THIRTY-FIVE

*W*E BEAT SCAT to Semper Fi by about a half hour. While we waited, I placed a call to Agent Hong with ICE.

"We found the sawmill where Cabby's been cutting the Brazilian rosewood," I told him. "And there's a bonus. Turns out Villar is also smuggling the bogus Chinese oil pipe for Holbrook Construction."

"Don't suppose you'd like to tell me how you figured that out?"

"Villar told me himself."

I heard a choking sound on the other end of the line.

"Damn. Nearly drowned myself with a Coca Cola. Wanna run that by me again?"

"I slipped up a few days ago. Gave my card to a guy at a Gamblers Anonymous meeting who ratted me out to Villar. He's been on my trail ever since. While we were checking out the sawmill, he showed up with a bunch of his mob buddies."

"Can't be true," Hong said. "If it were, you wouldn't be breathing."

"We caught a break. That fellow Dickens you met last night had a tracker on my car. He called the cops. They broke up Villar's party, but he promised a rain check."

"Time for you to go into Witness Protection, Gallegher."

"Forget it."

"Don't see another option. If Villar wants you dead, you're already breathing someone else's air. Let us put you up somewhere safe for, oh, maybe the rest of your life."

"Not going to happen. I made a promise to Cabby. I'm seeing it through."

"It's your skin. I'm not going to be much help. Neither is Boulware. We got hold of the security videos of the shipyard around that rust bucket, the Rio Gaucho. Picked up several shots of Villar and his crew boarding and un-boarding the ship. From your description, it looks like your friend Jacks was with him in one or two of the shots."

"Were the videos time-stamped?"

"Sure were. The most recent that shows your buddy was yesterday afternoon."

"How'd he look?"

"Hale and hearty, from what you can tell. It's not what you'd call theater quality video, but he wasn't being roughed up and he was walking under his own power. When you called earlier today, I couldn't talk because Boulware and I were getting our asses chewed out. Seems we're trespassing on another agency's case. I was going to call you in a bit, once I figured out where we stand, but the short version is, hands off on Villar."

"Want to run that by me again?"

"Some other agency wants him worse than ICE or DOJ and they have dibs. The poop is they've been working a case on him for a couple of years. They're about to spring the trap. We've been told to stand down."

"Not the sort of news I'd hoped for," I said.

"Can't be helped. My boss looked like he'd been worked over with a Louisville Slugger when he pulled us off the case. He was fit to be tied, but all he could do was say he was sorry. So, you've got no support. If I were you, I'd reconsider my Witness Protection offer."

"No dice. Now I know Cabby's still alive, I need to find him. But there's more. I've been working under the assumption that Bob Holbrook has been dealing with Villar for cheap Chinese oil pipe. Something Villar told me this afternoon makes me question that assumption. Now I think it's being traded right under his nose."

"How, exactly?"

"From what I've been told, Holbrook is sort of an absentee landlord on the worksite. He'd rather spend his time drinking and whoring on his yacht out in the Gulf. The way I figure it, the transfers have been made while Holbrook is away. I told Villar that Holbrook was selling him out to the feds in return for immunity. Villar looked a little puzzled. He said Holbrook had nothing to sell."

There was a long pause on the other end of the line, until Hong said, "You just got that boy killed. You know that, right? Villar thought he was pulling a fast one over on Holbrook. Now he thinks Holbrook's found out about the pipe. Bobby just became a loose end."

"I'm way ahead of you. Dickens, my partner Chick, and I are at Semper Fi right now, waiting for Scat Boudreaux to get back. We're going to the Holbrook worksite to get him away before Villar shows up. Then we're headed to the Rio Gaucho to get Cabby."

"Officially, I should tell you to lay off."

"I think you already did."

"I have no standing here, Gallegher. I've already shredded my career by trusting a civilian in San Francisco. I don't feel like falling in the same pile of shit twice. How long before you make your move?"

"Maybe an hour. Once Scat gets back, we'll be on the road

within minutes."

"Can I get you to delay?"

"For what?"

"I can write up a report, include all the details you've given me, forward it to the chief of the investigation at the other agency with a hard-on for Villar. Maybe they can expedite their arrest. We might be able to wrap this all up without putting you or your buddies in harm's way."

"Do what you need to," I said. "Holbrook's crew is working on some land right off Lake Saint Catherine. Once Scat gets back, I'll forward you the exact location. We're going in, with or without support, in about two hours. Once we get Holbrook in the clear, I'll call you back. You get some kind of response from this other agency, you let me know."

"I'll do what I can, but my advice to you is to wait and let the Feds handle this one. I have only one request."

"What?"

"Don't fuck me on this deal. I'm hanging by a thread as it is."

CHAPTER THIRTY-SIX

I HADN'T BEEN OFF the phone with Hong for two minutes before it rang. It was Quentin Wardell.

"What'cha got, Q?" I asked.

"You wanted me to research Kellen Kenzie."

"I did."

"How deeply do you want me to go? Because I can tell you, there isn't a great deal available in most resources. Mr. Kenzie appears to have taken great pains to keep his life as private as possible."

"Probably because he spends so much of it on the dark side of the wall with all the other rats."

"How colorful. You sound out of sorts."

"Things are a little tense right now."

"This sounds like a story I'd want to hear."

"And I'll be happy to tell it to you," I said. "Presuming I'm still breathing tomorrow."

"Oh, my."

"Can you collate all the data you do have and send it to me as an email attachment? I'll look it over and see if there's anything useful in there."

"Please, dear boy, do be careful. If anything were to happen to you, I'd lose one of my prime sources of entertainment."

It sounded shallow and crass, but I could hear the genuine sentiment behind it. Quentin had spent most of his life with little more than books and documents to keep him company. For the most part that was enough for him. On occasion, he yearned for real human company. Most of the friends he could have called for companionship had long since moved to the wrong side of the turf. He had lived a life of heart-stopping danger vicariously through my adventures. My stories might even have been part of why he had lived so long.

"Don't worry," I told him. "I'm not dead yet. I have a lot of things left to do before I am."

"I'll send you the file," he said.

I thumbed the phone off as Scat walked through the door to the warehouse. He carried his gillie suit, which looked like a pile of shredded rags, over his arm. His face was still covered with green and black camouflage grease. He had shaved his head clean to the scalp. He saw us standing around and blinked a couple of times, as if he had forgotten exactly why he had returned to Semper Fi. Given the way his head worked, it was entirely possible he had.

He ignored Chick and Dickens and focused on me.

"Sitrep," he barked.

I'd been around him long enough to understand what he wanted. I told him about our encounter with Villar and how I might have inadvertently placed Robert Holbrook in mortal danger.

"If I'm right," I finished, "Villar will take a small hit team out to the pipeline site and eliminate his loose end. Probably soon. Maybe tonight. Was Holbrook on site when you left?"

"He'd just arrived. The foreman . . ."

"Al Garlock," I said.

"Guy who looks like a prison gun bull?"

"He was one at one time."

"Not a surprise. He was waiting at the company trailer when Holbrook drove up. They went inside. You called about ten minutes later. They were still in the trailer when I left, maybe an hour ago."

"We need to get there right away," I said. "For all I know, Villar is already on his way."

"How bad is this dude?" Scat asked.

"Maybe as scary as Lucho Braga back in the day."

"Then we go loaded for bear," Scat said. "Hang loose."

He grabbed a shopping cart and disappeared into the warehouse. I took the opportunity to call Merlie.

"Are you all right?" she asked.

"For the moment. Things are ratcheting up pretty quickly. If it goes well, I might find Cabby Jacks tonight."

"And if it doesn't?"

"Let's be optimistic."

"What you're doing tonight. It's dangerous, isn't it?"

"Merlie," I said.

"Yes."

"We've been here before. I've always come home. Tonight's not going to be any different."

"Then I shouldn't tell you I love you, like I might never get to say it again?"

That stopped me for a second or two.

There was a time, before I met Merlie, when I didn't give a damn whether one of my perilous dalliances took me off the game board permanently. You can get to a point in your life, especially if it has been as misspent as mine, where you no longer care about anything but the rush of adrenaline and the pounding in your head. The action is its own reward. You're so in the instant that nothing in the future, even the future one heartbeat away, matters. Later, after the fight is over and you lay in your own bed and have the chance to recognize how closely you had come to the wrong side of the grass, there might be a glimmer of fear.

Scat himself, reflecting on his time in combat, had once said to me, "Before the firefight, there ain't no reason to be scared, because a million things might happen and you cain't keep track of all of them. When everything shifts up into the heavy metal rock and roll, you're so focused on surviving, there ain't no time to be scared. Once it's over and you've survived, there ain't no fuckin' point in being scared, because you're still breathing and the other damn sumbitch ain't, which was what you came for."

"Tell me you love me because I'm coming back and you can't wait to see me," I said.

"Oh, I do. Be lucky? Just one more time?"

"Count on it. I love you, Merlie. I'll call you when it's over."

"Don't call. Just show up and tell me it's over. I'll be waiting."

We left it there. I punched the END button and stowed the phone in my pocket as Scat rounded the corner with the shopping cart loaded so heavily he had to strain a little to push it.

"First things first," he said. "What kinda ordnance d'you think the bad guys was carryin'?"

"Just sidearms," I said. "Thirty-eights or forty-fives. I didn't see any rifles or shotguns."

"Alrighty then, this should do." He lifted several packets wrapped in plastic from the cart. "Interceptor body armor, what you civilian pukes call vests. Discontinued by Uncle Sugar's Army, but still plenty serviceable. Got these on a huge discount. Kevlar lined with armor plates. Long as your Brazilian buddies ain't using cop-killer rounds, this should stop anythin' we're likely to encounter. Extra-large for you, Gallegher?"

"I'll have to try it on."

"What about you, sonny?" he asked Chick. "You look like a medium. Who in hell are you anyway? Never saw your face around here before."

"Name's Chick Kasay," he said, offering his hand. Scat ignored it.

"Take this then," Scat said, handing him the vest. "What about you, Mr. Federal Agent?"

"Large for me," Dickens said.

"Finest kind." Scat yanked a box from the cart and opened it, pulling out an automatic carbine.

"Okay, kid," he said to Chick. "Don't suppose you know what this is."

Chick reached for the weapon and said, "M4A1 carbine. Ten-point-three-inch barrel for close-in fighting, gas operated, magazine-fed rifle. Single shot to full auto, flip of a switch. This one configured for the four-point-five-six, or the .223 Remington rounds?"

Scat was temporarily silenced. That made two of us. He looked over at me. I shrugged.

"You pull a ringer in on this mission?" he asked.

"Beats me," I said. "I'm as surprised as you are."

"You familiar with this weapon?" he asked Chick.

"Used one similar in The Sandbox," he said. "Uh, you know it's illegal to own one of these if you're a civilian, right?"

"Sonny, I ain't your typical civilian," Scat said. "How about you, Mr. Federal Agent? You ever fire one of these?"

"No," Dickens said, "but I'm familiar with the M16 that preceded it. Used one in Nam."

Again, Scat looked at him quizzically. "You was in-country?"

"Yeah."

"What'd you say your name was again?"

Dickens took the rifle from Scat and said, "Sergeant Charles

B. Dickens, USMC, Third of the Ninth, India Company, Bien Hoa. Want my serial number?"

"Not necessary, Sergeant. Bien Hoa, eh?"

"Yeah."

"Nineteen seventy-three?"

"Actually, I arrived in November the year before. We were gone by March."

"Don't I know it? Think you can handle the M4? Been a long time since you was in the jungle."

"I'll adjust, unless you have an MP5 lying around. That's what I used in the Secret Service."

"Cain't help you there, Sergeant. Got an FN P90 you could try, if you don't mind using a five-point-seven armor piercing round."

"Show me," Dickens said. Scat led him back into the layers of shelves at the rear of the warehouse.

"The Sandbox?" I said to Chick.

"Operation Iraqi Freedom," he said, as he started to strip the M4 on the table between us. "Did two tours. It wasn't by choice. I was a reservist, just doing it to pick up some spare change and play soldier one weekend each month. Next thing I knew I was in the desert dodging IEDs and eating MREs. Then I was stop-lossed. What can I say? I got screwed. Kind of hoped I'd never see that sort of action again. What I get for taking up with people like you."

"Who in hell *are* you?" I asked.

"I'm not a lot different than you, Gallegher. Just a musician with a talent for finding trouble. Once this deal is over, I'm in the wind."

"How come?"

"No offense, but this is more than I signed on for. I've seen my share of dying and I don't cotton to seeing a lot more. Hell, I'm still a kid. Once I filled you in on the Dalbergia, I probably should have faded into the background."

"You could leave any time," I said.

"My nature, I'm afraid. No problems. I'm used to sticking my nose in where it doesn't belong, and I'm used to getting it smacked. Maybe Shorty's stories about you caught my interest. I wanted to see if you're the real deal. Anyway, I'm in, for better or for worse. Once we're done, you need to find a new partner at Holliday's. No offense."

"None taken."

"So, you do this a lot?"

"More than I'd like."

"Makes you a special kind of crazy, doesn't it? And what's up with those two?"

He pointed to Scat and Dickens, who were hunched over a weapon on a towel-draped table on the other side of the warehouse. They appeared deep in conversation, and for an instant I saw Scat smile. I had never seen him smile before, in all the years I had known him. It was kind of spooky.

"Kindred spirits, I suppose," I said.

"And what's the deal with this Scat Boudreaux character? He seems a little . . ." Chick twirled a finger at the side of his head.

"It's a long story. I'll fill you in over a beer before you hit the road."

Scat clapped Dickens on the shoulder and headed my way.

"What about you, Gallegher?" he asked when he reached us. "I know you ain't particular to carbines. You're a pistol boy, if I recall correctly. Which reminds me."

He reached into the shopping cart and extracted several shoebox-sized parcels. He handed two of them to each of us.

"Glock 19 and a holster on a Bianchi web belt for each of us. This pistol is an ugly little fucker, and it ain't available in nothin' but nine-millimeter, but it's effective, light, and a baby could pull the slide on it. Strap it on, make sure it fits right. Listen to me, now. I'm not going in with you."

"Why not?"

"Dispersion of forces. Tactical advantage. I got me a nice little nest in the woods with a clear view of Holbrook's trailer and most of the worksite. I'm gonna lie low there with a sniper rifle in case your South American buddies show their faces. Things start to go south, I'll be in a position to lay down suppressing fire and maybe take out a few of them for you."

"Sounds like a plan," I said, as I started to wrap myself inside the vest.

"One more thing," Scat said, reaching into the cart. "We need to stay in touch."

He pulled out four small boxes. "In-ear radios," he said. "We each wear one. They're all on the same frequency and voice activated. No button to push if you want to talk, so make sure nobody else is speaking before you open your mouth."

He distributed them to us, one by one.

"Here's my suggestion," he continued. "My position in the woods will give me clear vantage to almost everything happening in the worksite compound. If I tell you to run somewheres, you hightail it there and stay put. I tell you to hit the deck, you chew dirt. You follow my lead, we might all sleep in our beds tonight."

"That's fine with me," I said. "Preferably we get in, get Holbrook out, and get back to the city without Villar and his pals crashing the party."

"Yeah, and maybe we'll all shit gold bars and retire young. One more thing. I won't have time to call out names if we walk into a firefight. Don't forget your number. I'm One. Gallegher, you're Two. Sergeant Dickens, you take Three. Junior here's Four."

"It's Chick," Chick said.

"No, sonny, tonight you're Four. Didn't they teach you anything in The Sandbox?"

I caught a flash of anger in Chick's eyes, but it quickly subsided. I imagined he'd had a lot of practice reining in his emotions.

"All right then," Scat said. "Like they said on that airplane a few years back, let's roll."

CHAPTER THIRTY-SEVEN

*S*CAT HAD A van parked behind Semper Fi. It was a fifteen-year-old Chevy painted flat black. As soon as he opened the side door, I could see he'd fitted it with additional plating.

"Quarter-inch thick boilerplate welded two and a half feet up from the floor along the entire perimeter," he said. "Reinforced ballistic bumpers, composite run-flat tires, quarter-inch ballistic-resistant polycarbonate replacement windows, fuel tank armor, composite floor protection, the works. Even has a gizmo in the back that can lay down a smoke screen."

"It's a war wagon," Chick said.

"Got a fuckin' sweet sound system, too. You like Charlie Daniels?" Scat said. "Load up, boys."

We dropped Scat off near the end of the oiled dirt access road to the Holbrook site. I drove us the rest of the way into the compound. It was almost dusk. Work must have been over for the day. Several pipeline workers collected around the trailer Garlock had told me the other day was the kitchen. The trailer door was open. I could hear zydeco music playing from inside. Three men sat at a picnic table alongside the trailer, playing cards. They had a small portable television on the table, which appeared to be showing a baseball game. I couldn't tell who was playing.

I parked the van next to Holbrook's office trailer.

"Chick, you and Dickens go to the mess trailer and tell those men to head into the city for the evening. Tell them whatever you need to get them on the road. I don't want any collateral damage should Villar show up. Also, check the bunk trailers. Might have a few workers sleeping in them. I want them gone, too. Then position yourselves so you have a good view of the office trailer here. Got that, Scat?"

I heard a tinny response in my ear, as Scat radioed from his position in the woods. *"Sounds like a plan, Slick. I'll give you guys a heads-up if I see any cars inbound."*

Chick headed off toward the lighted mess trailer, but Dickens stayed behind. He pulled the radio from his ear and gestured for me to do the same. I removed my earpiece and placed it in my pocket.

"Gallegher, I think there's something you should know. I haven't had the chance to talk with you in private. If Villar shows up, things could get confused and messy. I need to fill you in on a couple of things."

A minute or so later, he placed the receiver back in his ear and retreated toward the mess trailer to join Chick. I didn't like what he had told me, but there wasn't time to process things. I stepped up to the porch on Holbrook's trailer and opened the door.

Holbrook and Al Garlock were seated inside. Holbrook sat in the plush button-and-tuck leather chair behind his desk. Garlock lounged on a couch along the side wall. There was a half-empty glass of liquor in front of Holbrook. Garlock held a shorter, wider glass in his hand. He started when I walked in the door. I pulled the Glock from my holster and pointed it at him.

"Easy," I said. "I'm Pat Gallegher. I was here a few days back."

"I remember you fine," Garlock said. "I also remember what I said I'd do if you showed your face around here again."

"What is this, anyway?" Holbrook asked. "And why are you in that get-up?"

"I don't have a lot of time to explain," I said. "Let's say I screwed up and as a result your life is in danger."

"What in hell!" Garlock shouted.

"Both your lives," I clarified. "Mr. Holbrook, I have information that someone on your crew, probably Garlock here, is ripping you off."

"That's absurd," Holbrook said. "Garlock runs this entire operation."

"So you said last time. You made it clear you don't have a real clue what's going on around your own job site. Here's what's happening. You order your pipe from Pennsylvania. Sometimes, after it arrives, a boat cruises up Lake Saint Catherine loaded to the gunwales with cheap Chinese knockoff pipe. This always happens when you're off on your yacht, leaving Garlock to run your show. The boat is operated by a Brazilian gangster named Villar. He trades his cheap inferior pipe for your good stuff, pays Garlock a bonus, and sails off with your good pipe to sell to the highest bidder elsewhere. The Chinese stuff looks like the real thing from the outside, but it's at greater risk of a failure down the line."

"You've got a lot of balls, making accusations like that!" Garlock roared.

Outside the trailer, I heard a truck rumble to life.

"That sound is your crew, heading back to the city for the evening," I said. "I brought some people here to help me. They gave your boys the night off. Remember Garry Sharp? I found him. Before he left, he and Garlock had a yelling match out on the pipeline.

Some of your other workers told me it was over the pipe, and Sharp and Garlock nearly came to blows. Sharp discovered the problem with the pipe using his equipment. He even heard the transfer take place one night while you were away. Garlock was here, though. A couple of your employees told me he locked them in their trailers. Whether he's the actual intermediary with Villar or not, he knows what's been going on."

Garlock started to rise from the couch, but I pointed the Glock at the middle of his chest. I growled a little, to reinforce the point. He sat back down and glowered at me.

"I don't know who you think you are, barging in here and making wild accusations," Holbrook said, trying to look tough from behind his desk. "You don't know who you're dealing with. You don't know who I am!"

"Cut the shit, Bobby," I said. "You're Kellen Kenzie's son-in-law. Garlock told me the last time I visited. Who do you think hired me? You don't get it, kid. Garlock's been stealing from you. In the process he's been stealing from your in-laws and risking an environmental disaster to boot. I had a run-in with Villar this afternoon."

"Bullshit," Garlock said from the couch. "If you'd come up against Villar, you wouldn't be standing here tonight."

An expression of epiphany appeared to cross Holbrook's face.

"Wait," he said. "You know about this Villar character?"

"Sure he does," I said. "And Villar knows all about you. There's more. Up until this afternoon, I assumed you were complicit in the smuggling scheme. You might say I tried to buy my way out of a jam by telling Villar you were selling him out. I told him you had decided his pipe program was too risky and you were going to inform the Feds."

"Oh," Garlock said to Holbrook, "you are in the shit now."

294

I said, "You both are. But yeah, Holbrook, he's right. I blew it. Villar told me you didn't have anything to trade. He knew you weren't part of the scheme, but I gave him the impression you'd discovered what he and Garlock were up to. Now he thinks Garlock ratted him out to you. That makes you a liability. Villar's certain to come looking for both of you. We're here to get you someplace safe before he does."

"Are you crazy?" Garlock said. "There's no place *safe* from this guy. You've killed us and yourself in the bargain."

He launched himself at me from the couch. Reflexively. I raised the Glock halfway up and unintentionally squeezed off a round that grazed Garlock's kneecap. In the narrow confines of the office trailer, the report from the pistol sounded like a cannon going off. Garlock spun, off balance, and curled into a fetal position on the floor, yowling like a kicked alley cat.

"What in hell?" I heard Dickens call out in my earpiece.

"I'm fine," I said. "Garlock tried to get to me. I had to discourage him. It's a flesh wound."

"It hurts like fuck!" Garlock yelled.

"It's a flesh wound that hurts like fuck," I clarified. I turned back to Holbrook. "We don't have time to negotiate this thing. If I don't get you out of here right now, Villar is going to kill you."

I turned to Garlock. "If you promise to stop being such a dick, we might bring you along, too. Or, you can stay here and try to talk your way past Villar."

"Don't worry about me. Villar and I have an arrangement. You have totally burned yourself," Garlock said.

"Yeah. Okay. We'll settle this later. For now, we need to boogie."

"*Got a big negatory there,*" Scat said in my ear. "*Looks like we stayed too long at the party. There's an SUV headed up the dirt track toward the trailers. We got company.*"

295

CHAPTER THIRTY-EIGHT

*H*OLBROOK AND GARLOCK couldn't hear Scat's transmission, so I had to relay it to them.

"Someone's headed toward the compound," I said. "They're driving an SUV. Are you expecting anyone tonight?"

"No," Holbrook said. He glanced at Garlock.

"Don't look at me," Garlock said. "I don't know who it is."

"*Correction,*" Scat called out over the radio. "*Make that two SUVs. They're already past my position and headed for the trailers.*"

I pulled a shade aside in time to see two Cadillac Escalades turn off the oiled dirt track into the compound. The front one skidded a little on loose dirt, kicking up rooster tails of dust. They parked side by side about twenty yards from Scat's war wagon. The doors opened, and four men climbed out from each truck. Each carried a small carbine-like rifle.

The compound was arranged in a semicircle of trailers, roughly the size of a baseball diamond. Holbrook's trailer was situated right in the middle. The men from the SUVs gathered in the space between the vehicles, huddled as if trying to decide what to do next.

"I don't see Villar," I said.

"Maybe he didn't come," Garlock said. "Figured you weren't

worth his time."

"He isn't after me," I said. "You're having a hard time dealing with that. He wants you and Holbrook. He doesn't even know I'm here."

I looked out the window again. A ninth man climbed from the nearest SUV to join the group meeting in the middle. Even from eighty or ninety feet, I could see the scar running across the right side of his face.

"He's here," I said. "He was laying back in one of the SUVs. Probably waiting to see if anyone reacted to his arrival."

"I'm leaving," Garlock said.

"The hell you are," I said. I leveled the gun at him again.

"Fuck you, Gallegher. You aren't going to shoot me. Not on purpose."

"You can't walk," I said.

"I can hobble. Like I said, Villar and I have an arrangement. I'm a lot safer out there than I am in here with you."

I kept the Glock trained on him, but we both knew it was a bluff. I had already shot him once, by accident. I wasn't about to do it on purpose. We both knew it.

"You go out there," I said. "Go ahead. Do it. I don't give you a minute and half before Villar cuts you down. You don't seem to understand the meaning of the words 'loose ends.'"

Garlock grasped the door handle, testing my resolve. The only choices I had were to shoot him and give away our position or let him go and allow him to give away our position. Either way, Villar was going to know in about thirty seconds where Holbrook and I were.

The splotch of blood on Garlock's pants spread a little. I grabbed a roll of duct tape from the table next to the door and I tossed it to him.

"Wrap some around your knee," I said. "The pressure will stanch the bleeding and the tape will help support your leg. Maybe you won't bleed out before Villar decides you're expendable."

Garlock tore a long strip of duct tape off the roll and began wrapping it around the wound.

"Scat," I said. "Do you have a shot?"

"*Negative*," he said in my ear. "*They're all bunched up between them SUVs. Four, can you move to the last trailer on my far left?*"

There was a brief delay before I heard Chick's voice.

"*Oh. Four. That's me. Yeah, I think I can make it.*"

"*Don't make yourself a target,*" Scat said.

Garlock opened the door and stepped out onto the wooden stoop. He looked back at me with a self-satisfied smirk, as if he was proud he'd guessed right about whether I would shoot him. I slammed the door behind him.

"Soon as Villar knows we're in here, they're going to concentrate their fire on the trailer. We need to put as much stuff between us and them as we can, to shield us from the bullets. Help me."

Garlock stood on the stairs to the trailer for few seconds, as if waiting for Villar to acknowledge him. Holbrook slid his desk against the wall facing Villar's crew, and then lifted the sofa on top of it. I heard Garlock hit the steps outside.

Garlock yelled out, "Holbrook and Gallegher are inside. Somehow, Gallegher found out about the pipe."

"*Four in position,*" Chick's voice said in my ear.

"Come on down," Villar yelled to Garlock. "We'll deal with your boss once you're clear."

Holbrook and I had every piece of furniture in the trailer stacked against the front wall.

"Get on the floor," I said. "No matter what happens, unless I tell you, keep your head down."

Holbrook flattened prone against the cheap all-weather carpet. He covered his head with his hands, lacing his fingers across the back of his skull. I peered out the shades again. Garlock limped his way across the dirt toward Villar's SUVs.

Scat's voice crackled in my ear. "*Four, when I give you the go, you pepper those SUVs with a full clip. Strafe 'em good. Soon's you're empty, break to your left for cover.*"

"*Ten four,*" Chick said.

"What's the plan?" I asked

"*Gonna try to scatter them, see if I can't pick off a few,*" Scat said.

"*What about me?*" Dickens echoed, almost overlapping Scat.

"*See if you can get to the backhoe, Three,*" Scat responded. "*Try to position yourself behind the blade. Damned backhoe blade will stop a bazooka round.*"

Garlock limped across the compound toward the SUVs.

"You hurt?" Villar yelled to him.

"Gallegher shot me in the knee. It grazed me, but it's bleeding."

"Who else is in the trailer?"

"Gallegher and Holbrook. Gallegher's been talking to someone on a radio," Garlock said as he drew within ten feet of Villar.

"Thank you," Villar said. He raised an automatic pistol and squeezed two rounds into Garlock's chest. Garlock jerked with each impact and crumpled into the dirt. Villar stood over him and put two more rounds into his head from three feet away, raising a red mist that slowly settled back into the dust.

"Jesus," I said.

"What?" Holbrook said from the floor.

"Villar executed Garlock. He knows we're in the trailer. Hunker down. It's going to get busy here in a minute."

From outside the trailer, I heard Villar shout, "Gallegher! I told you we were sure to meet again! Once more, you have seen fit to insert yourself into my business."

Staying silent wasn't going to make any difference. I needed to buy time so Scat could arrange Chick and Dickens where he needed them.

"Luck of the draw," I yelled back.

"Not so lucky for you, I think. On the other hand, I like you. Killing you isn't necessary. You are a resourceful man. I admire that. Perhaps we are kindred spirits."

"Think again!" I shouted.

"I will make you an arrangement. You give me Robert Holbrook and I will give you an opportunity to survive this night."

"Like the arrangement you had with Garlock?"

"Garlock failed me. He had the opportunity to become a wealthy man. He threw it away by telling Holbrook about the pipe. In my organization, failure comes at a high price."

"*This is Three,*" I heard Dickens say in my earpiece. "*I'm in position at the backhoe.*"

"Everyone hold your fire until they start shooting," I said into the radio.

"*Check One,*" Scat said.

"*Check Three,*" said Dickens.

"*Four,*" Chick said.

"How about this?" I shouted. "Holbrook and I walk away from here and you go fuck yourself!"

"Such bravado!" Villar said. "So like your historical comrades at the Alamo. And this situation is so similar. You, trapped inside an indefensible trailer, with my team outnumbering you. As I recall, that day did not end well for the defenders of the Alamo. You again earn my admiration. Your friend Cabby Jacks spoke so highly of you. He told me once you started looking for him, you would never stop.

Such tenacity in the face of overwhelming odds is to be respected. I will take no pleasure in killing you, as I took no pleasure when I put two bullets into Cabby's head."

His words hit me like a pile driver. I slumped to the floor, trying to catch my breath.

"*Slick?*" I heard Scat in my earpiece. "*Stay crispy, boy.*"

I couldn't find the wind to reply.

"I am sorry to be the bearer of such sad news," Villar continued. "I understand you and Cabby Jacks were close."

"What did you do with his body?" I yelled.

"It is on board my ship. It was necessary, I am afraid, to store him in the refrigerated meat locker. We will give him a burial at sea on our way back to Rio."

"Meaning you'll dump him overboard as soon as you're in international waters."

"More or less correct. Do you wish to know why I killed him?"

"Why?"

"Because he was a traitor. He was no different than Garlock. He betrayed my confidence. I found out that he planned to turn me over to the American authorities. And I killed him because you wanted him so badly. Sooner or later, your snooping was bound to cause problems for me, so I simply removed Mr. Jacks from the equation. Sadly, there was no way to let you know before now. And here we are. You in your aluminum Alamo, and me out here."

I reviewed my options. There weren't many. I glanced over at Holbrook, who raised his head from the carpet and looked at me with an expression of fear.

"I'm open for suggestions," I said to him.

"I'm way out of my depth," Holbrook said. "Seems to me you have an edge in experience here."

"Yes, it does," I said. "Scat!"

"*Right here, Slick.*" Scat said in my ear.

"Light 'em up."

"*Ten four. Strafe 'em, kid.*"

I stood and peeked through the blinds, as I heard a burst of full-automatic rifle fire from Chick's M4 echo through the compound. The windows in the SUV closest to the far trailer crazed and then collapsed, spraying Villar's men between the trucks with pellets of broken glass. I heard a brief, truncated scream and two of the men collapsed in the dirt.

Villar dropped to the ground and crabbed around to the front of the nearest SUV. I took the opportunity to crack the door to the trailer and squeeze three shots in his direction. One hit the radiator, which released a cloud of steam that blasted the side of Villar's face. He rolled away, clawing at his left cheek.

Two of his men darted around the rear of the SUV, trying to put as much steel between themselves and me as possible. They had no idea they were running directly into Scat's line of fire. I heard two rapid-fire whipcracks from the woods. One of the men started to run, but only made it few feet before stumbling and falling face-forward. He didn't move again. I couldn't see the other one, but I heard Scat over my radio.

"*Splash two!*" he yelped. I presumed that meant the other shooter had died behind the SUV, out of my sight.

"I think Chick got two," I said into the radio. "We have five left, including Villar."

"*I'm on it,*" Dickens' voice called out through my earpiece.

"*Four. I'm positioning behind the trailer next to you, Gallegher. I think I might be able to draw a bead on the guys between the Escalades,*" Chick said.

I heard a diesel engine rumble in the distance.

"The backhoe," Holbrook said.

"Oh, hell," I said. "He wouldn't."

"Guess I never mentioned I did a little work with heavy equipment in my youth," Dickens said. *"The controls haven't changed much. Tally ho!"*

The remaining Brazilians who stood next to the near Escalade began to barrage the trailer with gunfire. Holbrook and I hugged the carpet behind our makeshift office furniture barricade as shards of aluminum and glass rained down on us. Then, as quickly as it had started, the gunfire stopped. I heard the backhoe draw closer and closer. I peeked out the door and saw Dickens raise the backhoe blade parallel with the cab, as a shield against incoming gunfire. He seemed to gain speed as he headed toward the SUVs, which—since it was a backhoe—meant he went from a mild lumber to a jogging pace.

"We need to get out of this trailer," I told Holbrook. "One of my guys is providing a distraction. When we break for it, you stay in front of me. Maybe my vest will protect both of us."

I watched until the Brazilians behind the near SUV turned their attention from the trailer to the backhoe. They began firing in Dickens' direction. Bullets ricocheted off the blade in every direction. Some simply flattened against the steel and dropped into the shovel.

There was nothing in the worksite for hundreds of yards except sand, a little scrub, and mosquitoes. The only real cover available was the trailers themselves, Garlock's truck, and Scat's van.

Then I remembered the pallet of steel pipe on the far side of the trailers.

"Got it," I said. "I have just the place."

I held the door to usher Holbrook out. The sun was setting. Villar's men were preoccupied with the advancing backhoe, so we had barely enough time to sprint to the pallet of pipe. Even so, one of them got a shot off in my direction. It hit me in my body armor right between the shoulder blades. It felt like a punch from Rocky Balboa and knocked me on my stomach. For a second or two, I thought it had broken my back because I couldn't seem to make my legs work, but I discovered I was only stunned, and only a couple of feet from the pallet. Holbrook grabbed me and helped me scramble behind it where I sat grimacing and trying to huff a little air into my lungs.

"*You good, boy?*" Scat called out over the radio.

"I feel like I just got run over by a cement truck," I said.

"*Yeah. Hurts like a sumbitch, don't it? Now you know how it feels. You gonna have a big ol' bruise tomorrow, you.*"

"Hope this is the good stuff," I said, as I patted the steel pipe.

I looked over the pipe in time to see the backhoe ram the side of the nearest SUV. Between a three-ton Escalade and a twenty-ton tractor, there was no contest. The SUV began to slide toward the one on the other side of it, trapping Villar's men between them. Realizing they were about to become part of a human trash compactor, they began to scatter.

From behind me, I heard several three-shot bursts from Chick's M4. One Brazilian spun, clutching his chest and dropping his weapon, before he curled into a fetal position in the dirt. Another crouched in front of the nearer Escalade and tried to return Chick's fire. Dickens stood in the cab of the backhoe and took him out with an automatic burst from his FN P90. The other two Brazilians tried to make a break for the trailers. Chick took them down within seconds.

Villar had taken cover behind the far SUV. He stood and ripped off three shots in quick succession. Dickens was flung backward into the seat of the backhoe, his face contorted in pain.

I was about forty feet from Villar, which is about my limit with a handgun. I'm no marksman. The fact is, I hate guns, but I do know

305

how to point one and pull the trigger, and I was motivated. I stood, steadied my Glock on Villar, and emptied the magazine.

I hit him at least twice, which isn't bad for me. He dropped to his knees and tried to keep from going all the way down by bracing himself with his arms. After a few seconds, he seemed to collect himself. I dropped the magazine from my pistol and slammed in a fresh one. Villar was trying to get to his feet. I could see twin crimson florets high on the high right side of his chest, just under his collarbone. I had stopped him, but I hadn't landed a killshot.

"Don't!" I said, leveling the Glock at him. "Stay down. Please. I don't want to kill you."

He grinned as he pulled himself up on the bumper of the Escalade. His face was ashen, but he managed to wink at me.

"The difference between us," he said. "I do want to kill you."

He tried to raise his carbine. I heard a quick burst of automatic fire behind me, from the cab of the backhoe. Villar's neck and lower face burst in a shower of blood and bone, and he collapsed against the front of the SUV.

"I count nine," I heard Scat say over the radio. "Looks like we got 'em, boys."

Dickens slumped out of the backhoe and rolled over into the dirt next to the treads. I knelt beside him. There was a damp crimson patch at the point where his vest ended under his left arm and it was growing. His skin was nearly white. He was trying to put on a brave face, but I could see the terror in his eyes. He reached across his chest and grasped my hand. He had trouble breathing, and he took a wet gasp between almost every word.

"It's bad, isn't it?"

What was I going to say? He was right.

"You know," I said.

"Yeah. Reckon . . . I do. Jesus, Gallegher . . . you couldn't . . . have asked . . . for Fenster?"

He tried to chuckle at his joke, but it came out as a bloody gargle, and a few seconds later he grimaced. His eyes fixed on a point far beyond any world I knew, and he was gone.

I sat by him until I became aware of Chick standing behind me.

"He's dead?" Chick asked.

"Yeah."

"Damn. That sucks. He was a good man. Only met him last night, but I can tell."

"Yeah," I said. "A good man. Taken out by a miracle bullet."

"*Uh, guys,*" Scat said over our radios, "*We got more incoming.*"

"More cars?" I asked.

"*No. A chopper.*"

I couldn't hear anything at first, but I've long since realized that Scat's senses are all more heightened than the average joe. Within a few seconds, I recognized the *thwop-thwop-thwop* of helicopter blades. A minute later, a Stratus chopper swooped in over Lake Saint Catherine and hovered over the Holbrook worksite.

"Federal agents! Lay down your arms!" commanded a voice over the helicopter's PA system. "Drop the weapons and get down on the ground. Now!"

CHAPTER THIRTY-NINE

"WHAT DO WE do?" Chick asked.

"Drop your gun and your ammo pouch," I said. "Don't give them any reason to think you're hostile."

We both tossed our weapons into the dirt about six feet in front of us and knelt in the sandy soil around the pallet of oil pipe.

"You too, Holbrook," I said.

The chopper descended and put down about a hundred feet away, well clear of the bullet-ridden SUVs and Scat's war wagon.

"All the same to you guys," Scat radioed, *"I reckon I'll sit tight here for the time being."*

As the rotating blades of the chopper slowed, two figures emerged and strode across the compound toward us. They were dressed in desert combat fatigues, body armor vests. They carried automatic carbines.

"Boulware!" I called out. "You can fly a chopper?"

"Shut the fuck up, Gallegher, while I try to figure out what kind of shit you've gotten me into this time."

It was difficult to see distinctly in the dusk, but the other figure was as tall as Boulware, and maybe half again as wide.

"I see you brought Agent Hong with you," I said.

"Shut your mouth and assume the position. All of you!" Boulware commanded. Chick, Holbrook, and I all stood, turned, and leaned forward against the pallet of pipe. Boulware frisked all of us, but I could tell his heart wasn't in it. Once he was satisfied we weren't hiding any weapons on our bodies, he told us to turn back around.

"Someone tell me what's happened here," he said.

Holbrook stepped forward and offered his hand. Boulware ignored it.

"I'm Robert Holbrook. I own the company building this pipeline. Mr. Gallegher here arrived a while ago and told me my life was in danger."

Holbrook explained in detail how he had been duped by his construction manager, and how we had saved him from certain death at the hands of Villar and his henchmen. Boulware grunted once or twice to convey he was following the story, but he showed no expression of approval.

While Holbrook told his story, Agent Hong checked the carnage around Villar's SUVs. He walked up as Holbrook finished and stood in front of me.

He sighed once or twice, and then he flattened me with the fastest overhand right cross I'd ever seen. It sounded as if someone struck a gong in my head. I saw stars for a few seconds as I sat sprawled in the dirt.

"God damn it!" I said. "I've already been shot tonight. Was it necessary to pound me?"

"That's for killing my career," he said. "You're carrying the weight for both you and another asshole in San Francisco who got me transferred here. God only knows where I'll land next, if I still have a job in a week."

I didn't say anything. I didn't even try to get to my feet to retaliate. I figured I owed Hong the satisfaction of one sucker punch.

Besides, I wasn't entirely sure I could take him.

Boulware knelt next to Dickens. He removed his DOJ cap and appeared to be praying.

"He was a sellout of the first order," Boulware said. "But he was a good agent back in the day."

"He was a good man today. He saved all of us by ramming Villar's gangsters with the backhoe," I said.

"Sounds like him. Always the showboat. I don't mind telling you, Gallegher, you just stuck our dicks in a blender. We appreciate you sending us your location, but I do wish you'd have minded your own business and let us mop up Villar and his crew."

"If I had, both Holbrook and Garlock would be dead, and Villar would be in the wind."

"We were coming," Boulware said.

"You were late."

Boulware walked ten feet away, placed his hands on his waist, and spat into the dirt. "All right," he said. "This never happened. What we got here is nine dead Brazilian gangsters and one brave construction manager and an equally courageous Borglund Security op who gave their lives to protect Kellen Kenzie's son-in-law. And where in fuck is that nutcase, Scat Boudreaux?"

"What makes you think he's here?" I asked.

"Like I believe for a second you could have done this on your own?"

I decided to go with the truth. "He's in the woods."

"Tell him to stay there. Better yet, tell him to disappear. I know he's here, but I don't want to see his goddamn face. Hong and I will be days clearing this all up. By the time our respective agencies are finished ripping us a couple of new rectums, we may both be applying to Borglund for a job. One thing is certain, Gallegher. You could screw up a wet dream."

"There's one more thing," I said. "A . . . well, a loose end to clear up, I suppose. I need a ride. I also need someone with a badge to run interference for me."

"You are not improving my opinion of you, Gallegher."

Then I explained, and Boulware's mood changed.

Boulware landed on the chopper pad at the Port of New Orleans and accompanied me to the gangway of the Rio Gaucho. We encountered token resistance from the crew, but a flash of Boulware's credentials, along with the firepower we both carried, discouraged them. I asked one of the men to lead me to the galley.

I found Cabby's body exactly where Villar had told me it would be, in the meat locker. He was wrapped in a sheet and placed on a low shelf. The two bullets Villar had parked in his head had caused so much damage, I had a difficult time recognizing him at first. People always look different when they're dead. The effects of high-caliber firepower don't help. In his jacket pocket I found a wallet with Cabby's driver's license, and that settled it for me. I found something else, too. It was a folded piece of notebook paper on which Cabby had written a message intended for my eyes only. I read it and was immediately filled with profound sadness.

"We're impounding the ship," Boulware told me back on the dock. "We'll see to it your friend is treated with respect."

"Thanks. If you don't mind, I'd like to go back to the Holbrook site, collect my guys, and go home."

"That I can do," Boulware said.

CHAPTER FORTY

I CALLED ROSS DUNCAN from my car on the way to Lake Pontchartrain to give him the bad news. I probably should have told him in person, but I had other priorities. He took it about as badly as I expected, but he found the grace in his grief to actually thank me for finding Cabby. I told him I didn't think I deserved anything resembling gratitude. He said I was the only one who cared enough to look for Cabby, and that was why. It didn't make me feel any better.

I think Fenster was shocked to see me stride up the gangplank to the Sweet Crude in my fatigues and a bulletproof vest covered with dried blood, strapped with an automatic sidearm. My face was still streaked with black grease.

He stared at me until I was almost on him. His hand began to drift under his jacket. I had the Glock out and leveled at his chest.

"Don't," I ordered.

He dropped his hands to his sides.

"This can't end well for you," he said.

"It didn't start so great, either."

I thumbed the release and let the magazine drop into the water. Then I jacked the remaining bullet over the side of the gangplank. I slapped the empty pistol against his chest.

"Your boss," I said. "If he's sleeping, wake him up. If he's fucking, tell him to pull it out and zip it up. I'll be in the salon."

I walked past him into the fine wood and brass salon where Kenzie had—essentially—bought me several days earlier. Nobody else was there. Over the bar, the television showed a replay of a basketball game from earlier in the evening, the sound muted. I walked behind the bar, poured two inches of single malt into a wide glass, and plopped down on one of the white upholstered sofas. The dirt and grime and blood and gore on my clothes probably ruined it forever. I didn't care. Not tonight. There were scores to be settled.

I sat for a minute or two, sipping the scotch. I work in a bar, but I don't often run across the good single malt stuff. It isn't in the highest demand in a low-rent place like Holliday's. It felt warm and smoky and smooth as I let it roll over my tongue and down my gullet. I resisted the urge to slam it back. Some things demand savoring.

Presently, Kenzie appeared at the hatch. He looked as if he'd dressed quickly. He wore a wrinkled golf shirt over a pair of khakis, and topsiders without socks. He gave me the once-over.

"You want a drink," I said.

"It's late, Gallegher."

"You want a drink," I repeated. This time he heard the menace in my voice.

"Okay." He crossed to the bar and saw the bottle I'd left open there.

"You should cap this after pouring. The alcohol evaporates."

"Sorry. If it goes flat, I'm sure you have a case or two in storage."

"At least. I'll send you a few bottles."

"Don't bother."

He picked up the bottle. "Laphroaig. Forty years old. This goes for about six hundred a bottle. You are clearly a man of refined tastes."

"Luck of the draw. I grabbed the first bottle I saw that said single malt."

"A fine choice nonetheless."

Claudine stepped into the salon. She wore a full-length quilted robe. For all I knew she was naked underneath. She looked scared.

"Have a drink, Mrs. Kenzie,'" I said.

She was scared. I read it all over her face, but I had to give her credit. She tried to look calm.

"A drink sounds nice," she said. "Kellen, you know what I like."

Neither of them seemed terribly disturbed by my appearance, or the havoc I was wreaking on their furniture. I guess it was a regular thing to entertain folk who looked like refugees from the final reel of *Apocalypse Now*. Once they had settled across from me, I took a sip of the Laphroaig and placed the glass on the table next to me.

"First things first," I said. "Robert knew nothing about the counterfeit pipe. In fact, he was never present when the transfers were made. Your son-in-law wouldn't know quality pipe from toilet paper tubes. It was Al Garlock dealing with Villar for the bogus pipe."

"That's a relief," Kenzie said.

"Bullshit," I said. "You knew all along. I've come straight from the Rio Gaucho. Please don't tell me you never heard of it. We have a lot to discuss. It would be a bad idea to begin with artifice."

I took a fragmentation grenade from inside my jacket and placed it on another coffee table in front of me.

"You know what this would do to your boat?" I asked.

Their expressions told me they had a good idea.

"This is the game," I said. "Truth or Dare. I'm going to tell you some stuff, and then I'm going to ask you some questions. You're going to tell me the truth or take the dare. The dare will always be the same. Sweat it out while you guess whether I have the balls to pull the pin. Are we straight on the rules?"

"Perfectly," Kenzie said. Claudine couldn't take her eyes off the grenade.

"First," I started, "Villar is dead."

"Who?" Kenzie asked.

I picked up the grenade and stuck a finger through the pin.

"Okay! Stop!" he said. "You made your point. Yes. I know who he is."

I placed the grenade back on the table. They didn't relax.

"Chuck Dickens is dead," I said.

Claudine gasped. It was the first truly human thing I'd seen her do. Kenzie seemed to take it in stride.

"I'm sorry to hear it," he said. "He was a good man."

"He went with me and some friends of mine on a rescue mission to save your son-in-law's ass."

"Was it successful?" Kenzie asked.

"Do you care?"

"This is your game. Your rules," Kenzie said. "I'm only trying to keep up."

"My friend Cabby's dead," I said. "Al Garlock is dead. So are a bunch of other people, but they all worked for Villar, so I suppose that's fine with you."

"I'm not sure I follow you."

"You do, but we'll get to it later. I feel bad about Dickens. You got one thing right. He was a good man. A brave man. Before he died, he told me a lot of stuff. If you researched me, you're familiar with Scat Boudreaux. Somewhere on this boat is a dossier on him, no doubt."

"I know about him," Kenzie said. "A resourceful fellow with an impressive history. Like yourself."

"Don't try to butter me up. It won't help, and it annoys me. There are a lot of things about Scat you don't know," I said. "One story in particular. You can't know it, because until now only he and I did. You know why they call him the Cannibal Commando?"

Claudine glanced across at her husband. Perhaps she had never heard Scat's frightening nickname. He dismissed her concern with a wave of his hand.

"I know the story," Kenzie said.

"Not all of it. There's what's in the official files, which were easy enough for you to access. Then there are the details, the minutiae. Scat spent months in a Viet Cong tiger cage, deep in the jungle, living off rice and water and whatever insects he could catch. At night, he peeled strips of bamboo from his cage, and over time fashioned them into knives. When he was ready, and the opportunity presented itself, he killed his guard, got out of the cage, and killed every VC soldier in the camp."

"And then he ate them," Kenzie said. "Yes. I know."

"Not everything. There was a VC colonel assigned to the camp. Fellow named Tranh. Real sick motherfucker. Loved to inflict pain. I mean, he got off on it. There was another American soldier in the camp, held in another tiger cage. His name was Riley. Something about Riley pissed Colonel Tranh off. Tranh delighted in putting Riley through the paces. It was like Tranh spent every day trying to think up new ways to teach Riley that his lifelong concept of pure hell was a spritely illusion. Over the course of months, Tranh killed Riley in little pieces. Every night, Scat lay in his tiger cage trying to ignore Riley's screams. Once in a while, Tranh worked Scat over, but Scat never seemed to provide the colonel with sufficient entertainment, because pain is simply another annoyance for Scat."

"How horrible," Claudine said.

"There's more," I said. "Tranh was out of the camp the night Scat made his escape. Could have been the luckiest night of his life, wouldn't you think? Scat trekked south through rice paddies and rain forests, killing and eating Viet Cong soldiers he came across in order to stay alive. That's why they call him the Cannibal Commando."

"I don't feel well," Claudine said.

"Understandable, but you can't leave. You and Kellen here are strapped in for the whole ride. Scat finally made it back to friendly lines. For a short while he was the sweetheart of *Stars and Stripes*, a genuine, gold-plated G.I. hero. Then the real story came out. He was cashiered into civilian life. His military jacket was locked away in the top secret vaults they stash inside other top secret vaults. Years passed. We lost the war in Viet Nam. The U.S. eventually reestablished diplomatic relations with our former enemies and began to trade with them. Over a decade or so, people began to forget what a shithole that country was. Most people, at least. Not Scat. He never forgot. Most people think Scat is a little crazy. Scratch that. Most people think he's a whole lot crazy. Maybe he is, but his memory is like a constant roll of high-definition video running through his head. He forgets nothing. About ten years ago, he took a trip to 'Nam. The State Department wasn't keen on him revisiting the scene of his 'atrocities,' but they knew they couldn't stop him without risking a meltdown. Believe me, the last thing this country needs is Scat irritable and on a rampage. So they let him go. Officially, it was supposed to be part vacation and part therapy for the florid post-traumatic stress disorder he wears like paint on his soul.

"He was actually on a mission. It took him a week or so, but he finally located Colonel Tranh. Like most soldiers after a war is over, Tranh had returned to civvy life. He owned an automobile shop in a town about thirty miles outside of Saigon. He lived over the shop in a three-room apartment. May not sound like much, but in Southeast Asia it's the gravy train. Scat paid him a visit one night, not long after dark. I'll spare you the details, but when the sun came up the next morning, there wasn't a square inch of the apartment without some scrap of Tranh's DNA on it. Scat boarded a plane the next day and flew home, like nothing had happened."

Kenzie took a nervous sip from his scotch and set the glass back down. "I didn't know that story," he said.

"It never happened. Not officially. Now, you may be asking yourself, 'What does this have to do with anything?' And you'd be right to ask. You see, since I returned from San Francisco, I've been troubled by the most amazing set of coincidences, almost like I was surrounded by serendipity. I hate serendipity. I hate coincidences. But what I hate most of all is being played for a chump."

I lifted my glass and held it with my index finger pointed at Kenzie.

"You, on the other hand, like to play people for chumps. There were so many coincidences. It was all too . . . too unlikely. Six months ago, Cabby showed up at my club, telling me he was tied up in some shady business, and asked me to find him should he ever disappear. I owed him, so I said I would. The day I get back from San Francisco, my everlasting love, Merlie, tells me she has a kid in need of surgery whose dad is missing. I start working two completely different cases. Somehow, they wind up related, almost intertwined. That sort of thing doesn't happen in real life, except it already did once, to me, last year. Cabby showed up at my club not six months after I made a huge splash in the newspapers as a consultant with a New Orleans murder case."

I pulled a slip of blood-stained paper from my pocket. "Cabby died yesterday. I found this on his body. He wanted to come clean."

I read from the paper.

Gallegher-

Things don't look good for me right now and I don't want you to think I meant to hurt you. For the last year, I been working undercover for Kellen Kenzie. I couldn't tell you what I was involved in when we talked a few months back. Kenzie hired me to get close to a bad guy from Brazil named Villar. I don't know why, but he wanted me to keep tabs on Villar's coming and goings. He also paid me to hire you to find me should I disappear, but he never told me why. I know you'll do your best. If I am in danger I don't know anyone I'd rather have trying to save me. If you're reading this, then it means you didn't get here in time, and things went bad for me. I knew what I was doing was risky, so that's all on me. Don't blame yourself. I went into this thing with eyes open. There's a guy runs an antique shop over in the Quarter named Ross Duncan. I left everything to him. Tell him my will is in a safe under my bed to make it all legal. Also, there's a letter in there I wrote to him some time back. Please see he gets it. Thanks, buddy. Your pal Cabby.

I dropped the letter on the table between us and let it sit there as Kenzie stared at it.

"This is where we get to the stuff Dickens told me earlier tonight. You read about me in the newspapers," I said. "You had your own security personnel with Borglund, but you knew they wouldn't do the tough stuff you wanted done with Villar. It isn't in their job description. You needed someone with the right skills and experience dealing with dangerous people, but you also wanted someone expendable, someone nobody would miss if things went due south."

"Why on earth would I do that?" Kenzie said. I hooked my finger in the grenade pin again. He tossed up his hands. "Okay! Okay! Sure. I hired Jacks to wheedle his way into Villar's organization. I wanted Jacks to keep an eye on him, keep me posted on his activities."

"Why? That's the only thing I haven't figured out."

"Oh, I doubt that. Clearly, you're smart and resourceful, but I still have my secrets."

"I may surprise you yet," I said. "What did you want with Villar?"

"It was business," he said. "I deal in oil. Like any business, it's a buy low/sell high proposition. Oil is plentiful in Brazil. Exports there have tripled over the last three years. As you may know, Brazil is also highly corrupt. Where there's corruption, there's the opportunity to get things at a discount. Villar is . . . *was* a smuggler first and foremost. He provided things people want. Drugs, ancient artifacts, oil—"

"Endangered rosewood."

"Precisely. He had criminal contacts in Brazil who could provide me with large quantities of cheap, cut-rate crude. We met several times, outlined the parameters of our business arrangements. I transferred a large amount of earnest money into this bank accounts."

"And he screwed you."

"In a manner of speaking. What we were doing was illegal, since Villar and his organization were, essentially, siphoning large amounts of oil from Brazilian pipelines."

"Large amounts?"

"Think tankers full. I didn't want to get greedy, so we agreed on one tanker ship a year."

"How would you make a killing off of that?"

"I didn't intend to make a killing. This was only one of the deals

I had on the table. It all accumulates over time."

I turned to Claudine. "You knew about this?"

She dropped her gaze to her drink.

"Claudine introduced us," Kenzie said. "At a party in Rio de Janeiro, about eight years ago. Yes. She knew. A tanker a year is easy to hide, when you're dealing in billions of barrels from legitimate sources. Then, Villar got greedy. He demanded we buy five tankers a year from him. I refused. Villar, in turn, blackmailed me. He told me I buy his five tankers, or he'd turn me over to the government here, let them know I was knowingly buying black market stolen crude."

"But that would implicate him as well," I said.

"There's no extradition from Brazil. Even if there was, I would imagine I would be a career-making prosecution for some eager young federal attorney. They'd almost certainly offer Villar immunity in return for his testimony. He had me in a tight spot. I decided to find a way out of it."

"By getting rid of Villar," I said.

"Right. In order to do that, I needed to find a way to keep tabs on him, a way that wouldn't point directly back to me. Through the late Mr. Dickens and Borglund Security, I was able to procure the services of your friend, Mr. Jacks. Inserting him into Villar's organization by way of the oil operation wasn't possible. Too obvious."

"You set him up as a conduit for CITES enjoined Brazilian rosewood."

"Exactly. It was a completely different deal, with no connection to me whatsoever. Mr. Jacks let it slip that he knew you. He told me you were some sort of detective, or vigilante, or whatnot. He said you could find people nobody else could find. I asked him if you would help a friend in trouble He told me that was what you did best, so I got him to make an arrangement with you to find him if anything happened to him. Jacks was reliable, and he was resourceful, but he was bound to slip up sometime. It was only a matter of time before he would screw up and blow his cover."

"But you couldn't sit around and wait, could you?" I asked.

"What do you mean?"

"I have another friend. He's very good at getting information on people. He hit the mother lode with you. You and Claudine here have been married for . . . what? . . . twenty-five years?"

"Twenty-seven."

"Right. Your original name was Claudine Renzi."

"That's public record," Claudine said. "There's no secret there."

"But public records can be mined. You have three siblings, Ms. Kenzie. Your brother Philip and two sisters, Naomi and Corinne. Am I right?"

"Yes," she said.

"Corinne Renzi was seven years older than you, if I recall."

"Still correct."

"She married three times. Her second husband was a man named Lawrence Sharp."

Claudine looked destroyed. Her gaze fell toward the floor. "Yes," she said.

"Lawrence and Corinne Sharp had two sons. George and Garry. We are particularly interested this evening in Garry. Your nephew. That would make his daughter Audrey . . . what?"

"I'm her great aunt."

"Right. I met with Carly McKee, Garry's ex-girlfriend, a few days ago. Audrey asked me to pick up her clothes and personal articles. Carly lived in a dump, a real shit palace. I went back to her place a couple of nights ago, and it was empty. My information guy told me she has a new place now, a spiffy one, right down in the French Quarter."

I turned to Kellen Kenzie. "You hired Cabby to keep tabs on

Villar through the rosewood operation. Villar wasn't stupid. He had you by the short hairs on the oil smuggling, but he needed more leverage. So, he made a deal with Al Garlock to substitute good oil pipe, your good oil pipe, essentially, for his cheap Chinese knockoff pipe. This much I know from Chuck Dickens. Here, it gets a little hazy. Your son-in-law is lazy and clueless, but you gave him a lot more credit than that. You thought he was crooked. So, you hired your nephew Garry to spy on your son-in-law, Robert. They'd never met. Why should they? You had no ongoing relationship with Garry. Holbrook had married into the family and had no history with any of your relatives beyond your daughter. How am I doing?"

"As well as might be expected. My congratulations."

"Wait. There's more. It was like a chess game between you and Villar. You make one move, he counter-moves. Like in a game of chess, sometimes you have to set things up three and four moves or more ahead of time. You play chess, Kellen?"

"Excellently."

"I don't doubt it. Once you had Garry on the payroll, you had your opportunity to go for the kill. You hired Carly McKee to sleep with him, knowing you were going to send him off into the boonies to work for Robert. When you did, you had her volunteer to look after your great niece, Audrey. You also saw to it that information on A Friend's Place was mailed to Carly every several days, so there were plenty of brochures for the shelter lying around. You told Carly to be a bitch to Audrey, with the goal of goading her into running away to the only place she knew to run, a shelter for runaway kids."

"It was a gamble," Kenzie said.

"And it worked. You had a child with a missing father staying in a shelter run by a social worker whose boyfriend specializes in finding missing people. It was inevitable that Merlie would ask me to find Audrey's father. You had me tied up six ways from Sunday.

First, you arranged for me to go looking for Cabby once he went missing. At the same time, you knew I couldn't resist a request from Merlie to search for Garry Sharp. One search led me to Villar, and the other also led me to Villar by way of your son-in-law. There was no way Villar could ignore me. Once I landed on his radar screen, you knew he'd try to take me out and I'd retaliate."

"With your friend Boudreaux," Kenzie said. "Your record clearly suggested that the two of you had a good chance of killing Villar."

"Thereby taking your head out of the noose."

"I applaud you, Gallegher. You are far smarter than I imagined. It's a mystery to me why you haven't been more successful in life."

"That's where you made your mistake," I said. "Smart rich people tend to believe that the two go together. To get rich, you think you have to be smart. Alternately, you believe people who aren't rich must not be as smart as you. This time you picked the wrong smart guy."

"So now you know everything," he said.

"Most of it."

"Then, may I presume we are done with that?" he said, pointing toward the grenade.

"Sure," I said. "It's served its purpose."

"As have you."

He stood and walked to the bar, where he poured himself another drink. Claudine seemed to relax. With all the secrets out in the open, and no explosives in the offing, she appeared to believe the situation had been defused.

"Unless . . ." Kenzie sat down again.

I knew what was coming, because I knew the way he thought. "Yes?" I said.

"You are everything your friend Cabby Jacks said. Very admirable. Incredibly brave. Outstandingly resourceful."

325

"Don't forget lucky. Luck played a huge part in it."

"Don't underestimate yourself. Not only did you survive an armed conflict with an extremely dangerous international criminal, you also figured out how you got into the conflict in the first place. I could use a man like you."

"That's what you do best. Use people."

"And I reward them handsomely for it. You mentioned luck. This could be your luckiest day, Gallegher." He waved around at the salon of his yacht. "You could say, this is the day your ship comes in."

He glanced over at Claudine, who beamed at his wit.

"The people at Borglund Security recognize the sort of opportunity I'm offering you. They all slaved at underpaid government jobs for years, acquiring skills that serve me well. They appreciate the material rewards I can provide for doing so."

"They're cashing in," I said.

"Quite so. On the other hand, they tend to be stuck in procedural ruts. They play by the book, even if the book is a little looser than they were used to at their various agencies. And, for better or worse, they don't actually work for me. They're hired help. They're beholden to Borglund. You, on the other hand, are a maverick. The only rules you obey are your own. You get things done when others can't. I admire those qualities. I would reward you handsomely if you would exercise them on my behalf."

"You want a killer on your personal payroll."

"You are not without experience."

I sat back and surveyed them. Kellen and Claudine Kenzie were moral twins. I could feel the waves of arrogance and privilege rolling off of them, like a bad odor.

"I'm going to have to decline," I said. "I don't see working for you as being a long-term proposition."

"And why is that?" Kenzie asked.

"A few minutes ago, I told you how Scat Boudreaux settled his score with Colonel Tranh. You didn't see how it was relevant. This is where we return to that subject. Scat doesn't like anyone. Well, that might not be entirely true. I think he likes me, maybe because I'm a consistent source of income for him. For some reason, he liked Chuck Dickens. They shared a history. I think Scat saw in Dickens what he might have become if Colonel Tranh and his Viet Cong buddies hadn't scrambled his brains. And now he knows you set up the whole conspiracy that got Dickens killed."

"How could he know that?" Kenzie demanded.

"Because I told him. Dickens told me all about it before Villar arrived at the work site. Scat also knows that you tried to set *me* up. I told Scat what you'd done. It took a quarter century, but Scat wiped the slate clean with Tranh. Scat holds a mean grudge, and he holds it forever. He has a curious penchant for his own kind of justice. You can't buy him off, and you can't stop him, and he's the most dangerous man in Louisiana. He may be the most dangerous man in the world."

"Are you threatening me?" Kenzie said.

"No. The time for threats is over. Our business is done. I'm giving you due notice. This is your life from here forward. You are not safe. You will never be safe again. Someday you'll turn the key to start this lovely watercraft. Scat will have rigged the bilge pumps so they won't purge, and you'll go up in a huge pretty fireball. Or you'll start your car and it will become an inferno. Or you'll try to go somewhere far away in your shiny private G5 jet and a Stinger missile will blow you out of the sky. Or maybe you'll be walking down the street when a thirty-caliber slug fired from a football field away will take off the top of your skull and cut all your wires. You don't know when it's coming, or where, but I can assure you it *is* coming. You will spend the rest of your potentially very short lives looking over your shoulders, both of you, terrified to flip every light switch, turn every key, walk down every sidewalk, and enter every room, vehicle, and building. You just became Scat Boudreaux's lunch, and you can never know when he's going to get hungry. If you are praying folks, I'd suggest you get right with your God, soon, because Judgment Day is coming."

"You can't be serious!" Claudine cried out. "This is monstrous."

"Why on earth would you do this?" Kenzie pleaded.

"Because I owed Cabby Jacks my life. When it came time to pay up I wasn't able to save him. Now, my debt to him is paid. In spades. Oh, and thanks for the car and the deposit in my Cayman bank account. Merlie sends her thanks for your generous contribution to the shelter. Maybe it will grease the skids a little for you in the Hereafter. I'm leaving now, since I have no idea whether Scat is already in the neighborhood. He isn't terribly concerned about collateral damage. I don't expect to see you again, except in the newspapers. Bet you make the front page."

I took the last sip from my glass of Laphroaig and walked up to the deck and out of Kellen Kenzie's snare. I stopped at the hatch to the main deck to turn back for one last word.

"By the way, I've grown quite attached to your great niece Audrey. I think it would be a nice gesture if you were to see to it she is provided for. That also might help you when it comes time to leverage your position with the Almighty. Bye now. Sleep tight."

CHAPTER FORTY-ONE

Six Months Later

*I*T WAS TIME to visit my money in the Caymans. I had convinced Merlie to take a week off and come along with me. The sands were coral pink under the razor sunlight, against a turquoise tropical sky. The colors clashed with her immodest sea-foam green string bikini. The Caribbean does that to people—takes perfectly rational social workers and turns them into debauched nudists overnight.

For all of which, I should add, I was mighty grateful, as I scanned the lush womanly curves barely concealed by the paucity of spandex she dared to call a swimsuit.

It had been a quiet six months, for the most part, compared to the cocktail blender kind of life that had been forced on me by Kellen Kenzie. I had only been asked to do one or two favors, mostly piddling stuff involving finding wayward wives whose husbands were too tied up in nefarious schemes to trust real detectives. In the meantime, I had worked assiduously on my triple-tonguing technique on the ancient Conn band cornet. I was no Al Hirt, but I was getting better at it.

I hadn't killed anyone since the shootout on Lake Saint Catherine. I considered that a plus in the spiritual development column.

On the other hand, the lack of side action had done a number on my cash flow, so it was time to visit my money in the Caymans. Even before I met Kellen Kenzie, I had a nifty little nest egg—a million more or less—salted away in a numbered account in the islands, courtesy of a finder's fee I'd claimed after recovering a considerably larger sum, long before I met Merlie. Kenzie's largesse—sociopathic and manipulative as it had been—had graciously increased my tiny fortune. I had a nice margin of mad money available for the frosting on my life cake.

Now it was time to dip into my little retirement account. I could have done it by wire transfer, but then I wouldn't have gotten to lie on these coral sands with a snappy babe in a sea-foam green bikini and drowsy lust in her violet eyes.

"Did I tell you?" she asked. "Audrey Sharp has recovered quite nicely from her knee surgery."

"Glad to hear it."

"She's doing so well, she's considering trying out for track and field at her school this year."

"We'll have to go see her run."

"Might be a bit of a road trip. She and her dad moved to Atlanta a few weeks back. It seems Garry came into a substantial amount of money."

"Uh-huh," I murmured.

"Don't suppose you had anything to do with that?"

"Maybe a little. Sounds like the Kenzies are trying to get right with the universe. I might have prodded them a bit."

She rolled over onto her stomach and gazed out over the crystal-clear waters of the Caribbean. "I could get used to this," she said, dreamily. "Doesn't feel like November at all. Do you think people live like this?"

"I imagine they do," I said. "But it would get old after a while."

"Like twenty or thirty years?"

"More or less."

"Shame to go back."

"Shame to spoil it all by staying. Besides, there are things to do back home."

She rolled over on her side and lifted her sunglasses to peer at me. She didn't know it, but when she did, her top slipped down enough to expose a quarter inch of her right areola. I considered telling her, but then she would have felt compelled to do something about it, and that too would have been a shame.

"You don't fool me," she said. "You don't want to miss your birthday party."

"I've reconsidered," I said, "Let's stay."

They say time and tide wait for no man. That includes hulking fifty-one-year-old guys named Gallegher. My fifty-second birthday was only five days away. I was anticipating it the way five-year-old kids dread tetanus shots.

I was irrevocably over fifty. The ache in my joints and thickening gray at my temples told me there were a lot fewer good years ahead of me than I had left behind. I had abused the good nature of my own body more times than I should have. It was beginning to show whenever I tried to stand after sitting for more than a half hour. I was beginning to wonder if I had lost the edge, and whether it might soon be my turn to draw the short straw in one of my infrequent adventures.

"Stop it," Merlie said.

I snapped back into focus. "Beg pardon?"

"I do not like what you're thinking," she said.

"Are you claiming telepathic powers, now?"

"We've been together long enough. I know that look. Fifty-two is not over the hill anymore."

"Easy for you to say," I said. "You're still three years away."

She sat up, grabbed her straw hat, and stuffed her suntan lotion and her paperback into a mesh bag.

"Come on, then" she said, as she stood, "Let me show you what a forty-nine-year-old chick can do."

Over the years, I've had them young and I've had them not so young. For my money there is nothing in a twenty-five-year-old hard bodied girl-woman to compare with the benefits of experience. Merlie was all softness and warm curves, and she flowed over me like thick syrup. She seeped into all my crags and crevices and worked out my kinks like nobody ever had.

Afterward, we collapsed on the bed in our tenth floor room, the windward breezes of the Yucatan Basin billowing the sheers in the open sliding door to the balcony, with the rhythmic splash of the clear Carib waves keeping time with my breathing, and she lay her head on my barrel chest, her cerise hair with its own occasional flecks of salty white spreading out like cooling lava, and she occasionally made this long *mmmmmmmmmm* sound, not actually a sigh, but nowhere near a moan. It was just contentment, I suppose. That made two of us.

It was going to be hard, going back. The islands are seductive, but they aren't real. If I wanted *real*, all I had to do was rent a car and drive back in the hills behind George Town, where I would find all the reality I could eat in the rows of shanties and tossed-together hovels where our waiters and housekeepers laid their desperate heads at night. For Merlie and me, the islands were an illusion, and a damned fine one, but they weren't for keeps.

It was going to be hard, but we were going back. In two days, I would be at Holliday's, playing on stage. She would be running A Friend's Place. Three days later I would turn fifty-two, and that was the way things were dealt.

As I drifted off to sleep, to the aroma of hyacinth and bougainvillea drifting in with the island zephyrs, I found comfort in one small thought.

We could always come back here to visit.

And it was true.

For I am, after all, one lucky son of a bitch.

About the Author

RETIRED FORENSIC PSYCHOLOGIST and college professor Richard Helms is the author of nineteen novels and numerous short stories. He has been nominated six times for the SMFS Derringer Award, with two wins; five times for the PWA Shamus Award; twice for the ITW Thriller Award with one win; and once for the MRI Macavity Award. A former president of the Southeast Chapter of Mystery Writers of America, and a former member of the MWA National Board of Directors, Helms was the 2017 recipient of the SEMWA Magnolia Award for service to the chapter. When not writing, Helms enjoys gourmet cooking, international travel, fine woodworking, rooting for his beloved Carolina Tar Heels and Carolina Panthers and just hanging with his grandsons, RJ and Cash. Richard Helms and his wife Elaine live in Charlotte, North Carolina.

CPSIA information can be obtained
at www.ICGtesting.com
Printed in the USA
BVHW030201050520
579210BV00001B/84